OVER
THE
FALLS

OVER THE FALLS

A Novel

REBECCA HODGE

NEW YORK

Published in the United States by Crooked Lane Books, an imprint of The Quick Brown Fox & Company LLC.

Crooked Lane Books and its logo are trademarks of The Quick Brown Fox & Company LLC.

Library of Congress Catalog-in-Publication data available upon request.

ISBN (hardcover): 978-1-64385-754-1
ISBN (ebook): 978-1-64385-755-8

Cover design by Nicole Lecht

Printed in the United States.

www.crookedlanebooks.com

Crooked Lane Books
34 West 27th St., 10th Floor
New York, NY 10001

First Edition: September 2021

10 9 8 7 6 5 4 3 2 1

To George, Austin, Daniel, Carson, Rose, and Bianca, in thanks for your love and patience as I wander through fictional worlds.

CHAPTER ONE

Bryn

Three buzzards circled in the distance, dropping lower each minute, confident they'd found a feast. The sight turned the warm June evening cold.

I grabbed my bag of delivery supplies. I hadn't been all that worried when I called my two goats into the barn and only one showed up. Thistle liked to wander, and she knew her way home. But the buzzards' presence converted my casual concern into a more urgent rescue mission. Thistle had more than a week to go before she was due to deliver, but goats weren't all that good at checking the calendar.

I called Tellico, my oversized mixed-breed hound, and we set out to search the endless acres of the front pasture, hoping to find her.

"So much for a quiet evening. Come on, let's see what's going on." Talking to animals was a direct result of my years living alone, but at times it made me feel like a full-fledged Tennessee mountain crazy woman. As always, Tellico ignored

1

my chatter but stuck close, his nose twitching as he checked every new scent.

I picked up my pace, heading through the pasture for the boggy area near the front gate. Tellico snaked through the tangled undergrowth with an ease I envied, while the snarled vines clawed and grabbed at my jeans, slowing me down.

I fought my way to the spot where the birds hovered and skidded to a stop. Thistle lay stretched on her side in a patch of swampy goo near the corner where my long gravel driveway met the paved state road. Her sleek red-brown coat was covered in mud, her breath came in short painful gasps, and she didn't even try to stand when she saw me.

"Easy, Thistle, it's okay."

A long slow wave of muscular contraction rolled down her side, and she gave a pitiful bleat. She must have been in labor for hours, stuck here and in trouble while I was locked in my home office, finishing the day's coding and meeting deadlines, but oblivious to her distress.

The buzzards settled on a nearby tree, three heads staring in my direction, foiled for the moment but not giving up.

"What's going on, girl?" I patted Thistle on the neck and set my bag down on a dry tuft of grass. "Goats are supposed to have an easy time delivering. Didn't you read the fine print?"

I'd acquired this goat and her sister the year before, in the hope they'd keep this unused pasture chewed down to manageable levels. When it became obvious two weren't enough to take care of the backlog, I decided to breed Thistle, my favorite of the pair. I was looking forward to having a kid around. A four-legged kid, that is. I'd been absent when they passed out the instinct necessary for mothering humans.

"Okay, girl, hang in there. Let's see if I can figure this out." I'd read the chapter on potential birthing problems once or twice, but in truth, I hadn't taken it all that seriously. Thistle would take care of things on her own, right?

Wrong. The idea of faking my way through a challenging delivery was ridiculous, but it looked like I had no alternative.

Another big contraction hit, so with a feeling of stunned disbelief, I pulled out my tube of K-Y, lubed up my hand and lower arm, and eased myself down into the muck. I slipped my hand inside, and in only a few inches my fingers ran into two hard lumps. Thistle's muscles gripped hard on my hand with every contraction, but after a minute I was able to sort things out by touch. Two hooves. Two legs. I pulled back out. There was unquestionably a baby goat in there, and it was trying its best to get out.

So why wasn't it happening? In a kayak I could judge a crisis in an instant and respond with certainty, but acting as a goat midwife was a blind leap off a very tall cliff. I closed my eyes and wished for magical powers.

My cell phone was in my back pocket, and this time of day, Landon was probably at home taking care of his own herd of goats. He'd drop what he was doing if I called, and in five minutes, he'd be here, full of encouragement, experience, and advice. He'd seen every sort of emergency there was, and I had no doubt he would know exactly what was wrong and exactly what I needed to do.

Tempting, but I didn't reach for the phone. In the three years since Landon bought the acreage next to mine, we'd mended fences together, traded tools, laughed over many a cold beer at the end of many a long day. He not only understood my mortgage worries, he knew how to get rid of tomato hornworms and the best way to nurture baby chicks. He answered my endless questions with patience, and relying on his knowledge had become second nature.

But he had ruined that easy comradery a month before when he'd asked for far more than I could give. My *no* had stunned him, and I hadn't seen him since. There was no way I could call him now for help.

A car came to a stop on the paved road out front, hidden by the shrubbery along the front fence. Not Landon—I knew the clatter of his ancient truck—but perhaps my wishful thinking had worked, and someone had swooped in to help. They didn't turn into the drive. Instead, a car door slammed, and the car sped off at once. Not a rescue after all, probably someone pitching garbage or getting rid of a litter of kittens—I'd have to check once things calmed down.

But then footsteps crunched toward me on the driveway. Unexpected visitors were rare out here, particularly someone who was simply dropped off roadside. I peered in that direction, but Thistle chose that moment to scramble, her legs flailing, trying to stand. She couldn't get any traction, but she did manage to coat me with another layer of muck.

"Easy girl. Calm down." If she kept thrashing like that, there was no way I'd save her and her baby.

"Hello? Are you Bryn? Bryn Collins?" The voice came from the driveway. A boy's voice. One that cracked as he choked out the question.

I glanced his way long enough to see a gangly form silhou-etted against the low sun. I kept looking for an adult, but he was apparently alone. What in the world was he doing here?

But explanations had to wait. "Yeah, I'm Bryn. Hey, give me a hand, would you? If you can hold this goat still, I can maybe get this kid out."

"What?" His incredulous tone made it sound like I'd sug-gested a leap to the moon. But he took a few hesitant steps closer, moving toward the wire electric fence.

"Not that way. You'll get shocked. The gate's in the corner there."

He headed in that direction. Thistle settled down, and I didn't have time to worry about the boy. I knelt behind my goat again and this time slid my hand in farther in my attempt to figure out what was wrong. Two legs, okay, that was good. The book said there should be a head stretched forward to rest on those legs, creating a nice compact package for delivery. Maybe the head was twisted back somehow?

Water from the bog was soaking through my jeans and T-shirt, a chilling damp, and a strand of hair escaped from my ponytail, stinging my eyes. I felt my way between the two legs, expecting them to lead to a chest, neck, and head, but my hand just kept sliding between them. I was elbow deep at this point and utterly confused. *What the hell?*

Slow footsteps came closer, on this side of the fence now, the boy's shoes making wet sucking sounds in the mud. Tellico ran to greet him with a wagging tail, but I didn't even give him a decent look. "Grab onto her halter, would you? Don't let her get up."

"You're kidding, right?" He waited, as if he thought I was going to let him off the hook, but after a long moment, he came closer and hung a small backpack on a bush. He stood as far away as possible and grabbed the side strap of Thistle's halter. He was leaning so precariously I was afraid her slightest movement would cause him to tumble flat. Not much help, that was for sure, but at least he was trying. Thistle calmed a little despite his obvious nervousness.

I tried to remember all the scary illustrations I'd seen in the goat manual. Head bent back? No, that wasn't it. Rear presentation? Not that either. Curled with four feet presented? Nope. Twins? *Oh no, that must be it.* "I've got two legs here, but they belong to two different kids."

Tellico gave a tail wag, but the boy didn't seem overly impressed. "Uh, isn't it going to be hard for them to get out with you in the way?"

Smartass. Like I was here in the mud, breathing essence of goat for the fun of it. "Yeah, yeah, I'm working on it. Hang on."

I could picture the problem now—twins, both trying to come head first, had each gotten one leg into the birth canal, plugging up the works. They may have been stuck this way for hours, and it was possible neither of them was still alive. A strong surge of guilt paralyzed me. I should have confined Thistle to the barn. Should have checked on her every few hours. Should never have bred her. Should have had some damn sense.

My first attempt at breeding, and all I'd bred was death. A foul sourness coated the back of my throat.

Stop it. Do something.

I forced myself back to the present. Now that I could visualize the twins, the lumps I was feeling made sense. I squirmed around until I got a hand on the chest of the kid on the left, trying to remember the illustrations in the manual and hoping I was doing the right thing. I slowly pushed the kid back inside, vetoing its effort to exit.

Every contraction was a vise clamping hard on my arm, but I finally got that one pushed out of the way. The twin on the right immediately slid toward me to fill the gap. I ran my hand along its neck to make sure its head was straight, and my fingers brushed against its muzzle. A wet tongue wrapped around them for an instant, and a fizzing joy bubbled up through my chest.

"It's alive. At least one of them is."

The boy merely grunted, but he took a step closer, as if perhaps now I'd said something he was willing to pay attention to.

I pulled my arm out, and as if on cue, a huge contraction delivered the first kid. A moment later, the next spasm delivered the second. In only a few minutes, two wet, furry creatures were struggling to their feet beside me, fighting to get their balance, their long awkward legs skewed out at crazy angles.

Amazing. I'd read the manuals, seen videos online, but I never expected an actual birth to give me such a spectacular rush. I was wet and muddy, weary and marveling, but all I could do was sit in the muck and grin.

Thistle, still shaky, struggled to her feet and began licking her twin daughters. The kids gathered close and searched out her udder.

"How do they know?" The astonishment in the boy's voice reflected all the magic I was feeling, both of us floating on the same incredulous buzz.

"Wonderful, isn't it? It's all in the hard wiring."

I got to my feet, holding my goopy arm out to one side as I tried to brush off chunks of mud with my free hand. Homesteading always gave me plenty of chances to ruin my clothes, but this time it had been totally worth it.

I turned and looked full-on at my visitor for the first time, and the shock of what I saw sent sparks through my body far worse than what the electric fence would have inflicted.

Sawyer.

This boy looked like Sawyer, but of course he wasn't. Sawyer would be pushing forty now if he were alive. But the powerful resemblance was unsettling. Same ice-blue eyes. Same white-blond hair. Same whorl over the middle of his forehead, the one Sawyer hated because he could never get his hair to lie flat in front.

This boy had a left-sided dimple like the one I used to tease Sawyer about. He was watching the twins nurse hungrily, and even the way he was standing, with one foot slightly in front of the other and his hips canted to stay balanced, was an exact match to my ex-fiancé's stance.

Ex-fiancé, not ex-husband. While he and I were busy designing wedding invitations, discussing reception menus, and debating a final guest list, my younger sister, Del, got pregnant.

And Sawyer was the father.

This boy, my reluctant birthing assistant, had to be the fourteen-year-old result of that pregnancy. Sawyer's son. My nephew. If Sawyer and I had had a son, this is what he could have looked like.

A stab of wrenching loss lanced through my chest, making it difficult to breathe. I gave myself a hard mental kick. Hadn't I just been thinking I had zero instinct for motherhood? But see-ing him there, right in front of me, ripped open wounds I'd fool-ishly believed were well healed .

I snapped myself back to reality and took another look at the boy.

Nowadays, my mother knew never to mention my sister or her family—I'd threatened to stop paying her cable bills if she said a single word. But she had spoken of my nephew when he was born. I pulled up the vague memory. "You're Joshua, right? Joshua Whitman?"

He looked startled that I recognized him. Perhaps he didn't even know about his striking resemblance to his father. Sawyer had died in a plane crash two years after he'd been born, and Del probably hadn't wasted any time before moving on to someone new. I should have felt better when I heard the news of Sawyer's death, knowing he was permanently out of the picture and out of my life, but instead, a fragile hope of reconciliation had shat-tered. It was a hope so unfounded in reality, I hadn't even known it was there.

The boy nodded. "Josh, not Joshua."

He gave me a careful once-over, no doubt itemizing the scraggly hair, the filthy clothes, my one arm coated in mud and the other still dripping lube and amniotic fluid. Del had always been a perfect-hair, perfect-nails girly girl, and it was obvious from Josh's face that I didn't measure up.

"So, Josh, who did you come with?" I looked down the drive-way again, still unable to believe he'd arrived alone. Had Del—or somebody else—just dumped him off? When I heard the car leave, I'd thought *garbage* or *kittens*, and the idea of treating this boy that callously dismayed me. Fourteen-year-olds did not travel from Memphis to the eastern end of the state alone.

He looked away, silent, staring across the pasture toward the orchard, where neat rows of Winesaps hid the house, barn, and creek from view. The silhouette of the Blue Ridge Mountains shadowed the horizon on all sides, their presence usually a soothing comfort. At the moment, with the son of my ex-lover unexpectedly on my doorstep, it was hard for me to pull much solace from my mountains, and it didn't look like they offered much reassurance to Josh either.

I waited for him to answer. His eyes dropped, and he studied his soggy tennis shoes. "I came by myself. Mom said if I needed help, I should go to my Aunt Bryn. She gave me your address." He gave me a searching look that was so like Sawyer's, I flinched. "I didn't even know I had an aunt."

I shouldn't have been surprised—Josh's existence was something I'd done my best to forget, so there was no reason for Del to say much about me. But his last words were a fist that punched hard—sharp and unexpected. It was one thing for me to disown my sister—heck, I was the injured party in all this; I was justified—but it was something else to discover she had also disowned me. "Surprise. Here I am."

What a mess. Here alone. Needing help. Was he in trouble? Was he a runaway? Did I need to call the police? The last thing I needed was a fourteen-year-old puzzle on my hands.

Typical Del, dumping her problems on someone else. For the first two decades of her life, that *someone else* had always been me, two years older and constantly told to take care of my

precious baby sister. During the past fourteen years of oblivious-
ness, I hadn't missed that responsibility for a single minute.

I made a valiant effort not to let my irritation show. This kid
had nothing to do with all that history. "When exactly did she
tell you about me?"

"Right before she left." Josh looked more than a little lost
and confused, his shoulders slumped, his expression dazed.

The phrase *before she left* sounded like more bad news, and I
dreaded hearing the details. Runaway or not, he must have been
traveling all day. Another few minutes delay wouldn't be fatal.
"Well, you made it here okay, and that's a start. We'll get it sorted
out, but first let's get these goats back to the barn."

Josh picked up his pack and slung it over one shoulder, but
he took a step backward when I scooped up the kid closest to me
and thrust her into his arms. "Yuck! It's all wet!"

I almost laughed, but I managed to convert it into a small
choking sound. I admit, maybe I was a little happy that he didn't
like it. Heck, I hadn't asked him to show up unannounced. I
hadn't asked for reminders of the past. He could take what came.

"Welcome to farm life. Here, put one arm under her chest and
use the other to support her hindquarters." I helped him make the
adjustment, and the four-legged kid settled in tight against the two-
legged kid's chest. I picked up my bag of supplies and the other
twin. Thistle nuzzled my leg, bleating for her babies. "It's okay, girl,"
I told her. "Just follow us back to the barn."

Josh looked uncertainly at the leggy bundle in his arms.
"Hey, something's wrong with her eyes. She looks like a space
alien."

I leaned over to look. Nothing was wrong. "You mean her pupils?"

"Yeah. They're rectangles. It's creepy. Aren't they supposed to be round?"

"That's normal if you're a goat."

Normal. A normal, peaceful life was what I craved. Was that too much to ask for? My need for *normal* was why I lived on my own, why I'd given Landon an emphatic *no.* I was a talented expert when it came to avoiding complications. But Josh's unexpected appearance had flipped my day from totally normal to utterly bizarre.

We started toward the barn. Thistle stuck close, wobbly and still upset but determined to keep up. The buzzards flew down to investigate, and I had the satisfaction of knowing I'd cheated them out of their meal. Despite an unexpected nephew and a conniving sister, the day was not a total disaster.

At least not yet.

CHAPTER TWO

Josh

I followed Bryn on a dirt path through scratchy weeds, carrying the wriggling goat, with Bryn's dog close beside me. My stomach had been hurting the whole long drive, and the goat's funky stink made it worse. All day I kept telling myself that once I got here, everything would be okay. But now I was in a strange place with a strange aunt, holding a strange animal. Now I was here, and nothing was okay.

The path widened underneath tall trees, and Bryn dropped back to walk beside me. She took one of those deep breaths like when I have to write an essay for English class. "What's going on? Where's your mother? And how did you get here?"

I only knew the answer to the last question. "Uber."

"You Ubered across the entire state? I didn't know that was even possible."

"It wasn't easy." Yeah, okay, I was a little proud I'd done it. Some of my friends didn't even have the app. "Nine rides. Four hundred miles. I promised big tips, and I had a note Mom wrote a long time ago. *My son has permission to ride with you. If questions, call.* Three of the drivers called, got her voice mail, and drove me anyway. The other six just looked at the note, shrugged, and told me to get in."

"How did you pay for it?"

"I didn't. It's linked to Mom's credit card." Mom was going to shit when she saw the bill, but hey, she was the one who told me to come.

"So why are you here? Does your mom know? Do you need to call her?"

Too many questions. Her voice was calm and quiet like when she talked to the goat, but the answers made my stomach twist. "I don't know where she is. And her phone is off. It's been off the whole time she's been gone."

"Gone?"

"Gone a whole week."

"A week?" Not so calm and quiet anymore. She stopped walking, stared at me, and her face went all scrunchy. "She abandoned you for *a week*?"

She made it sound like Mom had done something awful. "She didn't *abandon* me." I said it hard, and she turned kind of pink like she'd gotten the message. "I was with neighbors. I've stayed with them before."

Jill and Francie. In and out all day and night, their apartment smelling like the locker room at school. I'd heard them talking the night before, saying a week of babysitting was too long, especially now that summer vacation had started. They mentioned child services, a major hit to the gut, and I knew I had to jump. "I left this morning before they were awake."

"You didn't tell them you were going?"

I shook my head. She didn't get it. They probably hadn't even noticed I was gone yet.

"Okay then. Let's get the animals settled, and first thing we do is call those neighbors."

Yeah. Go ahead. Call them. But that wasn't going to find my mother.

We arrived at a little barn with a rust-streaked sheet-metal roof. Chickens fluttered around in a pen on the left, and there was another goat making a lot of noise in a fenced corral on the right. The goat who had just dumped the babies was reddish-brown, the other one was black, and they both had long floppy ears that were even bigger than the ones on Aunt Bryn's dog.

Bryn unlatched the goat pen. "Tellico, stay out." The dog sat down at once, panting with a long pink tongue. Pretty good, listening like that.

We carried the babies in, and the mother goat followed. We set down the little ones, and they ran straight to her to nurse. At least they had a mother.

"This one is Thistle," Bryn scratched the goat on her forehead, and Thistle lifted her head for more. "The other one's Kudzu."

Like I care.

"We'll have to think of names for the little ones."

We? Yeah, right.

"I'll put the chickens up for the night, and then we'll go to the house."

"I'm hungry." Maybe food would help things seem not so strange. "I got one of the drivers to stop at a McDonald's, but that was a long time ago."

"Okay. We'll put dinner on the list."

She went to the other side of the barn, and I could hear clucking sounds. I stayed with the goats.

The baby I'd carried came over and sniffed at the legs of my jeans. I bent to give it a pat, and it sucked on my fingers like it was still hungry. I wiped my sticky hands on some straw, took out my phone, and snapped a few pictures of the goats.

The gurgling of some sort of creek or river sounded close by, and the air was cooler here than in Memphis and smelled wet and green. Beside the barn was a beat-up truck, the kind with four doors in the cab and a short cargo bed in back. It had a kayak strapped on top, a fancy kayak like I'd seen once on an ESPN special, so I left the goat pen and took another few pics. Marcus would like them; he was into all that water stuff, always going off fishing with his dad and sending me snaps of what he caught.

I'd made it the whole way here, I'd found Mom's sister, and I was seeing mountains for the first time—my ears popping when the road twisted up and up on the way here. But Mom says you always have to watch out for the bad news, and around here I didn't have to look all that hard. I had no real idea where I was. I had to watch goats being born and carry one through a field. And it was possible my aunt was certifiably crazy living out here. Out here I hadn't seen any houses, any stores—any anything. Out here, something creepy bad could happen, and nobody would ever know.

I shouldn't have come—that was already too obvious—but I wasn't sure what to do next. Bryn—Aunt Bryn? —had mentioned food. And her dog acted kind of nice, sort of like

Marcus's dog, Henry, who carried his own ball with him every-where. This one stayed right beside me every minute, like he would leap to my defense if I needed it. That might be because he could smell the Snickers bar I'd had in my pocket earlier in the day, but maybe he really liked me.

It was my growling stomach that made up my mind. I could stick around long enough to eat and see what happened next.

Bryn got done with the chickens and led the way to a cabin made from old gray logs stacked on top of each other, like in pioneer days. Old-timey except for a big satellite dish on the roof. I took a few more pics, the sun low in the sky and the shadows long. The mountains surrounded us like a giant's fence, maybe walling something out but maybe just trapping us in, and I was glad to head indoors.

We went into the cabin through the unlocked back door, into a little room with coats on hooks and muddy boots in a scrambled-up pile. The dog came with us.

"Leave your shoes here." Bryn dumped hers onto the heap, and I added my wet tennis shoes. She washed her arms and hands at a deep metal sink in the corner, waited while I did the same, and handed me a fluffy towel. We went into a long narrow kitchen—bare countertops and pots hanging on the walls—way bigger than our kitchen at home and a lot more sparkly. Bryn pulled a cell phone out of her pocket. "These neighbors. Do you have their number?"

I pulled up a snapshot in my head that showed the list of numbers on the fridge at home and read the right one off. Her eyebrows went up when I didn't need to look it up, but she punched it in and got Jill.

"Hi, my name is Bryn Collins, and I'm Del Whitman's sister. Josh showed up at my house, so I wanted to let you know."

I could hear Jill saying something, her voice short and snappish, but I couldn't hear the words.

"Yes . . . He's right here . . . Well, yes, of course I'll take care of him now, but . . . Yes, but . . . No, but . . . I see . . . Uh-huh . . . Wait—don't hang up. Do you have any idea where Del is? . . . Okay, yes. Thanks."

Pretty much what I expected—Jill was probably doing a happy dance at the news I was gone—but Bryn's face was red and her lips were tight by the time she finished. "Your mother left you with those people *on purpose*? I could have been anyone. She didn't even ask where I live." She gave another one of those long I-don't-want-any-part-of-this sighs.

She wasn't going to help. I could tell. That whole long drive for nothing.

My chest got small and tight, making it really hard to breathe, like the time in third grade when I came home from school and couldn't wake Mom up. Her hand was ice cold. Her face was the wrong color. Her chest jerked when she breathed, like it was getting stuck every time. I was scared she was dying, and I was scared she'd kill me if I ran up a doctor bill, but I called it in anyway.

The ambulance guy told me I saved her by getting help, and I knew from then on it was my job to take care of her. But shit, I couldn't take care of her if I couldn't find her, could I? I stared out the window. Dark had come on fast, and I could see only a hint of the black shapes of trees.

"Can I have something to eat?" The words spilled out sounding sad, and I cleared my throat. I hadn't meant to sound that way.

Bryn came over, hesitated, then put a hand on my shoulder. I barely felt it, like she wasn't sure if it was okay to touch me.

"I'm not mad at you, Josh. It's just . . ." She cleared her throat like that would clear up her words. "Look. Your mom and I haven't talked for a long time. A really long time. Since before you were born. I don't spend much time around kids, so you're going to have to help me out." She gave my shoulder a squeeze that felt more normal. "Everything is going to be all right. We'll work on this together."

"Yeah. Okay." What else could I say? She didn't know much. Nothing was going to be all right.

She grabbed an apple from a fancy wooden bowl on the counter. "Start on this while I roll through the shower. Then we'll fix dinner and figure out what happens next."

I took a big bite. The apple tasted good. Dinner would have tasted better.

"If you've got a different shirt in your bag," she said, "take that one off, and I'll dump it in the washer with my stuff."

"Okay."

She left with my sticky goat shirt. I could hear the shower running, so I got up and gave Tellico a pat, and he thumped his tail. He came with me, and I had a look around. A living room, also very neat and picked up. A woodstove in the corner—awesome. No TV—prehistoric. An open door in the hall led to an office, and there I faced enough electronics to stock a Best Buy.

She had three different computers on three different work-stations, all with sticky notes on whiteboards above them and pads of paper with writing beside them. One Dell, one Mac, and one that didn't have a name, maybe home built like Chris's dad put together as a demo for the school science fair. Each one of the computers had two big monitors, and a fancy chair on wheels could cruise from one station to another. She could play some awesome games with this gear.

A bookcase was crammed full of programming manuals: Python, Java, C++, Rust, Swift—a little of everything. I'd done some basic programming at the YMCA computer camp one summer, but even the teacher there didn't have all this stuff.

The router in the corner had a slip of paper taped to it, with an access code. I entered it into my phone. The cell signal was crap out here, but internet would help.

A piece of paper thumbtacked to the wall said "In Case of Emergency" and had a list of names and phone numbers. I stared at it for a few seconds to file it away. Grandma's number was on it. Mom's wasn't.

By the time Bryn was done with her shower, I'd loaded my pics up to Instagram and texted Marcus that I couldn't play *Fortnite* with him. I looked up goats—yes, Bryn was right; they had rectangular pupils. One point for my aunt, zero for me.

Bryn looked better without a coating of mud, and a little like Mom with her wavy black hair and dark brown eyes. Instead of her Great Smokies T-shirt, now she wore one with Calvin and Hobbes that said "Some days even my lucky rocket ship under-pants don't help." Ha. Someone wearing that shirt was supposed to help me? It didn't inspire confidence.

"Still hungry?"

"Always."

She smiled an almost-laughing smile, and in that moment she looked exactly like Mom despite the offbeat T-shirt. My heart gave a jolt that hurt.

"What sort of food do you like?"

"Hamburgers?"

She shook her head.

"Pizza?"

"Takes too long for the dough to rise. Need to plan ahead on that one."

I'd never thought about pizza as something you made yourself. Didn't she know you could just call? "Okay, what do you have?"

"How about spaghetti?"

"Yeah, okay."

Bryn did a lot of banging around with pots and pans. I played Alto's Odyssey on my phone and tried not to think about the way it was when I ate dinner with Mom. She wasn't home most nights—working evening shift or out on a date—but sometimes she'd stick a Stouffers in the microwave, and it was nice to have her there on the couch with me. Even if that meant she got to choose what we watched on TV.

The food smelled promising. Bryn brought my plate to the table, and I poked through the lumpy sauce with my fork. "Where are the meatballs?"

Bryn looked at me like she'd never heard of meatballs. "It's a sauce put up from last year's garden. Roasted red peppers. Zucchini. Tomatoes. I'm vegetarian. No meat."

Oh good. Now I was going to starve to death. I stared at it, doubtful, but there wasn't anything else, so I ate it. Okay, it was better than I expected, sort of spicy and sweet both, but really? No meat?

It was a quiet meal, nobody talking, like when you get stuck having lunch with the new kid at school, and you spend the whole time watching the other person and pretending you're not. Except Bryn didn't even pretend—she kept giving me odd looks, like she was trying to figure something out just by studying my face.

I ate two helpings and Bryn ate one. Did vegetarians eat dessert? I decided it was better not to ask.

Bryn drummed her fingers on the tabletop, just like Mom did when she couldn't make up her mind. "Does Del go away like this often?"

"For a weekend. Yeah. But usually not by herself." Usually she was with whatever guy she was hanging out with at the time, and the guy was always the one paying. "She comes back late sometimes, but never more than a day or two. And she always calls."

"Does she still work at the bank?"

"The bank?" I'd never heard anything about a bank. That must have been when I was little. "She's a cashier at the Kroger."

"Would anyone there know where she went?"

"I don't think so. When she didn't show up, I called the store and told her boss she was really sick." I was the one who always called in for Mom if she was going to miss her shift. She never remembered until a day too late.

"Why do you think she told you to come here to me? I mean, why me and why now? She left for other weekends and didn't tell you about me."

I shrugged. If I knew any of this, I wouldn't have had to come, would I?

I couldn't start tearing up in front of a stranger, so I knocked my fork to the floor and bent down to give myself a minute. Tellico beat me to it, and that distracted Bryn, taking the fork from the dog and getting me another one even though I was done eating. The food hadn't helped my stomachache at all, and her questions about Mom made the hurt spread up to fill my chest.

The day Mom left, she looked straight at me to make sure I was listening. *"If anything happens that scares or worries you, I want you to go to your Aunt Bryn."* She used her toughest voice, and she grabbed a piece of junk mail from the pile on the floor, scribbled out the address, and stuffed it into my backpack. *"Promise me. Promise."* She stared hard at me, the Mom stare of death that meant she was serious.

So, I promised.

And I'd spent the past week waiting and worrying.

"So, why did your mom tell you to come here?"

She wasn't going to drop it. "I don't *know* why. But she did." It came out snarly, and I waited for Bryn to get pissed, but no.

Bryn glanced at the clock on the microwave. "It's too late tonight, but tomorrow we'll make some more phone calls, see what we can learn. If we can't figure anything out, we'll go to the police and get them to help. Sound like a plan?"

I didn't like the idea of going to the cops, but at least she wasn't talking about social services yet, so I nodded.

Bryn got up and came over to me. "Try not to worry. I'm sure your mom is okay."

She gave me a quick hug, but it wasn't anything like Mom's hugs. Mom's hugs were so fierce on my ribs it made it hard to breathe, and they smelled nice like the flowers in her perfume. This ordinary hug hardly felt like a hug at all, and it just smelled like plain old tomato sauce.

CHAPTER THREE

Bryn

A restless night left me tired and frazzled. I was frustrated, I was worried, and most of all I was angry. Not an ordinary who-dinged-my-truck anger; this was hot, murderous anger, deep-rooted anger, the kind of anger that sizzled in my head and made my hands twitch. Josh's arrival had reignited the Del-Sawyer inferno I thought I had damped down to cold ashes, and I wasn't feeling very rational. Normally, I would calm down by heading for the nearest lake with my kayak to let a quiet hour of paddling work its magic, but instead I had to stay here at home and decide what to do about Josh.

Josh, the personification of Sawyer's bitter betrayal.

Josh, the irritant forcing me into action.

Josh, the teenager caught in the middle, who hadn't meant to destroy my precarious balance. He was alone. He was family. I needed to help if I could.

The sun was barely up, but I rolled out of bed, pulled on a shirt and jeans, and checked on my nephew in the living room. I had settled him on the couch with a quilt and a pillow, but he had moved to the floor in the night and was sound asleep with one arm wrapped tight around Tellico's fuzzy chest. His face was smooth, all tension and worry gone, and in that moment he looked deeply vulnerable. An unexpected sympathy forced my frustration back into its cage.

I'd responded that way to Del when she was a baby—she'd been helpless and needy, a beautiful doll who smiled and cooed whenever I held her. I would have done anything to please her and even more to protect her. But that was a long time back. Now, if Del herself had been on my doorstep asking for help, I would have slammed the door and thrown the deadbolt.

Even though she'd disappeared, it was hard for me to get seriously worried. It had only been a week, and her track record of reckless decisions made it likely she was simply off partying somewhere. The real question at the moment wasn't whether I believed she was in trouble; it was how much I was willing to invest in her son. *Their* son.

I headed to the kitchen for my first mug of hot tea. I tried to be quiet, but Josh wandered in behind me, sleepy-eyed and yawning.

"Want some tea?"

He looked appalled, as if I'd offered something toxic. "A Coke? Coffee?"

I shouldn't have been surprised. Del had never been a poster child for healthy choices. "I'm sorry, I don't have any soda. I think I've got some coffee somewhere." I rooted around in the cupboard for my ancient jar of instant and stirred up a rather murky-looking cup.

He took a tentative swallow, made a face, and pushed the cup aside. "What's for breakfast?"

I'd heard that teenage boys were bottomless pits. Fruit and yogurt weren't going to cut it. "How about some eggs and toast?"

"Sure." He glanced around the kitchen, where I'm sure he noticed there was zero evidence of food in progress .

At the moment, I couldn't do anything about finding his mother, but at least I could tackle breakfast. "Come on. We'll get the eggs."

I grabbed an empty basket, and Josh followed me out the door with quick steps and a surprised expression. Tellico bounced along the path ahead of us, snuffling for evidence of any rabbits that had passed by overnight.

Cumulus clouds drifted across a Crayola-blue sky, shifting the light into a moving patchwork at our feet, but Josh didn't seem to notice the day's beauty. A mourning dove gave its distinctive coo, and he jumped and looked around for the source, not even noticing the bird on a nearby stump. I wasn't sure where he and Del had been living, but it must not have included much time away from the city.

Mornings were when I most enjoyed being alone, and the presence of a clueless teenager left me uncertain how to act. My normal routine was to check the creek before going to the barn. Who knows? Maybe he'd learn something. "Come this way. I want to show you something before we go for the eggs."

I veered right, away from the barn path, and paused under the ancient black gum tree to listen. "Hear it? That soft humming?" It hadn't yet warmed enough to lure the workers out, and the sound was the hum of pent-up energy.

Josh's forehead crinkled, and he peered into the branches, looking for the source. "What is it?"

"Bees. This old tree is hollow, and they've been busy in the orchard. I haven't figured out a way to get the honey without breaking my neck or destroying the tree, but I haven't given up yet."

Josh pulled his arms in tight as if protecting himself from a possible sting.

"It's okay. They won't attack if we leave them alone. Come on."

I led the rest of the way down the path to Walker's Creek. The water was high from heavy spring rains, and it tumbled noisily over and around the large granite boulders that dotted the streambed.

Josh kicked at a stone and looked downstream. "I saw your boat on your truck. Can you take it out here?"

"This creek is too shallow to paddle. In about a half mile, it joins the Tellico River, and that's big enough for the kayak." Josh glanced at Tellico, and I nodded. "I found him as a puppy along its banks a few years ago, half starved and covered in mud. It's how he got his name."

Josh took a few pictures of the creek with his ever-present cell phone. "My mom told me once that my dad used to kayak sometimes."

Sawyer had kayaked more than "sometimes." Sawyer was world class, had lived for the water. He was the one who taught me to love paddling, and in our four years together, we'd camped our way up and down the Appalachians, going wherever there was good whitewater.

"Life is not a spectator sport." He'd lived the motto, repeating it a thousand times, urging me to take risks and try new things. But I'd learned the hard way that life was far safer on the sidelines.

I swallowed the caustic memories and tried to keep any bitterness out of my voice. "Yes. He was one of the best paddlers I've known."

Josh whirled to face me, one hand lifting in my direction as if asking for more. "You knew my dad?"

I'd blown that one. If Josh hadn't known I existed, of course he wouldn't know the rest. Now that I'd opened that doorway, I was stuck. "I knew him."

"How did you meet him? What was he like?"

"We met in college. He was nice. You remind me of him." Josh reminded me of the Sawyer I'd loved. Not the Sawyer who haunted me now.

I talked fast to avoid further questions. "I wanted to show you this creek because it's fine to come down here whenever you want, but don't get in the water." Josh frowned, not liking my change of subject, but he let me get away with it. "The current is faster than it looks, and once you get farther downhill, you hit whitewater. There's a small waterfall where you could get hurt."

Whitewater. Yet another thing Del had stolen from me. The weekend after I learned about her and Sawyer, still reeling from their deception, I'd gone on a whitewater trip with friends. Sawyer and I had planned to go together, and his absence was a disturbing presence every minute of the day.

I made mistakes. Read the river wrong. Flipped, got trapped, nearly drowned.

My companions had dragged me to safety, but there had been a black moment when drowning felt right.

The two events—the crushing weight of the broken engagement and the killing pressure of water against my chest—became so tangled in my head I couldn't think of one without getting stuck in the other. For the past fourteen years, I'd paddled my kayak only on the calm surfaces of the local lakes, leaving the whitewater thrills to those who didn't understand the risks.

I'd let my silence go on too long, and Josh opened his mouth as if he was determined to ask more about his father. I cut him off. "Here. Let me show you something else." I led him upstream to where a muddy patch gave easy access to the water. "Animals like to come here to drink. There are almost always new tracks in the morning. Let's see what we can find."

That distracted him, at least for the moment. I pointed out several sets of deer tracks and a jumble of marks where a raccoon and her babies had washed their dinner. A fox had wandered by and so had a pair of rabbits. Josh picked up on the details fast, and when he found more deer tracks on his own, he gave me a triumphant grin.

"There's a bobcat around here too," I said. "I've seen his tracks for months, but I haven't spotted him. They tend to be pretty solitary."

Josh looked around him, wide-eyed, then scanned the nearby low-hanging tree branches as if he expected to find a cat lurking there, ready to pounce. "A real bobcat? You're making that up, right?"

"Don't worry. They only go after small animals." Like me, they preferred to avoid people, and like me, they were damn good at it.

Josh gave another nervous glance around him. It was nice to have someone to show this stuff to, even if his arrival had screwed up my day. But between bees and bobcats, I wasn't making him very comfortable.

We walked back to the barn without any further mention of Sawyer. I let the chickens out of the coop and propped open the gate to their pen.

"Won't they run away?" Josh stepped out of their path, and the flock bustled out and headed toward the orchard, where they did a great job of catching bugs.

"No, they forage, but they don't go far."

As usual, Annabelle, my geriatric Rhode Island Red, hunkered down in a sunny spot just outside the fence instead of scurrying off with the others. I went over and scratched her back, my fingers sliding easily over her smooth feathers.

Josh ran a cautious finger along her neck. "Why doesn't she go with the rest?"

"She's my oldest, and she sticks close to home nowadays. She's the only one left from my first year of raising hatchlings, when I gave them all names starting with *A*. Her name is Annabelle. This year's youngsters are all *H*'s: Hilda, Henrietta, Helen, and Hermione."

"I didn't know chickens liked being petted."

"Don't tell the other chickens, but Annabelle is my favorite. She loves people."

I gave her a final scratch, and she ruffled her feathers. "Come on, I'll show you how to collect eggs."

We gathered more than a dozen from the nest boxes, and Josh peppered me with questions along the way: Aren't there chicks inside? Doesn't it make the chickens mad to take them? Are they safe to eat? At least it seemed to sidetrack him from thoughts of his missing mother and long-dead father.

I turned Kudzu out to graze. "I'll keep Thistle in for a few days with her babies. Do you want to feed her?"

"Okay." Josh headed for the open bale of hay and tossed in enough for five goats.

I had to laugh. "You sure you gave her enough?"

Josh turned pink, scuffed his toe through the dirt, and patted each of the kids in turn. "She's eating for three, right?"

"Good point. Come on. Let's go fix that breakfast."

We walked toward the house, but the familiar rumble of Landon's truck coming up the driveway slowed my steps. It had been four weeks since I'd seen him. I missed our usual visits, but I wasn't at all sure what to expect. No one liked rejection, and he had every right to be pissed. At best, this meeting would be awkward, but maybe having Josh there would keep things civil. "Hang on a minute."

Josh gave me a questioning glance and stopped beside me. I couldn't decide whether the flutter in my belly was apprehension or excitement.

Landon parked in the same spot he always did, and got out.

"Morning." His cautious voice matched his hesitant smile. I guess I'd given him plenty of reasons to doubt his reception, but maybe his presence was a step toward at least a baseline reconciliation.

"Hi." It was all I could manage.

Landon gave Josh a curious look, went to the back of his truck, and lifted out the ice chest I'd loaned him a year earlier. "Thought you might be needing this."

He knew damn well I didn't need that ice chest—he was only looking for an excuse to test the waters. Well, fair enough. We couldn't go forever without speaking.

"Thanks." The word came out sounding reasonably sincere, and I gave myself credit for good acting.

Landon headed for the back door without another glance in my direction. Josh and I followed him inside, and he placed the chest in the pantry.

He turned to Josh and reached out for a handshake. "Hi. I'm Landon Mitchell. I live on the farm next door."

Josh looked surprised, as if he wasn't used to being treated as an adult, but he shook Landon's hand. "I'm Josh, Bryn's nephew."

"Nephew?" Landon gave me a quick "what's up?" look. One late night, after far too much merlot, I'd told him the whole saga of Del and Sawyer, so he knew I made no claim to being an aunt.

He composed his face and turned back to Josh. "Good to meet you. It's great you can visit with your aunt. Where are you from?"

And that's all it took to draw Josh in. He started explaining his situation in detail, every word tinged with his worry about his mom, the worry I couldn't yet embrace. Landon focused on Josh to the exclusion of all else, as if what he was hearing could fundamentally change his world. When I was on the receiving end of those intense looks, I always ended up sharing more than I intended.

I scrambled eggs and toasted half a loaf of bread under the broiler. Those two settled at the kitchen table and worked their way through Del's disappearance, Josh's Uber saga, and the successful delivery of the twin goats. Josh's description of the delivery emphasized the grosser aspects of the process, but I was impressed by the details he'd noticed.

I kept glancing their way while I cooked. It wasn't often that I watched Landon from the sidelines, out of the direct beam of his personality. Tall, tanned, and athletic, he looked like the farmer he was, but many who'd known him for years in that role didn't realize he was also a master woodworker—a true artist.

The furniture he crafted sold in galleries for premium prices, and I always felt I should apologize for my houseful of yard-sale rescues. He'd given me a beautiful walnut bowl inlaid with tiny flecks of turquoise that I used for my apples. It sat center stage on the counter, a glowing contrast to the rest of my well-worn kitchen equipment, and I thought of him every time I saw it.

He was even more of a homebody than I was, and avoided travel as if it was contaminated. He preferred to read about the rest of the world instead of exploring it, focusing instead on his livestock and his wood creations, and that was an attitude I had no problem understanding. I wasn't much different—home was the space I could control.

I'd lost plenty of sleep since I'd met Landon, indulging in carnal imaginings while being careful not to act on them. The casual relationships I drifted in and out of never matched the intensity of what I suspected Landon had to offer, and the temptation to make something happen between us was a constant pull. But Sawyer had taught me too much about heartbreak, and I kept my relationship with Landon firmly platonic.

Four weeks earlier, Landon had rocked our uncomplicated friendship and possibly damaged it beyond recovery.

He spoke the words that tore me up right here in this kitchen, a confession that came out of nowhere. I thought he'd come by just to say hello, and I was happy when he stayed to help stack hay. We came in for a drink. He gave me a searching look and then calmly said, "I've fallen in love with you."

"What?" I momentarily lost my balance and cracked my hip hard on the edge of the counter. Not the most romantic response I could have given, but he'd caught me off guard. I'd worked hard to convince myself such a thing was out of bounds, and now the blunt option of romance had my head spinning.

"I've fallen in love with you, and I want to be more than friends." This time, he said it with more determination. He came closer. Much closer. He took my hand.

His touch was an electric shock. A sexual promise that hit every nerve ending.

He leaned in for a kiss, and I met him halfway, my body overruling my brain. The next few electrified minutes proved my imagination was only a feeble imitation of reality. It was a serious kiss. A promise, not a ploy. That kiss galvanized every fiber and every cell, a disorienting jolt I hadn't felt in years.

Was it two minutes? Five? He pulled back at last. I was so dizzy, his arm around my waist was the only thing that kept me from falling.

"We'd be great together, Bryn." Landon ran his thumb along the line of my jaw and gave me a look that should have melted all hesitations. "And I'm not talking about farm chores."

Part of me wanted to grab hold of him and never let go. Ravish him on the kitchen floor like a scene from some low-budget movie. I could see what our lives could be like together. Friends. Lovers. True partners.

But instead of feeling a rush of joy, my chest tightened. I couldn't breathe. Thoughts of Sawyer's betrayal swelled fast, and a wave of sheer panic took me out. I slipped out of Landon's arms, my lips still tingling. I gave him my answer. *No.*

I had hoped we could turn back the clock and stay friends, layering some sort of pretend-it-didn't-happen veneer over the whole brief encounter. But Landon quit calling and stopped coming by. I hadn't realized how empty my life would feel without him until he was gone.

Now, here he was at my table, patiently answering Josh's questions about goats. Acting like nothing was wrong.

Good. We were moving on. Maybe we really could go back to the way things used to be.

I served breakfast, pouring coffee for Josh and tea for Landon and me. The goat discussion wrapped up, Josh started wolfing down food, and Landon pulled the conversation back to the matter at hand. "So, Josh says you're going to phone around to see if anyone knows about your sister, and then go talk to the police. That's the plan?"

I slid the honey his way. He drank his tea so syrupy it could almost hold a spoon upright. "It seems like the best approach."

"I hope your sister's okay. I know you must be worried."

I glanced at Josh and chose my words with care. "There's probably a simple explanation—a damaged cell phone or a broken-down car." Or she was drunk or stoned or holed up with a new lover. Josh was worried, so I needed to follow up, but this was probably a whole lot of fuss about nothing.

Landon opened his mouth as if to discuss it further, but he, too, gave Josh a glance and caught himself. "Hopefully, you'll get some answers soon." He reached for the platter of scrambled eggs at the same moment I did, and our hands brushed against each other.

A surge of heat caught me unawares, and I pushed the plate in his direction, unexpectedly flustered. Too many temptations, that was for damn sure. So much for a return to the old low-key friendship. Josh raised his eyebrows and looked back and forth between Landon and me with a knowing smirk.

I gave him a don't-even-go-there glare. "We'll start calling as soon as we're done here."

We ate. Still flustered, I put too much pepper on my eggs, and the inside of my mouth heated up to match my blush.

As soon as Landon was done, he got to his feet. "Time for me to get back to work." He carried his plate and silverware to the sink and loaded them into the dishwasher, as at home in my kitchen as he was in his own. "Thanks for breakfast. Nice meeting you, Josh. Hope to see you again while you're here."

Josh grinned. "I'm sure Aunt Bryn would like that."

I knew there was some reason I'd never wanted kids.

"Thanks for bringing back the ice chest." I, too, could be pointlessly polite.

Landon lifted a hand in farewell, gave Tellico a pat, and headed out, his truck rumbling its way down the driveway. I watched him leave with mixed emotions, wanting my space but wanting him to stay, wanting the benefits of a relationship but without the heart-wrenching complications. It was easy for me to criticize Del's life—the way she dumped her son and disappeared without a word—but in moments like this, I had to wonder whether the path I was choosing was equally foolish and doomed to failure.

CHAPTER FOUR

Bryn

With Landon gone, Josh and I took care of the rest of the dishes and started toward my office to get down to business. But Tellico stopped, looked toward the front of the house, and barked before we got there. I stepped to the window, wondering if perhaps Landon had forgotten something.

But it wasn't his truck returning. A black sedan bounced its way along the final stretch of driveway and came to a halt. Maybe this had something to do with Del? I could usually go weeks without visitors, but in the past two days my homestead had turned into a major crossroads.

The man who climbed out of the car wasn't familiar. Mid-thirties, salon haircut, clean-shaven. He was dressed for the city in slacks, a carefully tailored dark jacket, and polished dress shoes. He looked wildly out of place on my homestead, but he surveyed his surroundings with a take-charge air of confidence, as if he belonged.

I opened the front door and stepped onto the porch in my sock-clad feet. "Can I help you?" Tellico stood beside me, a deep rumbling growl sending a clear warning.

Josh came out and stopped a little behind me. "Oh no." His whisper whipped me around—this stranger's visit must indeed have something to with Del—but Josh shook his head and studied the floorboards. The dismay on his face didn't offer much reassurance.

The man gave me a piercing inspection, raised one eyebrow at the dog, and then focused his attention on Josh. He gave a small nod, as if checking off an item on an invisible checklist. Tellico snarled when the stranger was about five feet from the porch steps, and the man stopped. The dog usually had good instincts. I was inclined to agree with his distrust.

The man smiled in a way that was so polite and perfectly executed, it looked as if he had practiced in front of a mirror. "Hello, Bryn. It's been awhile, hasn't it? I'm looking for Del." He gave Josh an equally fake-looking grin. "Hi, Josh. Where's your mother?"

I looked harder, but I would have sworn I'd never seen this guy before. Josh straightened and faced the man down, but he was careful to stay two steps behind me. "I don't know where she is. We're trying to find her." He spoke slowly, as if reluctant to share even that much, and his voice had a faint tremor.

The man's studied expression slipped for an instant, giving me a flashing glimpse of anger that disappeared as soon as I saw it. "I didn't come all this way to listen to bullshit."

My apprehension ramped up fast, but I wasn't about to let him harass a kid. I put on my tough-girl face. "Who are you? Why do you want Del?"

The man's lips tightened, and he shook his head in mock dismay. "You don't remember me? I would have thought that night would be etched in in your memory." He pointed his index finger at me with his thumb raised, an imitation gun, and he slouched forward into a stoop-shouldered stance. *Try and call the cops and I'll shoot.*"

Carl. Carl Griffith. The memory came roaring back, so vivid that a wave of nausea rolled through me. *Carl.* I could see the resemblance now. The scuttling, perpetually stoned degenerate I remembered was still there, thinly disguised now by the new clothes, the new car, the new attitude. Carl had gone to high school with Del and me. Hanging out with him was one of Del's worst mistakes. The last time I'd seen him was fifteen years earlier, and it was a real gun in his hand then, a gun he pointed at Sawyer when he spoke those words.

My attitude toward Carl's arrival took an abrupt U-turn. This wasn't some arrogant stranger looking for Del for benevolent reasons; this was a lethal predator looking for prey. The Carl Griffith I'd known couldn't even spell the word *benevolent*, much less understand its meaning.

Much of what I knew about Carl was more rumor than fact. The kid who'd taunted him for his outdated shoes junior year had his car windshield beaten in with a baseball bat. The girl who turned him down for prom never returned to school, and people reported seeing her in town on crutches. Teachers stepped aside to avoid him; burly football players turned tail and hurried away. Whenever something violent happened, Carl was there on the periphery, watching. He was the sort who was rarely accused but always suspected.

Now, it was me he was staring at.

I kept my eyes fixed on Carl but reached back to touch Josh, double-checking that he was still safely behind me. "Carl. You've changed." Bullshit. Evil like that never changed.

He resumed his confident persona and gave a self-satisfied sneer. "I've moved up, but I see you haven't." He looked around at my farm with the sort of expression I'd direct at a putrid land-fill. "Living in a dump. I always knew you'd go nowhere."

I resisted the urge to snap back. Messing with Carl was like nudging a boulder onto a slope already poised for avalanche—the effect was far out of proportion to the action. "Why are you looking for Del?"

His forehead wrinkled as if he was considering possible answers. "She and I have a business arrangement. She took something of mine. I want it back." He looked at Josh. "You're her kid. You have to know where she is. Tell me."

"I don't . . ." Josh started, but I shook my head, and his voice faded to a stop.

I'd believed Del's disappearance was only her normal gar-den-variety irresponsibility, but if it involved Carl, I had to take it more seriously. And I needed to try to keep Josh out of the direct path of Carl's anger.

I took a step forward to the very edge of the porch, squared my shoulders, and sharpened my tone, faking a confidence I didn't feel. "Del's not here. I haven't seen her in years, and Josh already told you he doesn't know anything." There was no way I was going to ask what Del had taken. I didn't want to get involved in this mess. But part of me knew it was already too late. "If we hear from her, we can pass on a message."

Carl's fixed smile disappeared, and his eyes narrowed. "Tell her to call me. If I don't hear from her in the next week . . ." He gestured around him, a sweeping arm that encompassed my cabin and barn. My homestead. My life. "You've got, what, a volunteer fire department out here? How long does it take them to respond? An hour? More? Old wood buildings. Animals. A kid. You should be careful. Very careful."

He spoke the words without any bravado, as if they were a statement of simple fact and not a bone-chilling threat.

And then he just stood there, looking at me, but his calmness made the warning far more intimidating than it would have been if he'd screamed it in rage. From a stranger, the threat would have been concerning. From Carl, it sparked a deep-seated fear. I had no doubt he meant it. No doubt at all.

He gave another little check-box nod. Message sent. Message received.

I struggled to find my voice. "You can't threaten us that way."

He laughed. It was another link to the Carl I recalled from years back—a scraping laugh that sounded too much like fingernails on a chalkboard. "Who's going to stop me? Del jumps when I tell her to. Even your precious Sawyer believed me and did what I wanted when I pushed the right button and pointed out what mattered to him. He thought he was so holier-than-thou, but I showed him."

He wasn't talking about something that happened when Sawyer and I were together—I would have known. This must have happened later. "What the hell are you talking about? You mean you threatened to hurt Del and Josh to get Sawyer to do something?"

His fake smile came back. "Well, what really brought him in line was my promise to hurt *you*."

What the hell? In the end, Sawyer only viewed me as a piece of insignificant history. He wouldn't have lifted a finger to protect me.

Carl looked pleased at my confusion. "One week. Seven days. The only reason I'm giving you that much time to find Del is because we're such old friends." He sneered and turned toward his car, but instead of getting in, he circled around the far side of my truck, where I couldn't see him.

I couldn't chase him without shoes. I held the door open for Josh. "Get in." He did as I asked, but he was moving like a machine, stiff and on autopilot. His bleak face belonged to someone years older. "Watch him out the front window." I dragged Tellico in with us, closed and locked the door.

I raced through the kitchen, bolted the back door, grabbed my boots and a six-inch kitchen knife. Landon was always telling me I needed a gun, but until that moment, the suggestion had felt overly dramatic. I was no expert with a knife, but I'd use it if forced to.

I ran back to Josh. "How do you know Carl?"

Josh stayed glued to the window. "Mom used to date him. Not anymore, but he still comes around." His voice was even, but his face was colorless.

There was a hell of a lot more going on here than an ex-boyfriend, and if Del was still foolish enough to date such a creep, there was no telling what kind of trouble she'd gotten herself into. My hopes that she was just somewhere partying shriveled up and turned to dust.

"See him yet?"

"No." Josh stared at the knife in my hand, the blade glittering in the sunlight that streamed through the front window. "He was heading for the barn, but I can't see it from here."

Thistle and her babies were locked in their pen, unable to run.

I was stuffing my feet into my boots and tying the laces, my fear making me fumble the simple task.

"Wait. There he is." Josh pointed. "He's getting back in his car."

The engine roared to life and tires crunched on gravel. I gripped the knife hard, unlocked the front door, and stepped out. "Stay here. Lock the door behind me. I need to check the goats." Josh nodded, so tense it was more of a jerk than a nod. I sprinted for the barn. Tellico ran at my side.

The goat pen was still latched tight, and Thistle munched calmly on her mountain of hay. The twins looked up at my hasty arrival and wandered my way to investigate. No problem here. Carl must have just been looking around, snooping where he didn't belong, but not out for damage.

I turned to head back to the house, and my eyes fell on a lump on the ground in front of the open gate to the chicken pen. A lump that shouldn't be there. A lump with dark red feathers.

Annabelle. My favorite. The chicken who sat quietly when anyone came up to her, waiting for a friendly back scratch. I walked toward her with reluctant steps, not wanting to know.

Her neck had been twisted into an impossible angle, and her lifeless body lay in a discarded heap.

CHAPTER FIVE

Josh

I thought Bryn was only checking the barn, but I waited and waited, and she didn't show and she didn't show. I stayed by the window, picturing that big knife in her hand, hearing Carl's snarling words and watching for him to come back, my mouth tasting like metal. But nobody came, and the front yard stayed quiet.

I worried, wondering if I should go look for Bryn, but finally she and Tellico appeared, coming from the direction of the barn. Bryn was walking slowly, and she still had that knife ready. Her hands were dirty, and her eyes were red like she'd been crying.

I unlocked the door. "Is everything okay? Are the goats alright? What did Carl do?" Something bad enough to make her cry. I hated it when Mom cried, and Bryn's tears were just as bad.

"The goats are fine." She stopped, cleared her throat, and swiped at her cheeks with the back of her hand, leaving long dark smudges that made her look even sadder.

"What happened? He's looking for Mom." If I'd known Carl was after her, I would have freaked the first day she was late coming home. "You need to tell me."

Bryn's lips tightened, thin and pale, like maybe she was too upset to say anything, but then she gave a big swallow. "He killed Annabelle. I buried her out behind the barn."

The red chicken I'd petted that morning. A sick feeling swirled through my insides.

I'd killed about a zillion people in my games, but I'd never touched an animal that was alive and breathing and then had it die. A chicken with a name, a chicken who liked to sit in the sun and have her back scratched, Dead? It didn't feel real.

Bryn locked the front door and headed to the kitchen. I followed. She washed her hands, then stood, twisting a towel, and stared out the window. "Your mom was dating Carl? They used to hang out long ago, but I thought she got her act together and quit seeing him."

"They dated maybe a year ago. It lasted about four months, then he broke up with her. He used to try and act like my buddy, clapping me on the back, slipping me five-dollar bills, asking *'Josh, how you doing?'* in a fake-happy sort of voice. He gave me the creeps."

He'd been okay at first, with a better haircut and better car and better clothes than most of the guys Mom knew. A wave of guilt rose into my chest, and I slammed it back down. I'd been happy when they started going out. I'd told Mom he might help us out.

But once Carl was around more, I could tell I couldn't trust him. He was always looking for an angle, like the guys at school who would punch you in the back or slam your locker door on your fingers if you didn't watch out every minute. He hung out with a bunch of scary guys—the sort with scars and tattoos and muscles. The sort with guns tucked into the small of their backs, bulging their T-shirts like oddly shaped tumors. Friends at school told me stories about what happened to people Carl didn't like—broken fingers, missing teeth, banged-up heads. And fires. Lots of fires.

"You said your mom kept seeing him after they broke up?"

"Yeah, he kept coming by." I wasn't going to tell Bryn, but he came by most often when Mom was low on pills. Which didn't make things too hard to figure out. "She acted upset before she disappeared. Do you think Carl was the reason?"

"The fact he showed up all the way out here makes me wonder. But how did he know where you were? Did you tell anyone where you were going?"

"No. I just left. I didn't even . . ." Oh. Oh no. This time the guilt flooded in fast, swamping me so hard I had to lean against the wall. "I posted pictures."

"Pictures of here?"

"Yeah. And of the trip."

Bryn set the towel down. "Come show me."

We went into her office, and I pulled up my Instagram account on her computer. Bryn clicked through my posts. I hadn't marked location on them, but she ran reverse image searches on a few of the photos.

She didn't say anything, but she didn't have to—I could see how easy I'd made it. The searches identified not only the city but in most cases also the street and the specific address of whatever I'd taken.

There were pictures I'd posted from Memphis, then Nashville, then Chattanooga. Pictures I snapped from the car or while I waited for my next ride. I'd taken an I-finally-made-it picture of Bryn's mailbox when I got dropped here, and a snap of Bryn's kayak that showed her truck and its license plate. It wouldn't take anyone long to put it all together. Heck, I could have done it myself with a little time.

"Marcus and I always post stuff. I didn't think it would matter." Carl finding Bryn was my fault. What happened to Annabelle was my fault. I was supposed to be helping, but instead I was just screwing up. I picked up a pen from Bryn's desk, drew a circle on the back of my hand, and colored it in, pushing down hard.

Bryn's lips tightened up skinny. "I don't know much about Instagram, but anyone who's a follower of your account can see all this, right?"

"Sure." They were always hounding us at school about social media privacy, but I never thought about something like this. I set down the pen and pulled up my list of Instagram followers, but it wasn't much help. Most were friends from school, but some were avatar pictures with made-up names like *Superdog* or *Mega15*. They could have been anyone. One of them could have been Carl.

"No more pictures online, okay? Not until we know what the hell your mom has gotten herself into."

She didn't seem mad at me, but I was mad at myself. Carl had killed Annabelle. He'd threatened to burn down Bryn's farm. Bryn had to hate me. She must just be good at hiding it. "No more. I promise."

I couldn't decide how much I should tell her. About Carl. About Mom. About her pills. I didn't want to get Mom in trouble, and I didn't want Bryn to change her mind about helping, but I also didn't want Carl to hurt anyone. Or burn anything down.

My head hurt with the choices, but I decided to wait. I could tell later if I had to, but I couldn't unsay the words once I let them escape. She'd only been my aunt for less than a day.

Bryn gave my shoulder a squeeze. "You can keep taking pictures—just don't share them with the world." She closed the Instagram screen.

Mom would have yelled. Bryn didn't, but that could change any minute. I took the chance anyway and asked about what was bugging me. "What did Carl mean when he talked about a gun and said *'Don't call the cops'*? And why did he say he made Dad do what he wanted?"

Now it was her turn to decide what to tell, and from the brick-wall look on her face, I figured I wasn't going to get much. "I don't know what he meant about Sawyer. And the rest . . . the part about the gun . . . the rest is complicated. I'll tell you about it later. Let's make those phone calls about your mom." She said the last bit like an order.

"Okay." It wasn't okay, and I wasn't going to let it drop. I figured my chances were better if I let her calm down.

I got why she was upset. I kept thinking about that chicken too. I was glad I hadn't seen her dead. Had he stabbed her with a knife? Had there been a lot of blood? I picked up my phone to find a game but set it down again. A game where I shot cartoon characters seemed sort of pointless.

Bryn pulled out her phone and called Kroger first when I gave her the number. She put Bill, Mom's manager, on speaker and asked if he knew anything about Mom.

"Do I know where she is? Hell no." He wasn't holding back—his voice was seriously pissed off, and he was yelling over the noise of shopping carts rattling in the background. "I can tell you where she isn't, and that's here working her shift. If you find her, tell her she can look for another job. And tell her not to even dream of using me for a reference." He clicked the phone off without waiting for Bryn to say anything else.

Bryn gave me a glance like she was sorry I'd heard it. But it was what I'd expected.

She ran her fingers through her hair, pulled a pen and one of her pads of paper over. "What about friends? Work friends, neighborhood friends, drinking buddies?" She paused a little before saying *drinking buddies*, like maybe I'd take it wrong, and I tried not to laugh. She had no clue.

I started giving her names, one at a time, along with the phone number. She wrote them down and called them. After the first three calls—Patsy, Phil, and Wayne, two "I-don't-know-where-she-is" answers and one voice-mail message—she gave me a puzzled look. "How do you know all these phone numbers?"

I hadn't been looking them up. "Mom made a list of people so I could find her if I needed to."

"Yeah, but you don't have the list with you."

I studied the cover of the Python manual sitting out on her desk. I couldn't think of a reason not to tell her and admitting this made me feel less guilty about hiding the rest. "It's kind of weird. I look at something. I tell my head to save a picture. Then I can take the picture out again later when I want to."

"A photographic memory?" It sounded like she didn't believe me.

I nodded. "You have that in-case-of-emergency phone list over there." I pointed. "I looked at it last night. The third name is John Miller, CPA." I gave her the phone number. "The last name is Melanie Richards." I gave her that number too.

She walked over to the list to check, but I already knew I was right. At school, I had to be careful. I never raised my hand, never acted like I knew the answer. The way this worked was too strange. Too different. I didn't like people to know.

Bryn checked the list, and while she was up, she also checked out the window, looking down the driveway as if she was still thinking about Carl, her teeth closed tight and her face sad and worried. She came back without saying anything, and we kept making calls to everyone I could think of.

At one point, my cell phone dinged, and I lunged for it—maybe Mom?—but it was only a text from Marcus, asking how long I was going to be away because he wanted me to come over.

I loved the days when I went to Marcus's house. His dad let us use the big plasma screen in their family room for games, and his mom baked cookies when I was there and fussed around with lemonade. Their house always smelled like something spicy, and when I stayed over for dinner, we ate at a table. With napkins. And some of the silverware, beside the plate, we didn't even need. My visits always felt like stepping into one of my books, where everything was shiny and new, and you had to pay attention to learn the rules of a different world.

But I was stuck here and couldn't go. My thumbs hovered over the screen, uncertain what to type. Mountains. Goats. Carl. A dead chicken. This was a book of its own, but not one where things were shiny. I finally replied to the text. *Sorry, I have to help find my mom. Don't know when I'll be back.*

Marcus would understand. He had been over at our place one Friday night when Mom came home late with her hand sliced up from broken glass. She'd been drinking and acted like she didn't even notice the cut, but there was blood all over her sleeve and dripping onto her leggings. Marcus looked scared, but he helped me get her cleaned up and bandaged, the two of us getting her to bed and tucking her in, making sure an empty bucket was on the floor close by her head.

"Does this happen all the time?" he'd asked, and the disbelieving way he said it made me worry he'd quit being my friend. But he didn't disappear, and it was kind of nice someone knew the way things were. He'd get it that I needed to find Mom.

I went back to helping Bryn, and by the time we finished, her list went down the whole page. No one knew a thing about Mom.

"Even people who saw her the day before she left don't know anything." Bryn slouched in her chair and flipped her pen back and forth. "We left a bunch of messages, but I'm not convinced anything will come of them."

She did the table-drumming thing, then sat up straight with her shoulders back, like she was a soldier ready for inspection. She frowned, lifted her phone, and punched a number that was already programmed, not one I gave her.

I watched out of the corner of my eye, because she was so tense she wasn't even breathing. It wasn't until the sound of a voice-mail message came from the phone that she relaxed. "Hi, Mom, it's Bryn."

She'd called Grandma, which was sort of stupid, because Grandma didn't know anything about Mom. But maybe Bryn didn't know that.

She went on with her message. "Josh showed up here at my place . . . your grandson, Josh . . . and we're trying to find Del. Could you call me back as soon as you get this? You may be able to help."

She clicked off the call and stood up like she was glad to be done. "Come on. Now we go talk to the cops."

"Mom won't be happy about that." She always drove the speed limit, crossed the street at crosswalks, turned the other way if a police car drove by. She would freak if she knew we were going to the cops about her on purpose.

"Any particular reason not to? If nothing else, I want to report Carl and his threats."

There it was. Another chance to tell her more. Instead, I changed the subject. "Can we get some lunch in town?"

Bryn gave me a hard look, and I could tell she noticed I'd dodged the question. I waited for her to push back, but she let it slide. "Absolutely. Whatever you want. Let me grab my wallet."

She went to get her stuff, and I sat and patted Tellico. For an unknown aunt, she was pretty nice, but she was also pretty easy to fool. Double points for me, which should have been a good thing, but I couldn't make myself celebrate. All I kept thinking about was Annabelle sitting out there in the sun, happy and alive, never suspecting a thing.

CHAPTER SIX

Bryn

How dare this total creep come to my home, to the farm I'd built up for the past ten years, and threaten me? How dare he kill Annabelle?

This was Del's fault, all of it, and now I had yet another accusation to add to her account. I'd spent plenty of time over the years rehearsing everything I would say to her if I ever got the chance, and I'd pictured dozens of outlandish ways to punish her. I would shave her head. I would shred her favorite clothing. I would design a billboard that listed her cruelties. To hell with a scarlet letter—dousing her with scarlet paint was more like it.

But at the moment, Del was far beyond my reach, and Carl was all too real. He was the priority. For Josh's sake, I needed to find Del. For my sake, I needed to do it fast and recover whatever it was Carl searched for. I wasn't convinced the police could help, but it was foolish not to give them a try.

What would Landon say if he knew about Carl? I thought about calling, letting him know what Carl had done. But maybe that was too much pressure to put on a frayed and fragile friendship. He'd worry. I'd tell him not to. We'd end up arguing.

No point in calling. It was the right decision, but a small stab of disappointment highlighted how nice it would be not to always fly solo.

Time to get moving. Tellico leaped to his feet as soon as I picked up the truck keys. "Sorry boy, you have to stay here."

Josh gave the dog a pat, obviously reluctant to leave him behind. That dog was just what Josh needed. After growing up without pets, I was astonished to discover how much Tellico added to my life. He was the ideal listener, patient and never critical, and he was always delighted to see anyone who was willing to play.

"We'll be back soon."

Josh climbed into the passenger seat and immediately ran his hand over the carved wooden glove compartment panel, strikingly out of place in my battered truck. "Whoa. Where'd you get this?"

"Landon made it. Beautiful, isn't it?" I'd bought my truck used, and when I got it, the glove box was mangled—the panel that should have opened was badly dented and frozen in place. When Landon offered to fix it, I'd accepted gratefully, figuring he had some way of hammering out the metal so it would be functional. Instead, he'd created a wooden replacement—not a simple smooth panel like the original, but one intricately carved to show the landscape of my homestead—the mountains, the orchard, the barn, my cabin.

Josh ran a finger across the long line of mountains. "I like it. Now he just needs to add some goats."

It was carved out of cherry, and the deep reddish glow of the finish made me think of the way my farm looked at sunset. When he showed it to me, he said, *"This way, wherever you go, you'll remember to come home."* This land was the first place that had ever truly felt like a home worth returning to, a place of retreat and comfort, my personal sanctuary. It wasn't just buildings that Carl was threatening; it was my very existence.

Landon's carving captured the peace of this homestead, but when I looked through the windshield at the cabin and barn, I had a sudden vision of what they would look like after a fire: black and twisted timbers, scorched fencing, my stone chimney standing as a lonely sentinel beside a burnt ruin coated in ash.

I thrust the image aside and turned down the driveway.

Josh was quiet as we started winding our way down the mountain, but not for long. "You said you'd tell me later. About Carl and a gun. This is later."

My stomach tensed just thinking about having to explain, but I'd told him I would, and if I didn't play fair, neither would he. It was weird that Carl had brought up that particular evening. I sorted through the details, trying to figure out what to say and what to keep to myself. "I told you I knew your father when I was in college, and we stayed friends after graduation."

"Yeah."

"Well, your mom knew Carl back then too, and one time the four of us were in a car late at night. A Saturday night, in the middle of a January ice storm. You know how it gets in Memphis—not enough ice and snow most years to justify the right road equipment, so when storms hit hard, it's a mess. This night, the roads were in bad shape."

"This was before Mom and Dad were married?"

"Right." Sawyer and I were engaged when it happened, but I wasn't about to tell Josh that. Sawyer was working for a bank in Memphis. I had a programming job in Nashville and had come to visit for the weekend. We got a phone call around midnight—Del had gone east of town for a party, her car wouldn't start, she needed a rescue. I wasn't happy about it—it was just like Del to strand herself—but Sawyer and I bundled up and went to pick her up.

We fought our way through the storm to the address Del gave, and it was only when we arrived that we learned Carl was with her. I was shocked—didn't want anything to do with him—but the two of them had climbed right in and were already huddled in the backseat of our car. It seemed simplest to just drive back to town and get rid of them.

"Your dad was driving, hanging onto the wheel like it was trying to escape, with me up front and Carl and your mom in back. Power lines were down, snaking along the roadsides like sparking deathtraps. The streetlights were out. A sheet of ice coated everything. The car slipped and slid all over the place, hard to control, veering from one curb to the other on the bad spots."

Josh twisted in his seat, hanging on every word.

"Your mom never told you any of this?"

"Never."

I couldn't help but wonder what else she had never bothered to tell him. "We were outside of town and coming back, and there was a car ahead of us in serious trouble. Taking curves too fast, fishtailing around corners—we hung way back, worried it might crash. The driver had to be drunk or stoned to drive like that. Sure enough, we reached a heavily wooded stretch of road with thick black ice, and that other car spun out of control. It did a three-sixty, smashed into a telephone pole, flipped into a ditch. Your father slammed on the brakes and slipped into a long skid—your dad yelling, *"Hang on, hang on,"* your mom and I both screaming, I was sure we were going to smash right into that other car, but your father got us stopped. The four of us got out of the car to check, but the driver of the other car was dead."

That was as neutral as I could make it for my fourteen-year-old audience, but my heart raced as I revisited that moment. Icicles hung from every tree branch. Steam rose in a scalding cloud from the smashed engine. Treacherous ice crunched underfoot. The driver had been thrown all the way through the windshield. His head landed on a sharp rock and his skull had cleaved open the way a jack-o-lantern fragments when dropped onto concrete.

Blood splattered the pavement, the grass, the telephone pole, everything within reach. I took one look, dove into the bushes, and threw up. Del went hysterical, screaming her head off, flailing around like a lunatic. Sawyer and Carl checked the car, making sure no one else was there. Both of them were acting tough but shaking bad.

"Back then, cell phones were expensive, and Sawyer was the only one of us who had one. He pulled it out to call for help, and that's when Carl pulled a gun and stopped him."

The gun appeared from nowhere, and I could still see that horrifying moment—the barrel far too close to Sawyer's chest, the expression in Carl's eyes a look of cold desperation. Del and

I huddled together, speechless, and Sawyer dropped the phone into his coat pocket and lifted his hands. *No problem, no problem. Get in the car and we'll leave right now.* We dropped Del and Carl in town, but I was still shaking by the time Sawyer and I returned home.

"Why did Carl tell Dad he couldn't call the police?"

I shrugged. "Not sure."

"Probably had drugs on him."

Exactly what I'd thought at the time, and I still believed it was the most likely explanation. I gave Josh a quick look. He'd thought of that in record time. He looked like he regretted saying it, and he got quiet and stared out the window.

That night of the wreck was the beginning of the end for Sawyer and me. A week later, I was stuck in Nashville for a conference, and Del went to Sawyer in tears, trying to forget the horrors of that mangled body. Two bottles of tequila and some mutual consoling followed, and Josh was the unexpected result.

I was never sure if she'd gone with seduction in mind. She'd always wanted whatever I had, and I wouldn't have put it past her to have plotted the whole thing. But intentional or not, Del had never apologized, moving on like pregnancy and marriage to Sawyer were ordained from on high. Sawyer was the one who'd been guilt-ridden.

I'd told Josh the story of Carl pulling a gun, but Carl had also said he'd threatened Sawyer later and used me as leverage. What was that about? I had no clue. But I needed to find out.

Josh and I reached the edge of Madisonville. It was the county seat, and I hoped its police department was large enough

60

to be of some help. I found an open spot, parked the truck, and we headed in.

A big room filled most of the compact cinderblock building, brightly lit, overly air conditioned, and smelling vaguely of bleach. A woman in a green shirt sat at a reception desk in front, and a man in uniform was working at a computer toward the back.

"Hi." I stepped up to the desk. The woman—a girl, really, with stiff, jagged hair and a half-dozen earrings—set aside a three-ring binder and gave me her full attention. "I need to file a missing person report. And I need to report a man who's making threats."

She nodded indifferently as if requests like this came in every day and pulled a multipage form out of the file drawer of her desk. "Fill this out, and then I'll have you talk to one of the officers."

Josh and I sat on a metal bench in the front of the room. He glanced around at the utilitarian surroundings and shrank into himself, looking profoundly unhappy to be there. I started on the paperwork, tossing questions his way when I hit the ones I didn't know how to answer. "Exact time when you last saw your mother? Address of her workplace? Social Security number?"

He rattled off the answers as fast as any computer, his instant memory retrieval coming in handy. The only question that stumped him was Del's weight.

"Do you have a picture of your mom?"

He scrolled through a long line of photos on his phone, found the one he wanted, and handed it over.

Seeing Del in that picture stopped me cold. It all came rushing back. The hopes I'd had for a sister who'd be a genuine friend and confidante. The loneliness of accepting the far crueler reality. The pain of growing up as the girl who could do nothing right in my parents' eyes with the kid sister at my heels who could do nothing wrong. With Del in the family, I was always the one who didn't fit in.

She looked older in the photograph than my memory of her, and her dark hair was longer and tinted with blonde highlights. But it was a classic Del snapshot, identical in spirit to dozens I'd seen in the distant past. Photo-ready make-up. Shoulder-length earrings. A short look-at-me dress with tall high-heeled shoes. She was holding a beer in one hand and a cigarette in the other. The last fourteen years of that sort of party-heavy life had taken its toll. New lines around her eyes showed through her makeup, her shoulders slumped forward as if exhaustion was the norm, and her skin looked drawn and pasty.

She was looking off to one side, and there must have been some man there, because she wore a smile that said it all—a seductive smile full of promises. It was a smile I'd seen often, a smile that lured unsuspecting victims closer before she devoured them whole.

"Is that one okay?" Josh asked.

I shook myself back into action. "This is fine." She hadn't gained an ounce. I penciled in five foot seven and a guess of a hundred and twenty pounds.

The front-desk person glanced through my completed form, got up, and took it to the officer in back. I watched from across the room, the hard bench more uncomfortable by the second. He read the form and spent some time on his computer. My confidence plummeted as the minutes ticked by, but at last he called us back. The chairs in front of his desk were no more comfortable than the bench, not designed to encourage anyone to linger.

"I'm Officer Steven Poole." A direct gaze and no handshake. A deep resonant voice that was oddly musical. He was in his late thirties, with blue eyes, thinning hair, and a thickening middle. He looked familiar, but I couldn't place where I might have seen him before. He reached into his desk and pulled out a pack of Juicy Fruit, and a memory clicked. He'd gone through half a pack of that chewing gum the day I met him.

"I'm Bryn Collins, and this is my nephew, Josh Whitman. I met you a few years back. You came out to my farm when there was a robbery down the road from my place." It had been Landon's house that had been ransacked—his computer, his TV, and everything else electronic, gone. The real value lay in his woodworking shop, but the thieves were only interested in things they could pawn in a hurry.

The officer gave me a closer inspection, his eyes puzzled, his brow creased. Then his face cleared. "I remember you. The kayak lady. You gave me some good tips about the local rivers. My son is getting good at all that stuff. Keeps bugging me about getting a better boat." A whiff of fake fruit smell wafted my way as he chewed on his gum.

It was the faintest possible connection, but his crisp official demeanor disappeared, and my pessimism backed off a bit.

"I'm sorry about your sister." He gestured toward his computer screen. "I've just been checking the files. Tell me what you know, and I'll do the same."

I walked him through the basics—my complete lack of knowledge, Josh's reasons for concern. He spent ten minutes talking to Josh, but there was nothing to be learned beyond the bare facts on the form. He had Josh message the photo to him, and he added it to the computer file.

He then gave me a pointed glance and turned to Josh. "Son, there's a snack machine in the back breakroom. Why don't you go get yourself something to eat and hang out there for a while?" Not a suggestion. A firm command.

Josh shook his head, obviously unhappy about leaving, but I pulled a few dollars from my wallet. "Go on. Let me finish with Officer Poole here, and then I'll come get you."

He frowned but got to his feet. "Yeah. Okay." He walked toward the breakroom with slow steps, turning two or three times to look back in our direction.

I waited until the door closed behind him. "What's up?"

"I'm sorry about this."

I braced myself for the worst. News about Del was never benign.

Steven gestured toward his computer. "Your sister has quite a few entries here. Noise complaints. Public intoxication. A bar fight. She got a suspended sentence for forging several OxyContin prescriptions and was on parole for two years. Finished that up three years ago."

The string of drinking complaints was no surprise, just business as usual, but the opiates were new and disturbing. In the distant past, she'd confined herself to pot and amphetamines, and Mom claimed she'd sworn off both when she got pregnant.

Maybe Sawyer's death had undone whatever good that relationship had provided.

How much did Josh know about any of this? He'd been pretty careful in what he said, and there were several times when I got the idea he was hiding something. I couldn't expect him to rat out his own mother, but he might know things that could help.

"All of that information is public record." Steven paused as if he was debating whether he should go on, but the kayaking connection must have paid off, because he didn't hold back. "What's not out in public is that there was also an investigation involving a possible theft at First National Bank in Memphis. It happened more than ten years ago."

"A *possible* theft?" Very weird. And it didn't sound like Del. Careless and impulsive, yes. A drug addict? Quite possible. But a participant in an organized theft? It didn't feel right. I knew Sawyer had pulled strings to get her some sort of clerical job at the bank branch where he was manager, but that put her in a file room, not a bank vault.

"The entry here is a bit strange. A safe deposit box was opened by a man who inherited it after his brother's death, but it was empty—totally cleaned out. He pitched a fit, claimed he'd been robbed, accused the bank employees of theft. They called it in, but the man stormed out before police arrived. Turned out the box had been rented under a false name, and the supposed brother used fake documents to claim it. Neither was ever identified. The bank requested an investigation anyway, and suspicion fell on the bank manager, who had been killed in an accident a few weeks before the theft was discovered. They looked into your sister, since the manager was her husband."

I slumped back into my chair. Sawyer. He was saying Sawyer was a thief.

It was hard to believe Sawyer would steal. Of course, I'd also believed he loved me. I'd believed he would never in a million years sleep with my sister. Maybe I was wrong about him from start to finish. Maybe I was just a fool to have trusted him about anything.

"So, is there still a search ongoing for whatever was in that box?"

Steven gave an emphatic head shake. "There's nothing to go on. No owner, no description of the contents. No case."

"I don't know what to think. I knew Del's . . ." I couldn't force myself to say *Del's husband*. Even after all this time, my throat shrank to the size of a toothpick and blocked those particular words from spilling out. I coughed to hide my stumble. "I knew the man who was bank manager back then. Emptying a safe deposit box doesn't sound like him. But I've been out of the picture for a long time."

Steven nodded and made a note on the computer. "The final note says your sister was dismissed from her job several months after the investigation was halted."

"That wouldn't be unusual." Maybe the bank was convinced she was involved in the theft, but it was equally likely it was just one more trip on Del's unemployment merry-go-round. Without Sawyer there to watch her back, dismissal would have been inevitable.

"At any rate, none of that helps with her current disappearance. I'll file the missing person's report and put out a bulletin for her car. I'll check for credit card transactions and watch for any Jane Doe reports. I'll ping her phone periodically, but with it turned off like it is now, that avenue's blocked. She left voluntarily, and she made arrangements for her son. Without any information about where she was headed, it's hard for us to do much more."

I wasn't sure what I had expected. Maybe some secret satellite system that could print out a map with a magical here-is-your-sister, X-marks-the-spot. Reality was far more disappointing. Josh and I couldn't do much more on the phone, and it sounded like sitting around waiting could be a long, worthless process. With Carl threatening action in seven days, we didn't have time to play around.

"One more thing." I launched into the story about Carl, which didn't take all that long to tell. In theory, Del's situation should have been intensely personal—my sister no matter what, right? —but talking about Carl proved far more distressing. This was the problem that hit closer to home, the one I needed solved. But I could tell by the look on Steven's face there wasn't much likelihood he could do anything concrete.

"Tell me again what he said about the fire. His exact words."

That was no problem. They were etched into my brain.

But Steven shook his head after I'd told him. "I know you felt threatened, but if you write those words down on paper, you'll see he can argue he was just expressing concern for your safety, not making an actual threat."

He looked Carl up on his computer. "There's a sealed juvenile file here, and then as an adult, he's got a long string of arrests but no convictions—assault, property destruction, one case of arson. I'd advise you to be careful. We can keep an eye on your place as part of routine patrols. And you can consider getting a restraining order, but the lack of convictions here makes me wonder if he gets other people to do his dirty work."

His tone was sympathetic, but it was sorry-to-let-you-down sympathy. "I know losing your chicken is distressing, but legally it's considered low-dollar property damage, and you didn't actually see him do anything. If he comes back, makes more direct threats . . . does something else . . ." His voice tapered away into silence.

I hadn't expected much action about Annabelle's death, but I'd hoped for at least some minimal help. Carl meant business, and a restraining order wouldn't slow him in the least.

Steven had ignored three incoming calls on his desk phone while we talked, and he'd been more than generous with his time. I got to my feet. "I really appreciate all this. And thank you for sharing the details of Del's history." Shitty details, but I'd rather know than not.

"If you learn anything else, please let me know. I'll do the same." He gave me a genuine smile. "Maybe my son and I will see you and your nephew on the lake some weekend."

"Absolutely." I headed for the breakroom. *Absolutely?* Not too likely. He was assuming Josh would be a long-term resident, but that was nowhere in the plan. Josh was going back home to his mother as soon as I could manage it.

The breakroom door had a clear glass panel on top, and I paused with my hand on the doorknob, the metal cold to the touch. Josh sat at a small Formica-topped table inside, an empty chips packet and a candy bar wrapper in front of him. His phone was on the table too, but for once he didn't have his face buried in a game. His shoulders were hunched, and his eyes were focused on nothing.

I hated seeing him so sad, lonely, and depressed. I wanted to wave a wand and fix everything for him. None of that was in my power.

I pulled on a lying smile, opened the door, and leaned in. "Hey. There's a café down the street that's supposed to have good burgers. Still hungry?"

He leaped to his feet, his chair rocking back so far it threatened to flip. "Yeah. Yes. Please."

Hunger, I could fix. But his mom had left him, and the glimpses I was getting of her toxic life weren't promising. Once we found Del and got her back, what sort of life would I be sending him home to?

CHAPTER SEVEN

Josh

We left the cops, and Bryn took me to a tiny restaurant on Main Street for lunch, the smell of actual meat on the grill making my stomach growl as soon as we opened the door. By the time I finished my second hamburger and Coke, I was no longer starving, and there was a big plate of cheese fries waiting.

Bryn ordered a portobello sandwich, which turned out to be a giant mushroom. No wonder she was so skinny. I just wished this place was closer to her cabin so I could come back for more real food.

She hadn't said anything about the police station, but I could tell by the way she kept staring out the window that the news wasn't good. I waited until she finished her food. "So, what did the cop say?"

She didn't look straight at me, a sure sign I wasn't going to get the full story. "They're going to do what they can. They'll put her description out, and they'll look for her car. They'll keep pinging her phone to see if it turns on again."

None of that ever worked on cop shows. "We need to go back to Memphis."

I'd been thinking about this when they kicked me out. Carl might also go back to the city, which sucked, but I'd still feel safer in my own apartment instead of out here. While Bryn talked to that officer, I'd been busy making sure her farm would be safe. She should take me home.

The mention of Memphis got her attention, so at least it was a start. "How would going there help anything?"

Well, for one thing, it would put me back in a house where there was pepperoni pizza in the freezer, but I didn't think that was the right way to start my argument. "Mom's computer is there. We can check her calendar. Look up her credit cards."

"The police are checking her credit cards."

I thought fast. "Yeah, but I bet they're checking to see where she is now. We could look at what she did before she left. See if anything looks different or gives a clue where she went. The cops won't know what's unusual. I will."

She gave a snorting laugh. "Nice try. We can do all that from my computer. I'm betting you know all your mom's passwords."

Ouch. One point for Bryn. I didn't even need Bryn's computer. I could do it all on my phone. I was the one who set up all Mom's online accounts. I was the one who kept an eye on the bank balance, watched out for bills, made the electronic transfers. When we had money.

Before I started taking care of things, we used to get nasty phone calls, and once the power even got turned off mid-winter. After that, I took over the bills. I couldn't imagine how Mom was managing somewhere out there without me.

Bryn thought for a minute. "How much do you know about your mother's legal problems?"

Oh. So that's what the cop wanted to talk about after he'd gotten rid of me. I sorted through possible answers. How much should I admit? "She had to check in with a parole officer for a couple of years, but that's done now."

She didn't act surprised. She looked me in the eye, one of those see-right-into-you looks that made me nervous. "Before she left, was she still doing drugs?"

And there it was. I studied the table for a minute. Ate another fry, but now it tasted cold and greasy.

Doing drugs. Saying it like that made it sound so evil. Davey's mom, upstairs from us, sometimes stayed in bed for days at a time, but Mom wasn't usually that bad. Michael's dad had been in rehab twice. Mom, never. So, okay, she always had a bottle of something in her pocket. She'd take cash out of the ATM, and the stash she kept in the freezer would get bigger. She'd get jumpy, and that meant the supply had gotten too low.

But she wasn't a bad person. She said the laws were messed up. Some people just didn't understand how she really needed medicine sometimes. I suspected my aunt was one of *some people.*

I glanced up at Bryn, who hadn't looked away since she asked her question. "If we went to Memphis, we could see."

It wasn't a real answer, and I waited for Bryn to get pissed at me, but she just scrunched her mouth tight and shook her head like she knew I was dodging. "Well, at least you're consistent. But you may be right. I'll think about it. There are probably things we can learn there that we can't figure out from here."

She handed her credit card over to the waitress and then checked a bunch of e-mails on her phone. I poked at the fries with my fork. On that long drive across the state to get to Bryn's farm, I had thought a lot about what she might be like. I decided she would probably be a lot like Mom. Boy, was I ever wrong.

She noticed things. Stuff like those raccoon tracks by the river. Mom would never have seen those tracks in the mud, and if she did, she wouldn't have cared. And Bryn had delivered those baby goats. She'd saved them. By herself. Mom took it for granted that other people should back her up. Bryn was the sort who tried to do everything on her own. She was definitely not Mom.

Now that I'd been around her more, she didn't even look like my mom any longer.

We went out to the truck and started back to the farm, and it was nice not to be hungry for once. I thought our little chat was over and I'd gotten off okay, but at a stoplight Bryn turned in her seat and gave me a careful once-over. "Do you know my mother? I mean, Del's and my mother? Your grandmother?"

Another trick question. I'd listened in on Mom's end of the arguments when she called Grandma for money sometimes, but I guessed that wasn't what Bryn was after. "She sends me birthday cards. Two Christmases ago, we drove to her house for lunch."

Three hours to get there, one hour to eat—just tuna salad sandwiches, not even a turkey or a pie—then three hours back. Grandma's tiny white poodle sat in its own chair at the table beside her and ate people food off a regular plate. Grandma gave me a jigsaw puzzle that was labeled for five-year-olds, and she gave Mom a check that Mom said wouldn't even pay for gas.

Mom said *"Never again,"* and she got no argument from me. "She's not like the grandmothers in books or anything."

"But you like her all right?"

This was not going in a good direction. "Not really. She doesn't like me. She smells funny. And she's . . . *old.*"

Bryn snorted. "She's always been old, let me tell you." She caught her top lip in her teeth and bit down hard. The light turned green and she drove on. "I was just thinking it might take a while for the police to find your mom. You might be happier with your grandmother than with me, and it might be safer there, what with Carl and all. She's supposed to call me back, and I can ask her."

"No!" I yelled the word so loud, it bounced off the windshield even louder. My hands turned into fists without me even telling them to. I'm not sure who was more surprised, me or her. "I need to stay with you, not her. Mom said you would help, and you need to come with me to Memphis, and we need to figure out where she is."

Bryn jumped when I yelled, and she gave me a worried look. "Josh, I'm trying."

"You're not trying—you're just doing the easy stuff." Even as the words came out, I knew they were unfair, but I couldn't stop. It was like something broke free inside and let it all escape. "You think you can stick me with Grandma and forget about looking for Mom."

"No, of course not. I'll keep looking. I'm just trying to do what's best for—"

"That's what they always say. *'It's what's best.'* Like they know. Then they stick you with some old woman who covers all her furniture in plastic and makes you sleep with three other foster kids who say they're going to cut your throat if you fall asleep." I bit off the rest. Couldn't believe I'd told her so much.

Bryn's eyes widened. "What are you talking about? When was this?"

I looked at my hands. Wished Tellico was there. "Long time ago. Mom had to be in the hospital, and social services put me in temporary care."

"You saved your mom." That's what the ambulance guy told me. Then when I got to go back home, the social worker said, *"Take care of your mom."* I'd been trying to do it ever since.

"They called Grandma that time, and she said she couldn't help. So see, you can't send me there. You need me. I can help. I can." My voice sounded wrong on those last words, like a little kid ready to cry. I blinked hard and turned to stare out the side window.

There was a long, long, quiet where I couldn't tell what she was thinking, and maybe Bryn didn't know what she was thinking either, because she kept fidgeting, shifting in her seat like there was no way to get comfortable. Finally, she reached over and gave my arm a pat.

"I'm not going to send you into foster care. I promise. I don't know what's happening with your mom, and I can't see the future, but for now, you're with me."

Uncertainty still hung like a cloud, but it was better than nothing.

Bryn drove on. She waited a few minutes like she expected me to say something, and when I didn't, she gave a loud sigh.

"Okay, you win. We'll let Steven—Officer Poole—investigate this afternoon, and while we're waiting, I'll arrange for someone to take care of things on the farm. If we don't learn anything more by tonight, we'll leave for Memphis in the morning. You and me. I've got a few days before I start my next programming project. Mind you—I can't be gone too long. Mortgage payments don't pay themselves."

Victory. "Memphis, right? You're not taking me to Grandma's?" I needed to hear it one more time.

"Not now. I can't promise it won't come up again, but for now, you're with me. Fair enough?"

It sounded like it was the only guarantee I was going to get. "Yeah, I guess. What about Tellico? Can he come too?"

"Sure, he can come. This should just be for two or three days."

Maybe if I scooted way over in my bed at home, there'd be room enough for him to fit there too.

We talked about goat names and other not-Mom stuff the rest of the way. We got back to her cabin, and Landon was there, leaning against his truck with Tellico at his feet. Waiting.

Bryn pulled her head back, looking surprised. She parked, got out of the truck, and walked over to him. "Hey there. What's up?"

Landon hadn't wasted any time. I went over to them real quiet so I could listen.

"Hi. I was worried." He stepped closer to her, his arms raised as if he wanted to give her a hug, but when he saw her face, he stopped, and his arms dropped. "Some guy threatens to burn you out? Of course, I'm worried. I wanted to see if you were all right. I'm incredibly sorry about Annabelle. I know how special she was."

"How in the world did . . ." She stopped. Looked around and found me squatting on the ground, half hidden by Tellico and trying hard to be invisible. "You. You called him? You told him what happened?"

I nodded and kept myself small. Carl had come here because of me. Bryn was in trouble because of me. And Landon's number had been on her emergency call sheet. It was obvious he really liked her, so what else could I do, locked away in a police breakroom? Bryn needed help, even if she didn't think so.

Landon gave me a nod, for certain on my side. "Don't blame Josh. And don't be stubborn on this. I'm glad I found out. How are you doing?"

Bryn's jaw tightened up, and she stood straight and tall, as if she was going to say everything was great, but then her shoulders suddenly dropped like strings had been cut. "I'm shaken. No other way to put it. Carl was a creep when I knew him years ago, but back then he was just a small-time punk, and he was after other people, not me. Now he's worse. Scary. Mean. Determined. He's real trouble. I'm taking him seriously."

Landon took another half step toward her, but when Bryn turned away, he stopped again. "Listen. I made a custom dining table last year for a guy who runs a security firm out of Chattanooga, and I just got off the phone with him. He's willing to rearrange appointments and come out this afternoon with his team since you've got an active threat here. They can install motion detectors. Cameras on the driveway, the house, the barn. Alarms. Remote monitoring. It's your call, but I hope you'll do it."

Bryn shook her head. "I can take care of myself. I don't need to be rescued."

The way she said it sounded fierce, but Landon didn't back down. "This isn't a rescue. It's one friend helping another. You need help. This is something I can do. Let me do it."

Bryn looked at her boots, then off toward the chicken pen, her face sad. Somewhere out there was Annabelle's grave. "I don't like the idea of somebody spying on me with a camera. Del missing, Josh here, Carl killing Annabelle, and now you want somebody recording my whole life? No way. It's creepy."

"You don't have to keep it forever. Just until you get all this straightened out. And you'll be able to monitor the video feed on your phone. I can move your goats to my place while you and Josh are in Memphis, and I'll check in on the chickens and the garden every day."

The word *Memphis* whirled Bryn back toward me with a death glare that would have done Mom proud. Yeah, okay, maybe telling Landon we were going to Memphis before I'd even talked to Bryn about it was worth a nasty look, but hey, it was obvious we had to go. I was just saving time.

Fortunately, the glare only lasted a few seconds, then Bryn's mouth twitched a few times, and she sighed. "I think I'm outnumbered."

I was surprised. Not just giving in, but pretty good-natured about it.

She turned to Landon, gave him a long, searching look, and then nodded. "Thank you. I guess this is the way it has to be. I'll go along with it, and I admit it will make me feel better if some security is in place while I'm gone. Make sure the bill comes to me."

"Yes, ma'am." Landon tipped an invisible hat, and Bryn almost laughed.

"I should know for sure about Memphis later tonight. And yes, if you can take Kudzu and Thistle and the twins in the morning, that would be great. It would keep them safe."

"No problem. I'll clear out a pen for them. Plenty of room."

She turned to me. "As for you"—I held my breath—"it's not your job to take care of your mom, and it's not your job to take care of me. It's supposed to be the other way around." She gave me one of her almost-smiles. "Thank you all the same."

At least I hadn't gotten yelled at. I stood up, and Landon came over. "Good job. Thanks for letting me know about Carl."

He gave me a quick fist bump and pulled it off pretty well for an old guy. He glanced back at Bryn. "You should reconsider a gun."

Her defiant headshake left no room for argument. "No."

"I figured." Landon pulled something out of his back pocket. "At least take this." What he held out to her looked like an over-sized pocketknife, but when he touched a button on the side a long sharp blade whipped out on its own. "It's a spring knife. Don't worry—it's small enough to be legal."

She hesitated a minute, but then she took it. "What the hell are you doing with something like this?"

He looked a little embarrassed. "After that break-in . . ." He left it at that. Bryn shook her head but slipped the knife into her pocket.

Landon must have had serious pull, because the security guys got there fast and started installing equipment. For me, the rest of the day was nonstop busy, with Bryn trying to get as much done as possible before we left. She tossed in a load of laundry, did some computer stuff, and had me straightening up the house, even though I didn't see much at all out of place. She mumbled under her breath at the security people, who were everywhere at once as they installed sensors at windows and doors. Bryn got fed up tripping over them and switched to outdoor tasks, dragging me along with her.

I helped take the kayak down off the truck, handed her tools while she fixed a hinge on the door to the chicken coop, learned how to pinch off suckers on the growing tomato plants. I didn't even have a spare minute to check Instagram.

Some of it was almost fun. I liked the goats a lot. The twins climbed all over each other like they were part of a tiny circus, and they liked it when I scratched them behind their floppy ears.

"You know, we really need to name them." Bryn was pulling together halters and leads for Landon to use while we were gone, bundling it all together real neat.

I thought about Bryn's real job when she wasn't hunting for a lost sister. "What about Python and Java?"

She burst out laughing, maybe the first real laugh I'd heard from her, and it made her face rounder and not so hard. "You're on."

"Python's the one I carried. She's the best."

"Totally. I can tell she's the really smart one."

She was teasing—the twins were so much alike it was hard to tell them apart—but I liked the way she said it anyway.

I also liked listening to Bryn, who just sort of talked along about nothing special while she was doing things. Not like I was a kid, but like I was a real person, although I noticed she talked the same way to Tellico and the goats. At least it gave me a break from worrying about Mom. We made pizza for dinner, and she told about how yeast does its bubbling thing.

"No way pizza crust is *alive*," I argued, and that got another laugh.

There were minuses too. The garden, for one. We spread mulch from the compost pile for weeds, and it took *forever* and smelled like shit. Didn't Bryn realize you can get all this vegetable stuff from the grocery? I dumped my fifth wheelbarrow of mulch, and I was sure my arms had stretched at least an extra five inches from the weight. "You know, there are child labor laws."

Bryn snorted like I was being an idiot. "Yeah, I've heard of such things, but they don't apply to boys who want to go to Memphis tomorrow. Keep going—we have plenty still to do before we get out of here."

I was glad we were heading back home to a normal apartment.

By the time Bryn called the cop, that Officer Poole, after dinner, I was worn out. I stared at my phone like I was playing a game, but really I was listening. Tellico was stretched out right in front of me, warm where he leaned up against my feet.

"Any news? . . . Uh-huh . . . And the car? Nothing there either?" She listened for a while. "Yeah . . . Okay. Well, Josh and I are going to Memphis tomorrow, and we'll see if we can find anything there that might help . . . Yes . . . I will. Thanks."

She hung up and sat there a long minute.

"You heard," she finally said. "We're going. We'll leave in the morning after we've fed the animals. It's supposed to rain tomorrow afternoon, so the garden will survive on its own for a bit."

At least there was a real plan, and all that work to get ready had been worth it. That should have meant I could worry less, but no. Annabelle dead. The cops. Bryn's questions about drugs. Mom's cell phone still off, her voice mail now full and not even taking any more of my messages. The worries piled up, and my insides tightened into a stone the size of a baseball.

To make things worse, Bryn's place was too quiet and too noisy both at the same time. No traffic sounds. No footsteps on the ceiling from an apartment upstairs. No music drifting in from out on the street. But once it got dark, it flipped, and jungle noise started up so loud it made my head hurt.

"What kind of birds are those?"

She gave me a look like she was embarrassed for me. "Not birds. Those are tree frogs and cicadas."

I seriously needed to get back to a city.

Bryn said she needed to do some work stuff, and she disappeared into her study. I looked through the books in the living room—boring—and after a while I wandered back to ask if I could use one of her computers since she didn't have a TV.

She wasn't doing computer stuff. She was sitting in her desk chair, hunched forward, looking at a photo album that rested on her lap.

I looked over her shoulder and saw a picture of my dad. Mom only had a few pictures of him at home, but I'd studied them hard. It was him. I was sure. "Where'd you get that?"

I hadn't tried to sneak up or anything, but she jumped like she'd forgotten I was in the house. She slammed the book closed. "Doesn't matter. This is nothing." She stood up fast and stuffed the album into one of the bookcases. "Are you all packed for tomorrow?"

Pack what? I'd only brought one change of clothes. She wasn't the sort to ask stupid questions like that. She was more upset by those pictures than she was letting on. "Yeah. I've got everything."

"Good." She wouldn't look at me. "I'm going to take a shower. Don't stay up too late. We'll try and get an early start." She waved me out of the office and closed the door behind us.

I went back to the living room and pretended to play a game on my phone. I waited until the shower started up, then hurried back to the office and searched for the album she'd been looking at. Bryn had stuffed it back behind the books in front, but I'd seen which shelf, so found it without much trouble. I closed the office door and sat down at her desk.

Nowadays, any pictures Mom snapped just lived on her phone, but she had some photos on paper from when I was a baby, and it was all paper ones in this album. I flipped through to see if I could find a picture of Dad like the one I'd seen, and I didn't have to look far. He was on just about every page. I turned to the beginning and started going through in order.

The pictures were pasted down tight on thick white pages, and under each one was handwriting.

Nantahala, 6/7/2004
Margery's birthday, 1/26/2005
Chattanooga festival, 4/20/2005

The pictures showed picnics and kayaking and parties, but none of them were of Dad and Mom. They were all of Dad alone or of Dad and Bryn together.

Holding hands. Smiling and laughing. Kissing.

Kissing? What the hell? Dad and Bryn? She'd said they were friends.

I found Mom in two pictures, real young and pretty, not all that much older than me, but she was in the edge of the pictures, not the middle. She wasn't standing near Dad in either one.

The pictures stopped at a page about halfway through the album, where there was a postcard pasted in. *Save the Date*. Save the date of June 16th for a wedding. But the wedding was for Bryn Collins and Sawyer Whitman.

I stared at the fancy card for a long time, thinking.

Dad and Bryn.

Dad and Mom.

It made no sense.

My stomach must have figured it out before my brain did, because it started feeling like I'd swallowed a handful of gravel. There used to be a framed thing at home Grandma made. It must have gotten lost the last time we moved, but it had the date of Mom and Dad's wedding in big blue letters. June 16th. Mom. Not Bryn.

A day from a few years back dropped into my head. Ben and I were finishing a level of *Zelda*, and his older brother, Keith, wandered around the apartment we had then, waiting for us to finish so he could take Ben home. "Hey," he said, when he got to that cross-stitch thing. "I thought your birthday was in October."

"Yeah." I hated it because it was just a few days before Halloween, so I always got stuck with costume stuff for presents.

Keith got a real snarky look on his face, and he laughed in a way I didn't like. "I get it. A love baby. Your parents *had* to get married."

That day, I hadn't understood. Now that I was staring at this postcard, maybe I did.

CHAPTER EIGHT

Bryn

I loaded the truck the next morning at half speed, more tired when I woke than when I went to bed. Revisiting those photos of Sawyer. Seeing Landon again. The two events had resurfaced in my dreams as a tangled mess—half erotic, half horror story. Sleep was the loser.

The moon hung low in the west, a waning crescent, setting later each day as it shrank into invisibility. Always a depressing time of the lunar month—the later moonrises made for dark evenings, and a daylight moon always seemed wasted, its light too feeble to compete with the sun. No wonder I was dragging.

I shook my head at my foolishness. The last thing I needed to worry about was the moon. The previous day, I felt bad about spooking Josh with talk of bobcats and bees. Now I'd give anything to worry only about such mundane risks.

I glanced at my phone for the twentieth time. No call or text from my mother. It's what I would have expected if I'd called about myself, but a call about Del? Mom should have tripped over herself to call back, eager to learn about her favorite daughter.

Del had always been her focus, the center point of Mom's orbit, but after my father died, Del became her obsession. Del was the cute one, the one who cared about hair and clothes and dating. The one who turned to Mom for advice, even if she never took it. I was the tomboy with my nose in a book, who questioned things Mom knew nothing about. Apparently, it was an easy choice. Del's lies and failing grades were shrugged off and ignored as thoroughly as my accomplishments.

I pulled up Mom's number and got voice mail again. Left another message, more pointed this time: *I'm calling about Del, not me.* Maybe this time I'd hear back.

I slipped the phone into my pocket, but it chimed at once, and I took it back out to check the incoming text.

No name. A number I didn't recognize. Six words: *One day wasted. Six days left.*

My mouth went dry, and my legs went wobbly. I leaned against the side of the truck for balance and read the message again.

How had Carl gotten my number?

Instantaneous rage swamped my fatigue. Carl was *not* in charge. I wasn't going to play this game. I blocked the number, turned off my phone, and stormed inside.

"You ready?" I snapped the question at poor Josh as if every problem on the planet was his fault.

A stupid question—he was pacing the living room, impatient and eager to be gone—and he looked at me in hurt surprise. "Yeah, I want to get home. Let's go." He and Tellico raced to the truck and settled in.

At least one of us had energy.

I armed the new security system and locked the front door. This new world of access codes, video feeds, and beeping monitors unsettled me more than I'd expected, but I dutifully checked my phone app and confirmed everything was working. For years I'd felt safe here. I rarely even locked the doors except when I went into town. Now here I was, jumpy and watching over my shoulder and worrying about the least little noise.

I hated Del for creating this mess. If I had any sense, I would stay put and barricade myself here at the homestead with Josh. I could stay on guard against Carl and close my eyes when it came to Del's disappearance. Let the police handle any search for her. After all, that was their job, right?

But Carl's threats were all too real, and locking myself away was no way to fight back. Instead of heading back inside, I climbed into the truck and started driving. What is it they say about eldest children? Responsible. Practical. Self-sacrificing. Maybe it was hard-wired; maybe I'd been raised to believe it. Despite my doubts about Del, I couldn't turn tail and hide.

Josh stayed quiet the first hour of the drive, but he fidgeted nonstop, like something was eating him. Started a game on his phone and put it down minutes later. Stared out the window. Picked up the phone again.

Would a good aunt ask what was bothering him or leave him alone? I figured it couldn't hurt to try. "What's the matter? You're acting like popcorn in hot oil. We're headed for Memphis—I thought you'd be pleased."

He gave me a long assessing look, but no answer.

I waited. I knew there were things he wasn't telling me about Del, but he acted like this was something new. Whatever it was hovered in the air between us, the issue so thick it was almost visible.

He finally faced forward and stared straight ahead out the windshield. "You said you knew my dad."

"Yes."

"You didn't tell me you were going to *marry* him." He slammed the words down, one at a time.

Shit. I tried to ease the sudden crick in my neck, but that only bought me a few seconds. "No, I didn't tell you. How did you find out?"

"Those pictures. The ones you were looking at last night. The ones you tried to hide."

A moment of outrage built over the fact he'd searched my stuff, but in his place I probably would have done the same thing. I stuffed my irritation aside and sorted through my answer. "Your father and I dated for several years in college. We planned to get married. We broke up. He married your mother instead. That's it." There. Just the plain bullet-point facts, as if I didn't care much either way. As if I could ignore the all-too-familiar sense of loss that washed over me as I thought about the plans Sawyer and I had made.

Josh grunted. "That's why you didn't talk to my mom all this time."

"Yes."

"They got married because Mom was pregnant. With me."

I hunted for the right words, hoping I could find ones he could hang onto. "They got married because they wanted to be good parents. Because they knew how much they would love you. They wanted to give you a family."

Maybe that was even true. Sawyer had always wanted kids, that was for sure, but he'd been as blindsided as I was when Del announced her news.

The spring after we'd found the wreck with its horribly dead driver, Sawyer had been unusually jumpy. Overly solicitous. Eager to please. He'd said all the right things and gone through the right motions but got antsy whenever I talked about wedding plans. I'd asked several times what was wrong, but each time he brushed me off. He didn't give me a single hint about the night he'd spent with Del.

In early April I came into town for a weekend visit, determined to force him to tell me what his problem was. I arrived at Sawyer's apartment, but we were interrupted at once by a knock. Sawyer slipped out of my arms to answer, and when he opened the door, Del waltzed in like she had every right to be there.

She had the same self-satisfied look on her face as the day she stole my high school boyfriend, and she glared at me like I was the one who was in the wrong place at the wrong time. I looked from her to Sawyer and back again, sudden apprehension making me queasy.

"Sit down," she said.

"I'm pregnant," she said.

"Guess who the father is." She said those last words in a voice of delighted triumph.

I started to laugh—how bizarre, how ridiculous, this had to be a tasteless joke—but then I saw the look on Sawyer's face. A pulverizing weight on my chest threatened to crack ribs, the pressure making it impossible to breathe. Stunned disbelief held me together, but I was shaking.

"Sawyer. Is this true?" I could hardly speak.

His face was a wordless answer. He gulped hard. "Bryn. I'm so sorry. I wanted to tell you . . ."

He stumbled to a halt because I was already up and moving, grabbing my weekend bag from the spot where I'd left it moments before, opening the apartment door, slamming it hard behind me.

I must have put one foot in front of the other, because somehow I ended up back in the car, back on the highway, peering at the interstate through a storm of tears. Sawyer's *"I'm sorry"* was the final blow. The pieces of who I'd been up until that moment shattered, tumbling into an irreparable heap.

Did Sawyer marry my sister only out of a sense of obligation? Out of a desire to protect his unborn son? I hoped so. The alternative—that he loved her, that he chose her over me with conscious intent and his whole heart—was still too painful to consider even all these years later.

That final scene with Sawyer was etched in my memory with vivid clarity, but I couldn't pass that damage on to Josh. "Look, all that stuff with your parents and me was a long time ago. No matter what trouble your mother has gotten into now, I know she loves you. You wouldn't be who you are if that wasn't true."

He licked his lips uncertainly but gave a small nod. "Yeah. Okay." He wiped at his face with the back of one hand. "I don't want to talk about it anymore."

Neither did I, but I tried one more time to imitate a good aunt. "Let me know if you change your mind."

REBECCA HODGE

He said nothing, just picked up his phone and started another game. And that was the way we left it the whole rest of the way to Memphis.

In the hours of silence, I forcibly set aside thoughts of Sawyer, but I couldn't stop thinking about Carl. I kept seeing the wreck. Carl then, with a gun in his hand. Carl now, threatening flames. Annabelle, her still-warm body limp in my hands.

A one-week deadline. Six more days to find my missing sister. A ticking sound in my head, counting down the minutes, made my skin prickle. I kept glancing in the rearview mirror, making sure we weren't being followed. He wasn't there—I knew he wasn't there—but the scared part of me half expected to find Carl lurking in the backseat of the truck, grinning as he planned his next move.

CHAPTER NINE

Bryn

It was late afternoon when we started seeing signs for Grace-
land. I exited the interstate and followed my phone's directions
to the address Josh gave me. We wound our way through downtown, the sky cloaked in heavy clouds and the streets clogged
with rush-hour traffic. High-rise office buildings towered everywhere, creating steel canyons that made me feel small and
hemmed in. It had been years since I'd been back to Memphis,
and I immediately wanted to leave.

Del's neighborhood, tucked in the shadow of downtown
opulence, looked long overdue for major renovation. Stately
southern red oaks lined broad streets, and broken slabs of slate
marked what had once been fancy sidewalks, but these were dim
echoes of a long-lost past. All the houses were in dire need of
paint, shingles, and basic maintenance. Plastic garbage bags
lined the street for pickup, half of them torn open, their rotting
guts spilling into weedy yards. Broken glass glinted along the

curbing. It was a neighborhood on the way down, and it looked like its residents were embracing the slide.

I cruised Del's block slowly, turned around, and drove back, inspecting each parked car and every shadowed doorway, worried Carl might be lurking. Josh gave me a quizzical look, but nothing seemed threatening. I found a space at the curb to parallel park and climbed out to stretch. Too much stress. Too much sitting. Too many hours of interstate.

"This one's ours." Josh pointed to a faded blue building. Their apartment was part of what had once been an elegant home, now crudely chopped into a fourplex. "Maybe Mom's back by now."

He sounded so hopeful, I wanted for his sake to believe it was possible. "Let's see."

A huge Doberman on a short chain barked incessantly from across the street. Tellico gave him a dismissive glance and followed us up steep steps onto the porch.

A thin calico cat sat on the broad railing. She eyed the dog but purred and arched her back when Josh gave her a pat. "Keeping an eye on things, Patsy?" He glanced my way. "She lives next door, but I feed her sometimes." The tiny cat yawned and stretched. When no food was forthcoming, she leaped off into the shrubbery and disappeared.

Josh used his key on the front door and then on their apartment door, which was on the bottom left. Tellico immediately went into overdrive, sniffing around the baseboards. Tobacco, stale beer, and a mix of heavy perfumes were what I could make out, those odors strong enough to mask anything more subtle. I tried to take shallow breaths, but I could taste the foul air in the back of my throat.

Josh looked around eagerly as soon as he stepped in, but the apartment was silent. No one home. His shoulders slumped, and he slammed his backpack to the floor with an echoing thud.

"How about a tour?" It was a weak attempt at distraction, but I couldn't think of anything better.

He made a this-is-stupid face, but he humored me and did his best. "This is the living room."

It had probably once been the dining room of the original house, and the chandelier looked out of place, centered over nothing, its chain shortened with a yellow zip-tie to give headroom. A worn flower-print sofa, a recliner in crackled green vinyl, and an enormous plasma-screen TV furnished the room. There may have been a table beside the couch, but the whole place was so cluttered with cast-off clothing, piles of unopened mail, and assorted empty pizza boxes that it was hard to tell. I wondered for an instant if the room had been torn up by someone searching, like in a detective story, but Josh seemed to find the chaos unsurprising.

"Here's the kitchen and my room. Mom's room is in the back."

The kitchen had lost out when the house was chopped in four, and all that remained was a narrow row of appliances and six inches of counter space. The floor sagged low in the middle, as if some sort of structural support had given way long ago, and the boxy pattern of the ancient linoleum was worn off in patches to expose underlying layers of crumbling brown.

Josh's bedroom, if you could call it that, looked like it had been created by knocking together a pantry and a laundry room. The marks left by old pantry shelves were still visible on one wall, and the laundry-room hookups were still present on another.

His small space was noteworthy, however, because it was as neat and well organized as Sawyer's bedroom would have been. The bed was made. A small bookshelf held a queue of battered science fiction paperbacks. Two plastic laundry baskets served as substitutes for a dresser, and the clothing in them was all carefully folded. The room was an oasis, a retreat for a kid who was trying damn hard to create some order in the midst of his mother's chaos.

Del's bedroom formed the back of the apartment, probably a maid's room in the original scheme of the house, and it was just as trashed as the living room. My standards were low, but not *that* low. I'd have to put in some work before I'd be willing to sleep here. A small bathroom with a miniscule shower completed the tour.

"Well." I looked around at the tight, cluttered space. It was hard to imagine anything less appealing. "We made it. Why don't we figure out some dinner, and then we can start finding out what we can about your mom's trip."

I opened the refrigerator, releasing a whoosh of stale air. Two six-packs of beer, one of Coke, a jar of mayonnaise, and a half-empty jar of pickles. In the freezer, a stack of frozen pepperoni pizzas on the left, and a lineup of ice cream on the right.

Josh lifted a stack of colored menus off the miniature counter. "We can do takeout."

It was the path of least resistance.

He flipped on the television and sprawled on the couch while we waited for a delivery from Golden China. I closed all the blinds, not wanting to advertise the fact we were there, and I started sorting through clutter, tossing clothing into one pile and mail into another. Small hurricanes of dust stirred as I worked, and the old wooden floorboards creaked with every step I took.

I cleared a heap of outdated magazines from beside the couch and discovered that, yes, there was indeed a table hidden there. On it, knocked flat, was a hinged silver frame, the same gift I'd seen my mother give countless times for weddings, graduations, and christenings. It was badly tarnished, but the color photos it held still glowed with life. On the left, a wedding picture of Del and Sawyer. On the right, a picture of the two of them holding a tiny newborn Josh.

It was a scalding reminder of the story I'd shared with Josh on the drive in, more searing than I would have expected. Sawyer looked solemn but handsome, and I had to admit he and Del made a striking couple. She'd always been the photogenic one, and she looked better in these photos than I would have. The realization intensified the burn.

Not for the first time, I wondered about their marriage. Sawyer was probably pleased to be a father, but what then? He was a neatnik who alphabetized the canned goods, set the table with a full place setting to eat toast, and ironed his button-down shirt each morning before leaving for the office. I looked around at the minimal progress I'd made on the living room chaos. It was hard to picture Del and Sawyer together under the same roof.

The food arrived, and Josh and I ate, the pungent smell of lo mein counteracting the background apartment stench, at least for the moment. We watched an old *How I Met Your Mother* rerun, its laugh track out of place in our current situation. Then it was time to get down to business.

"Your mom has a computer somewhere?"

"Yeah, it's over here." He shifted plastic grocery bags stuffed with heaven knows what away from a corner I hadn't gotten to yet. "I needed one for school, and when Kroger upgraded their system, Mom talked them into giving her this one since it won't work anymore on just a battery."

It was a laptop so ancient I was surprised it still worked at all, but it started right up after Josh plugged it in.

I handed it over. "You know your mom's password to log on?"

His focus remained half on the television. "Sure. Let me open what you need." He not only entered the start-up password but also logged in to Del's checking account and two credit card accounts, all without looking anything up. I could have checked all this from home, but it was somehow fitting to tackle the job with Del's clutter surrounding me.

I settled in to look through her finances, which told a straightforward story. Income came from Del's job and from Social Security payments to Del and Josh as surviving family. Outflow went to rent, cell phones, car payments, and a seemingly endless series of credit charges—department stores, shoe stores, online shopping. Lots of bars. Lots and lots of take-out restaurants. Josh's Uber rides were there, and I gasped at the total.

Credit card bills were paid with the minimum each month. One card was maxed out at ten thousand dollars and hadn't been used for a while. The other was close to its ceiling. I read through it all twice, with a focus on the past two months.

"Josh, turn off the TV for a minute. I want to ask you about a few things."

He obediently clicked off the set.

"So, is this everything? I don't see payments for electricity or gas or water."

"It's all part of the rent."

"You're watching cable. I'm on wireless internet. Where is that?"

Josh looked a little guilty. "The guy next door has a cable splitter and lets Mom get it for free. And the internet . . . well, the lady above us set up her wireless using *password* as her password."

I swallowed my impulse to spout some sort of lecture about honesty. This wasn't my kid.

"This is really everything?" I wouldn't have expected a boy Josh's age to know this level of detail about home finances, but that appeared to be the case.

"Yeah. Sometimes Grandma will send a check if Mom gets on the phone and cries, but usually that's when both the credit cards are maxed, and the money goes to pay down the balances."

"It looks like Del uses a card for everything—I'm seeing charges for less than a dollar. But the checking account also shows regular ATM cash withdrawals of two or three hundred dollars at a time. Usually right after the Social Security payments come in."

Josh looked away. I waited. He got up, went to the pile of mail I'd assembled, and flipped through it. He pulled out a credit card bill and brought it back. "We'll need to pay this."

Nice try. "Josh. Come on. I'm putting my life on hold to help you. Meet me halfway." I thought I knew where the cash was going. After hearing about the forged prescriptions, I'd looked up the street price of OxyContin—about ten dollars a tablet for the low dose, and seventy or eighty for each eighty-milligram whopper. Home-grown drugs weren't any cheaper. I hated to put Josh on the spot, but if we were going to find Del, I needed to know for sure.

He kicked the heel of one tennis shoe against the floor like he was trying to drive a decision into place. Finally, he sighed. "I'll show you."

I followed him into the kitchen. He opened the freezer and pulled out the four half gallons of ice cream—chocolate, vanilla, fudge ripple, and Moose Tracks. Del always used to reach for ice cream and a cigarette when she was upset. Another thing that hadn't changed.

Tucked in the back corner of the freezer was a pint-sized container of rocky road. Josh pulled it out and handed it to me. "She took most of it but left one behind. Probably by mistake."

The container had been washed out, and a plastic bag inside held a single tablet. I couldn't identify it just by looking at it—it had an irregular shape and no identifying code number. Probably counterfeit, cooked up in somebody's garage. But even without a label, the fact it had been hidden in the freezer told me all I needed. This was probably some sort of opiate.

I'd expected it. Sought out confirmation. But the full recognition was a hard kick to the diaphragm. Del was still taking illegal drugs even after her probation. She was my sister, and despite everything, I couldn't look at the situation as if she were a stranger.

This might explain Carl's involvement—his fury, his determination to track her down. It might even explain Del's disappearance. It unquestionably made Josh's future look even bleaker than I'd feared.

He picked at a loose edge of the Formica countertop with his thumbnail. "She used to take them on the weekends, mainly when she went out with friends. Then when she dated Carl, it got worse. Lately—" He stopped. Busied himself putting the real ice cream containers back in the freezer.

"Lately, she's been taking more?"

He nodded, not looking my way.

I reached out and touched his arm, not sure how such contact would be received, and Josh propelled himself toward me. He buried his head in my shoulder, and I gave him the strongest hug possible, hoping it would message all the right things. *I'm here. I'm solid. You can count on me.* I wished I knew whether I meant it.

It had been a very long time since I'd held another human being close this way, and a tangled knot in my chest unraveled a little, easing a tension I didn't know I carried. "It will work out. We'll find her. And when we do, we'll see what we can do to get her some help."

I felt his nod against my shoulder, but he made no effort to pull away.

If Del stopped spending so much on drugs, their financials would not be all that bad. There were lots of easy cuts she could make on the spending side, and the Social Security payments were enough of a boost on top of Del's salary that she'd be able to whittle down the credit card debt. Once those balances were paid down . . .

I jerked my thoughts to a screeching halt.

What the hell was I doing? Instead of trying to escape the spider's web, I was weaving its strands into a stronger chain. If I could find my sister, great. If I could help Josh, wonderful. But I couldn't fix the world. I couldn't fix Carl. And no one, no matter how well intentioned, could ever fix Del.

Josh seemed to suddenly realize he was still curled against me, and he lurched away, his face a brilliant red. Tellico flopped at our feet, and Josh dropped to one knee to pet him, avoiding my eyes.

I cleared my throat, a little sad that his reaction to my hug was embarrassment and an impulse to flee. "Come take a look at these credit charges. Nothing jumps out at me, but you may see something I don't."

He leaped up at once, acting relieved to move on from talk of drugs, and he followed me back to the laptop. I had gone backward through the charges Del had made, and he now started scrolling forward. He hit an entry dated a few days before she disappeared and stopped. "This one is weird. That was on a Saturday night, wasn't it?"

Martin's Bar and Grill. Forty-two dollars and twenty cents.

I checked the calendar on my phone. "Yeah, it was Saturday. What's weird about it?"

"Mom went out on a date that night. I mean, I thought it was a date—she was all dressed up, and she acted excited. She went out most Saturdays. That's why I didn't mention it. But she wouldn't have paid if it was really a date."

"It was the next Monday when she left?"

"Yeah. She had me take my stuff over to Jill and Francie's before the school bus picked me up in the morning, and I went to their place after school."

Josh was right. There could be a connection. The Del I knew would never have picked up the tab, or even part of the tab, if she was out on an actual date. "Do you know who she went out with? His name? Or what he looked like?"

Josh's eyes closed, his brow furrowed, his head dropped forward. I waited, and after half a minute his head snapped up. "I never saw him—she drove there. But she had me do a search online to find his phone number."

"She didn't know his number?"

"Nope. She said she'd seen him at the Kroger. Knew him in high school or something."

He thought again, and I wondered how his memory worked. Did he flip through pages in his head? Or jump straight to an image like a keyword search?

Regardless of how it worked, it only took a few seconds. "Got it. His name was Dave Bradford. Here's his number." He scribbled a phone number on the back of an envelope and gave me a look of triumph.

I couldn't recall anyone with that name from high school, but if he was in Del's class, two years behind mine, that wasn't too surprising.

Finding Dave Bradford might not be the answer to our problems, but it was a logical first step. And at the moment, it was the only step we had.

CHAPTER TEN

Josh

Mrs. Peterson, my language arts teacher, said one time that wishing for something is sometimes better than getting it. When Bryn and I got to Memphis, I started thinking she could be right.

I was home, and maybe that was good. But I kept expecting the door to open and for Mom to walk in, a six-pack in each hand, laughing and giving me shit for being worried. Without her, it was too quiet. Too calm. When I thought about Mom maybe never coming back, the apartment was way too empty.

Bryn didn't say much, but I could tell right off the whole place bothered her. She tried to get the air conditioner working, but it had been dead for ages. The window fans rumbled to life when she turned them on, but they just rearranged the dust. She piled the dirty laundry all in one heap, but I told her how far the laundromat was, and she sighed and didn't try to take it there.

She tossed out the junk mail and emptied ashtrays and scrubbed the stove, all of this going on while she tried again and again to get Dave Bradford to answer his phone. She left a whole bunch of messages, but he didn't call back.

When she thought I wasn't looking, she picked up those pictures Mom kept by the sofa and stared at them for a while, her face so sad it made me wish I knew what to do. Mom said she kept them out because I needed to remember I'd had a father, but Bryn looked at them like there was plenty she wanted to forget.

She left another *call me* message for Grandma, and her voice sounded as sad as the look on her face.

She didn't say anything more about Carl, but she checked out every car that drove down the street. When I took some of the leftover lo mein noodles out to the porch for Patsy, Bryn came with me and watched every minute. If Tellico growled at a noise, or the Doberman's bark got faster across the street, she got up and peered out the windows.

It made me jumpy, but I was glad she was taking Carl seriously. I double-checked that the doors were locked and made sure Tellico stayed close. Those movies where the bad guy is hiding in a dark corner and the people in the house don't know it were pretty fake, but I kept all the lights on anyway.

Landon Facetimed her late in the evening, and I muted the TV so she could hear.

"I moved the goats over this morning. They've settled in well." He made it sound like loading up four goats and hauling them around was no big deal, but I bet Python and Java were scared in his truck.

"Thanks so much. I owe you big-time for all this." At least Bryn didn't sound so sad when she talked to Landon. "I've been checking the security system app, and it seems to be working. It showed your truck going in and coming out again."

"Good. I'm more worried about you and Josh in Memphis than I am about things here. Everything okay? You haven't heard anything more from Carl, have you?"

Bryn opened her mouth to say something, glanced at me, and changed her mind. Had something else happened with Carl that I didn't know about? She looked around the apartment real slow and sidestepped the question. "I'm feeling a bit claustrophobic but hanging in there. We're trying to track down a guy who saw Del a few days before she left. Otherwise, not much to go on. Hopefully, I'll be back home soon."

"Do what you need to do. I've got things here."

They talked for a while about other stuff, and I quit listening. Bryn said goodbye and then sat there, holding the phone and running one finger around the edge of a cigarette burn in the arm of the couch.

"He likes you." Landon might as well tattoo it on his forehead. "Why aren't you two together?"

Bryn frowned and didn't look my way. "It's complicated."

Yeah, right. If Mom had a nice guy like him that interested, she would have been all over it. If Bryn kept on like she was, Landon would find somebody else for sure. But at least his call seemed to cut down on Bryn's worry a little.

*   *   *

The next morning, Bryn was up early. I came into the kitchen, and she was pacing back and forth, as restless as Mom when she needed a buy. "Let's pick up some lunch stuff and go out to a park for the day. Tellico deserves a run, and I'm going stir-crazy. I can't just hang around in this apartment all day waiting for Dave Bradford to call. If he ever does. Have you ever been to Meeman-Shelby State Park?"

"Never heard of it." What I wanted to do was find Mom, but since we had to wait, I was planning to get back to *Starfleet Command*. I would rather combat the Romulan plague and fight the Klingons while I sat on the couch with a Coke than get dragged out to some park in the middle of nowhere. "And we're probably safer here."

I thought Bryn would get the hint, but she barreled right on.

"Don't worry. You'll like it. I haven't been there for a long time, but it can't have changed much." She'd made up her mind. I don't know why she even bothered to ask me. "Come on. Help me get things together. Dave can call us there as easily as here."

So we went. And, okay, I was wrong—it was nice out there. The park stretched right along the Mississippi River, way bigger than the city park with the rusty playground I passed on my way to school. Here, there was a lake and woods and lots of room for Tellico to run.

We took a hike, following a trail marked with yellow triangles nailed to the trees. Bryn kept rattling off the names of birds and trees and mushrooms and stuff, like she thought I was taking notes or something, but I just liked walking and listening to the breeze. It talked in quiet sounds through the leaves, friendly in a different way than the wind in town. I couldn't see a single building anywhere, just trees, which was neat like that game *The Forest* I played a few times over at Marcus's house, but without the cannibalistic mutants.

At the lake, there was a boat rental place. "We should have kept your kayak on the truck."

Bryn looked at me curiously. "You want to go out on the lake? We can rent a canoe, and that way Tellico can come with us."

I'd expected her to ignore me—did she really mean we could do it? I guess the look on my face was answer enough, because she grinned, went inside, and made the arrangement.

We loaded the sandwiches and drinks into the boat and headed out. I was in front. I always thought you just sort of dragged the paddle through the water, but no. Bryn taught me forward, draw, cross-draw, stern pry, J-stroke—who knew canoeing was so complicated? She said I was a natural. Tellico sat in the middle of the canoe and looked around like he thought he was in charge.

There were trees standing on tall roots like stilts along the shore, which Bryn said were cypress, and tall birds tiptoed along the edge of the water, looking for fish—great blue herons. I could hear other birds in the trees, but sometimes the only sound was the splash of our paddles. Out here there wasn't even any traffic noise. Bryn claimed deer and coyotes lived here too, and I kept careful watch, thinking about her bobcat at home, but we didn't see anything except squirrels.

For lunch we pulled into shore at a sunny spot to eat, and Tellico went swimming and got me all wet when he shook himself dry. After, I stretched out on a big flat rock that was warm from the sun. I stayed still and watched a turtle crawl up on a log. Its neck was so long I couldn't see how he could fit it back into its shell, but when I clapped my hands, he tucked himself all the way in. Must be nice to have a hiding spot right there on your back.

Trees, sunshine, birds. A lake, a picnic, a dog. It was like one of those TV shows where there's a big happy family. But my family wasn't there, and a rocky feeling in my gut reminded me of it every minute. Maybe I shouldn't be here having a good time when Mom could be in trouble. Maybe I shouldn't have told Bryn about the pills. Maybe I shouldn't have even gone to her for help.

At least out here Bryn quit looking around for Carl all the time. "You've really never been here before?" she asked. We were getting ready to paddle again.

"Mom doesn't like mosquitoes." That seemed to satisfy her, but the truth was, I couldn't quite believe all this was so close to home and I'd never known a thing about it. Jackson Wallace was always bringing his Boy Scout stuff to school and talking nonstop about camping and hiking, but he was a jerk. Nobody I hung out with ever did stuff like this, but I bet Marcus would like it if he got the chance.

Bryn let me paddle in the back—the *stern*—after lunch. We went in circles for a while, but then I got the hang of things, and I was in charge, no matter what Tellico believed. By the time we got to the dock, my hands were stiff from holding the paddle, and my arms were aching bad, but I was pretty much a pro.

We turned in the paddles and life jackets and headed toward the truck. "Do you do stuff like this all the time?"

Bryn laughed. "Not all the time. I have a job, you know, even though I work from home. You just happened to arrive when I had a break between projects. There's the garden. And the orchard. And the rest of the homestead. But I go paddling when I can. There's a couple of lakes near home." We loaded Tellico into the back seat and got in front. "It's calming, being outside like this. I get restless if I'm indoors too much."

Restless. That was Mom. Always moving, always lighting a cigarette, or flipping TV channels, or fidgeting while she talked on the phone. Maybe when she was back home, I could get her to bring me here. Maybe it would help her too.

Bryn slid her key into the ignition but stopped and pulled out her phone when it chimed with a text. She opened the message and her eyes got real big. "What the hell?" She sounded scared and off-the-charts mad. Just that fast, the good feeling of the lake got erased.

She banged her door open and stepped into the parking lot, walking this way and that, looking around in all directions, her hands in tight fists. There were a few other cars, but I couldn't see any other people.

She'd dropped her phone on her seat with the text still showing, so of course I looked. It was a picture of Bryn and me with paddles and life jackets in our hands. I was talking and she was smiling, and we were walking along the dock. This dock right here. Someone had to have taken it less than five minutes before.

The message with the picture said: *Quit fucking around. Five days left.*

Bryn came storming back to the truck. She looked startled and not too happy when she saw the phone in my hand, but whatever. I would have made her tell me anyway.

"See anyone?"

She shook her head, her face tense. "They must have left before they sent the message."

"Carl?"

"Or someone working for him." She hit the steering wheel with the palm of her hand, hard enough that the whole wheel shook. "Dammit, I blocked the number so he wouldn't . . ." Her voice tapered off and she looked my way, but I guess she decided there was no point now in locking me out. "He sent a message yesterday, warning that we had six days. This one came from a different number."

So, someone was following us. All the way from Bryn's place back to Memphis? Maybe. But it would have been easier to follow from the apartment. Bryn had kept checking the rearview mirror, but maybe it wasn't as easy to spot a tail in real life as on the cop shows.

Creepy. Maybe someone was watching us right now. I looked around, which was stupid, but hey, I looked anyway.

Bryn was just sitting there, staring out the window. I guess nothing had changed—we already knew what Carl wanted—but it felt like plenty had changed. Like Carl could reach out and grab us whenever he wanted, no matter where we were.

The phone rang in my hand, and we both jumped. I tossed it to Bryn like it might burn my fingers.

She took a deep breath and answered. "Hello?" She listened, and almost at once she relaxed. "Thanks so much for calling me back." She gave me a thumbs-up, so I'd know it was Dave Bradford at last.

Maybe things were looking up for a change.

She explained about Mom being gone and told him she was helping me look for her. She asked about the dinner they'd had, but then she looked at her watch. "Five o'clock? Yes, I think I can make that. Yes, the one on Compton. I'll find it. I really appreciate it." She hung up and turned to face me. "He's got meetings now at work, and then he's leaving town tonight, but he said he'd meet me at a sub shop on Compton near his office. Do you know where that is?"

Now we were getting somewhere. I tried to force my worries about Carl into a box. I searched on my map app, pulled up directions, and looked at the travel time. "You can just barely make it from here by five."

"Not enough time to drop you and Tellico off first?"

"No. It's the wrong direction."

I could tell she didn't like that, and she sat there for a minute instead of pulling out of the parking spot.

Trying to cut me out again. "I don't want you leaving me at the apartment if Carl is watching us. Plus, this is my mom we're talking about. I should be there."

A flicker of pity came and went on her face so fast I almost missed it, but then she shook her head like it had never been there. "You've been great, Josh, really. We'd be nowhere without all your information. But it's because it's your mom that I'd rather you not hear all this. If the dinner with Dave is connected to the reason she left or the reason Carl's after her . . ." Her words drifted to a halt.

Enough. I was sick and tired of her treating me like a little kid. "What do you think I'm going to learn that I don't already know? That my mom has boyfriends? That she drinks a lot? Takes pills? I live with her. I know all that."

Bryn put the truck in gear and started toward the exit. "Yeah, okay, I get it. We'll see. I don't want to leave Tellico in a hot truck, so you may need to dog-sit while I go in."

There was no way I was going to be left out of this. No way. But I kept my mouth shut and gave Bryn directions to get there. She kept checking behind us, and so did I. I couldn't see anyone following, but that didn't make me feel any better.

We were about five minutes late. The sub shop had its own parking lot, and a man in khakis, a yellow shirt, and a dark blue tie sat waiting at one of the tables on the patio, without any food in front of him. Bryn got out and went to introduce herself, so I hopped out of the truck, grabbed Tellico's leash, and sat at the table beside her, like I belonged. Tellico stretched out by my feet.

Bryn gave me a dirty look and I gave her one back, but she didn't make me leave. "Dave, this is Del's son, Josh."

"Hi, Josh."

Mom had a lot of guy friends, but I had never seen this one before. He wore one of those super-fancy wristwatches with all kinds of dials built in. Nice haircut. Nice shoes. On the table beside him was one of those brand-new iPhones I'd seen online. Maybe this was all just for his job, but he sure didn't look like the sort of guy Mom usually went out with.

"Anything you can tell us would help a lot." Bryn leaned forward, focused and intent. "Del left town two days after you saw her, and we wondered if she said anything. Or if what you talked about could be connected to where she went."

"It's possible." He thought for a minute, sort of nodding to himself. "To be honest, it was all a little weird. Del and I used to hang out in high school, and then after we graduated, I dated one of her friends. Cindy and I doubled a few times with Del and Sawyer, must have been a year or so after they were married." He turned to me with a smile. "They brought a baby out to dinner once. That must have been you."

I nodded like I could remember that far back, but no way.

Dave checked his fancy watch. "Let me start at the beginning. In January, I went with some buddies on a ski trip to Aspen."

Bryn looked like she knew what he meant. I didn't know a place called Aspen, but skiing meant not around here.

"So," Dave went on, "one night we're out drinking, and I look across the room, and there's Sawyer, standing there big as life. Well, not Sawyer, obviously . . ." he glanced my way, and his words stumbled a little. "I knew he . . . passed in a car crash or something ages ago, so it wasn't him. But it looked a hell of a lot like him, and he had a tequila shot, salt, and lime lined up in front of him."

Bryn nodded. "Tequila was always Sawyer's drink, and he used to treat the whole process like a ritual. Shot in one gulp, glass turned over, salt off a spoon because he didn't like it on his hand, and just a quick lick of lime."

I filed the details away. If Dad did it like that, I'd have to try it one day.

"Yeah," Dave said. "Sawyer was the only person I'd ever seen do it that way, so when I saw this guy out in Aspen doing the exact same thing, it caught my attention, right? So, I go up and talk with the guy, and we laugh about the fact he looks so much like someone who's dead, like, you know, everyone has a twin somewhere, that sort of thing. And that was it."

"So, what? You called Del and told her?"

"No, I hadn't seen Del in years. But a couple of weeks ago, I stopped in at a Kroger to grab some wine on the way to a party—across town, not my usual grocery, right? And Del is working the express lane cash register, and we say *'Hey'* and *'How you doing?'* and all that. I mention I'd seen Sawyer's double, and I take my wine and leave, right?"

"Got it."

"A few days later, Del calls out of the blue, leaves a message, says she needs to see me. Says if I'll meet her, she'll treat for dinner."

He glanced at me, and I got the idea he was deciding not to say something while I was there, which was a pattern that was really starting to get old. But he went on with his story.

"I met her as we arranged. Del was always a lot of fun in the old days, but the only thing she wanted to talk about this time was this bit about Sawyer's double. What day was it, what bar was it, what else had I noticed about this guy—everything I could remember. It was weird. I was in Aspen the second week of January, but I couldn't remember which day it was. And the bar had all this Boston Red Sox stuff on the wall, which was odd enough out West I remembered it, but no way could I remember the name of the bar."

"Did she say why she wanted to know all those details? Or what else she was going to do?"

"No, she didn't say a thing." He gave another glance my way. "But she seemed to believe it was possible maybe this *was* Sawyer. And that's crazy, right? I mean, the car crash and all."

"Plane crash, actually. I don't know the details." Bryn stared at the street for a minute, even though there was nothing there but a crumpled beer can. "But it *wasn't* Sawyer, right? Even if you didn't know he was dead, you would have known this guy wasn't him?"

"Right. His nose was different. His chin wasn't right either. And, of course, he didn't recognize me in the least. It was probably just the thing with the tequila shot that made me think about Sawyer. You know how bars are, not much light, everything looks a bit off after a few drinks. But it was eerie, let me tell you. It made me think later about brothers adopted out to different families and never knowing about each other, that sort of thing."

I'd never thought about something like that. Dad was supposed to be an only child, and both of my grandparents on his side died when I was a baby. But what if he *was* adopted? What if Mom was out at this Aspen place, searching for my uncle? An aunt I didn't know about and now maybe an uncle. It was like a movie.

Bryn asked a few more questions, but Dave didn't know anything else.

His watch chirped like a bird, and he gave it a quick look. "Sorry, I've got to run. I've got a flight heading out later this evening. But, look, let me know how it turns out, would you? I hope Del's okay."

Bryn thanked him. I took Tellico back to the truck, but Bryn didn't follow. I looked back, and Dave was leaning toward her, talking fast. Then he waved and walked away.

"What did he say to you at the end?" I asked.

Bryn busied herself putting the key in the ignition and opening the windows for fresh air. "Nothing."

Uh-huh. "And where's Aspen?"

"Colorado."

I pulled up a memory snapshot from last year's geography test. One of those states with square corners. "How far away is it?"

"Far. Like, twelve hundred miles. Maybe more."

That's all she said. Bryn stayed really quiet the whole way back to the apartment, and I think she forgot to check behind us. I played a Childish Gambino song extra loud on my phone to bug her, but she didn't even tell me to turn it down.

Twelve hundred miles. A long, long way. And we only had five days. My worry circled twice around my belly and settled in to stay.

Finding Mom that far away was going to be just about impossible.

CHAPTER ELEVEN

Bryn

Aspen. The whole drive back to the apartment, I chewed on what Dave had told us, my panic over Carl's snooping set aside for the moment. If Del had heard the same identical-twin story from him that he'd told us, she would have headed straight out to Aspen. I had no doubt, no doubt at all.

Running off this way was classic Del, and her foolishness pushed all my buttons. When she was thirteen, she and a girlfriend had hopped a bus to Nashville to go to a Backstreet Boys concert, wandering home three days later like it was no big deal. When I was in college and Del was in high school, I got so many phone calls from Mom about Del's disappearances, I didn't even try to keep the stories straight—beach weekends, a multiday barhop, a girls' night out that somehow lasted four days. Now she'd graduated from days missing to more than a week missing, and I was convinced she'd expanded her range from cross-state to cross-country.

It would be just like Del to dream up a movie-of-the-week plot and convince herself Sawyer was still alive, and just like her to decide she needed to track him down and give him what for. Ridiculous. The drugs must have addled her brain. Sawyer wouldn't have been declared officially dead unless he was . . . dead. Dead, as in now he was a corpse. Dead, as in not breathing, not alive, not drinking tequila shots in a bar in Aspen.

I'd had plenty of proof Sawyer couldn't keep his pants zipped, but fake his own death and abandon his son? No way. No matter how fed up he might have been with Del, I couldn't make myself believe it. Del was just indulging in fairy tales.

So, there it was. My wayward sister was most likely in Aspen, and once again, the obvious choice was to call the police and let them start a search there. They could do their job, and I could get back home where I belonged. To hell with Carl—when the cops found Del, I'd simply let him know where she was and let the two of them settle things.

But I didn't reach for my phone.

Dave had pulled me back after Josh headed for the truck. "Listen, I didn't want to say anything in front of the boy, but you should know Del was in bad shape the night I saw her."

"Bad shape how?"

"High. Narcotic high—my sister went down that path; I know the signs. Serious signs, not a friendly fun-time buzz. She was tense, jittery, short of breath. She ordered a big meal and ate two bites. She's no first timer. She's well into it."

I added it to the list of things to toss in her face when I found her.

When *I* found her. Not the police. I hadn't realized I'd made my decision until those words hit home.

It wasn't just about Carl, although, yeah, okay, fear was a great motivator. It was the recognition that Del needed help. She needed treatment, not an arrest. And it was also because of Josh, the son I might once have had, a boy who deserved better than he'd gotten so far. The last thing he needed was a mother in jail. I couldn't set the Aspen police on Del's drug-littered trail until I'd given it a shot myself.

I could delay my next coding job. Ask Landon to hang in there a little longer, keeping an eye on things at home. It wasn't ideal, but I could make it work—I just needed to hustle. If I was going to keep looking, I needed to find Del before Carl lost patience, no question about that.

By the time we got back to the apartment, I was thinking about filling the gas tank and checking a map, wondering how long it would take to reach Colorado.

I circled the block as usual and once again saw nothing that looked worrisome. Checked behind me and didn't see anyone turning into the street.

Josh was acting just as paranoid as I was, turning around in his seat to look in all directions. "All the cars I see on the street belong here." It was the first thing he had said since leaving Dave.

"Good. Best to make sure." I parked the truck and we got out.

The front porch of the big fourplex ran the full width of the house, deep enough for tables and chairs if anyone had cared to furnish it. Since *decorate* appeared to be an alien word in this neighborhood, the porch was instead stacked at both ends with assorted junk—a dead refrigerator, a stack of tattered cardboard boxes, a child's crib with one side caved in.

All this clutter blocked the view from the street, and it wasn't until we were all the way up the front walk that I saw someone waiting. He had pulled an old wooden crate out of the junkpile, and he was sitting on it by the front door. He held a cigarette, and Patsy was curled in his lap, looking even tinier than usual compared to the manicured hand that petted her. I froze, one foot on the bottom step, cigarette smoke creeping down my throat in a choking swirl.

Carl. *Shit.* No need to follow us, he could have just headed straight here. I broke out in an adrenaline-charged sweat.

Tellico growled on cue beside me, and Josh gasped, his body tense and his eyes fixed on the cat.

Carl wore the same slacks-and-jacket style he'd had on at the homestead, still looking more like an executive than a drug dealer. "About time you got back. I've been waiting." He acted like we were late for a scheduled appointment. "I have employees and customers who depend on me. I need to get this mess settled."

He sounded so smooth—like some sort of Better Business Bureau member following up on a distribution issue. But the next minute, his attitude shifted. He glared at me, and his voice got nasty. "You're supposed to be the smart sister, so get with it. The clock's ticking, I haven't heard from Del yet, and now I get a photo of you screwing around in a park somewhere."

That answered the question of whether Carl himself had taken the picture, but it didn't make me feel any better to confirm there were other people out there reporting in to him. My thoughts were swirling, and I was still so dismayed by his presence, I couldn't think how to respond.

Maybe I was taking too long to answer, or maybe he'd planned it from the start, but he moved fast, pinning Patsy tight against his chest. She gave a startled meow, but Carl had her in a tight grip. He moved his cigarette, holding the lit end only an inch away from her face.

Whatever threat he planned to speak died in his throat because as soon as he seized the cat, Josh exploded.

"No!" Josh knocked me to one side and lunged up the stairs, grabbing for the hand that threatened the cat.

Carl dropped the cigarette and in one seamless move, he backhanded Josh, moving fast and hitting hard. Josh fell against the porch railing, one hand pressed to his cheek. Tellico barked in a frenzy and started to leap forward, but I grabbed his collar and dragged him back. I had no doubt his teeth could do some major damage, but that wouldn't solve anything. Patsy took full advantage of the chaos, wiggled out of Carl's grasp, and streaked away.

My heart pounded in my ears, and my face throbbed as if I were the one who'd been hit. My legs were shaking so hard I didn't trust them to move. The casualness with which Carl had struck was as distressing as the blow itself. "Josh, are you okay?"

"Guess so." He didn't sound very convincing, but I was going to have to wait to check for myself.

Carl was on his feet, and he came to the top of the stairs, his face an angry red. I backed up a few steps, but I still had to crane my neck to meet his glare.

"You said we had a week." I sounded more pitiful than I wanted to, but maybe that was okay. There was little chance we'd find Del that soon if we had to drive to Colorado, and I didn't want to tell him we were going. I glanced at Josh, who was standing now, looking angry but holding still. "It's only been two days. We're looking, but it's going to take more time."

"I don't have time." Carl glanced at Tellico, still tense and ready, and he made no attempt to come closer. "I don't think you're taking me seriously enough."

He pulled a lighter from his pocket and flicked it, the flame shooting higher than normal. He held it in front of him, staring at it, and for a moment he seemed to forget we were there. He was utterly mesmerized by that flame. Fascinated. Almost affectionate.

I'd never seen anything so profoundly disturbing.

He finally gave himself a little shake, clicked the lighter closed and looked back at Josh. "No chickens here, but this old house is all wood."

His words tossed me back to the moment I'd placed Annabelle into the ground, the rich black dirt cascading down on top of her, covering her beautiful red feathers. The fear that had kept me in check so far converted into hundred-proof fury.

"You killed Annabelle. And you stand there threatening cats and hitting children and tossing orders around like Josh and I have something to do with all this. Like it's somehow our fault Del's missing!" My voice saturated the street. "Back off. Back off, or you'll never find Del. Whatever the hell it is that you think she has will disappear for good. I'll make sure of it."

Josh gave a sharp intake of breath from his spot on the porch, a vote that I'd gone too far.

Carl stiffened, his face tightening hard and his eyes narrowing, a bird of prey eyeing his next meal. "Annabelle? It had a name? It was a chicken. A stupid chicken at that. She didn't even try to get away. Run over to the Piggly Wiggly and pick out a fryer. They're on special this week."

Pick out a fryer? "You bastard." I spit the words his way without thinking.

Now I really had gone too far. For a few seconds, Carl's anger crackled like an electrical charge, and if Tellico hadn't been standing guard, I think he would have lunged at me. I stood my ground, but that was only because I was too afraid to run.

The next moment, as if throwing an invisible switch, Carl's face relaxed into normalcy, once again a calm businessman, his fury stuffed inside. His screechy laugh made my skin crawl, the abrupt transformation even more unsettling than his anger.

"You've got more snap than your sister, I'll give you credit. But don't get too damn cocky. I can always find you when I want to. You and Josh both."

A ball of ice settled deep in my belly, the cold radiating outward to chill my skin. Any sensible person would leave it at that, but the question that had consumed me for two full days took this moment to ignore common sense and make itself known. "At the cabin—back home—you said you manipulated Sawyer into doing something. What did you mean?"

I held my breath, afraid the question would set him off again, but he seemed to relish the opportunity to brag.

"You three always thought you were so much better than me—you and Sawyer and Del. But you were the real fools. That night of the wreck? While you and your precious Sawyer were trying to get Del to stop screaming, I found a bag of cash and a gun in that wrecked car and liberated them. That's why I couldn't let Sawyer call the police. The fact the gun freaked you out was just an unexpected bonus. The three of you were so twisted you didn't even notice I was carrying a bag I didn't have when you picked me up. That bag held thirty thousand dollars, more money than I'd ever seen before. That money is what backed the start of my current enterprise."

That explained a lot. "And Sawyer?"

Carl opened his mouth, then closed it, and I got the sense he was deciding he needed to be a little more cautious in what he admitted. "That original funding source wasn't going to last forever. The bag of money also contained a key, and Sawyer turned out to be able to put it to good use."

I kept my face blank. Steven had told me about the bank theft—Carl had to be talking about a safe deposit key. He didn't know I knew anything about it, and I was happy to keep it that way.

Carl rattled on. "I backed Sawyer into a corner, and he helped me out. I had high hopes it was the start of a long and interesting partnership, but the idiot nose-dived into the Gulf. What a tragedy." Carl's smirk belied his words.

He shook himself. "Enough with the ancient history. You'd better get busy. I've got more important things to do than to keep chasing after you."

He came down the front steps, and I had to step aside to let him pass, dragging Tellico along with me. Standing so near him made me think of land mines and rumbling volcanoes and tectonic plates under massive tension. I'd never met a person so calm on the surface but so primed for explosion.

His half smile, his relaxed shoulders, the confident way he walked was all fake, an act he must have practiced for years, but he was careful to give Tellico plenty of room as he made his way down the walkway.

I turned as he headed toward the street, keeping my eye on him, and Josh joined me.

Carl paused when he was halfway to the curb. "Call me when you find her. Better yet, get her to hand over the two thousand eighty-milligram tabs she took. Or the money she got from selling them. I hired her to deliver across town, not to disappear with it."

In a single heartbeat, the shreds of anger that were still supporting me disappeared, replaced once again by overwhelming fear. I knew Carl was playing for high stakes, but I hadn't envisioned anything on this scale. He receded from view, down the street, but I was too stunned to watch where he went.

Two thousand eighty-milligram tablets of some sort of opiate? A street value of more than a hundred and fifty thousand dollars. No wonder Carl was pissed. No wonder he'd chased Josh across the state on the off chance he'd lead him to Del. We were in even worse trouble than I'd thought.

What the hell had Del been thinking?

I sank onto the front steps, and Josh thudded down beside me. His face was sheet-white, except for the red mark on his cheek where he'd been hit. *Del, you idiot.* I put an arm around Josh's shoulders, but I could think of nothing to say. We were caught in the middle with no easy way out.

Patsy crept out from the bushes and crawled into Josh's lap, keeping a close eye on Tellico as she snuggled in. Josh patted her automatically, but none of the tension ebbed from his body.

"How's the face?"

"I jerked back when I saw his arm coming my way. It's not too bad."

"Risky, jumping in like that."

He turned to face me, indignant. "I couldn't let him hurt Patsy."

"I know. You were faster than I was. I would have done the same."

So, what now? Even after this latest episode, after seeing another example of Carl's violence and discovering the extent of his investment, I couldn't just walk away. I'd already thrashed through the reasons I felt obligated to look for Del, but now I had to add another one: my own damn pride. If I let fear drive me into hiding, I'd never be able to look myself in the mirror again.

And I needed to find a way to make Carl pay for his evil. I couldn't do that if I disappeared into the mountains.

Josh gave a long shuddering sigh, and I belatedly realized he was close to tears.

"It'll be okay." I didn't believe it. I knew he didn't believe it either. "We'll find your mom. We'll get things settled."

Josh gave an impatient shake of his head. "No. You don't get it. All of this is my fault. All of it."

"Don't be silly . . ." I stumbled to a halt. He looked so stricken, so convinced, it felt cruel to shrug off his distress. "Tell me. How is this your fault?"

Josh wiped his nose with the back of his hand and looked at me with red-rimmed eyes. "Carl used to hang out at The Lantern, and some days I'd see him on my way home from school. He'd say hi, and he acted nice, and he had expensive clothes and a new car, and I thought he would be better than some of the guys Mom went out with."

He paused. I waited for him to pull himself together enough to keep going.

"So, one day, I pointed him out to Mom. I thought he'd be a step up; I didn't know they already knew each other. And then they started dating . . . and Mom just got more and more pills . . . and now Mom is missing . . . and Annabelle . . . and Patsy . . ." He couldn't go any further.

I gave him a major hug. Maybe a hug for him. Maybe for me. Holding on tight to someone at least stopped my insides from shaking.

Josh gulped his way into some semblance of composure.

"Look, Josh, none of this is your fault. Del and Carl made their own choices."

"But if I hadn't . . ."

"No *buts*. You can't take responsibility for someone else's decisions."

Easier said than done.

We sat there a while longer in silence, the evening's shadows creeping their way up the street, softening the decrepit details. Even the neighbor's Doberman was quiet for a change.

"So," Josh said at last. "Maybe one good thing about Colorado is it's a long way away from Carl."

I squeezed his shoulder. Indeed.

A proper aunt probably would have talked about emotional issues for another hour, tried to offer better support than what he could glean from petting a stray cat. But I was exhausted, and I was no kind of proper aunt. "What about ordering in some pizza?"

He shook his head as if thinking about food was ridiculous, but perhaps he was as eager as I was to avoid tough topics for a while, because after a minute he pulled out his phone. "Pepperoni for me and a veggie special for you?"

"Sounds good."

He tapped away. "Delivery in forty-five minutes."

Ordering the pizzas took Josh thirty seconds, probably a standing account linked to Del's magic credit card. How often had he been here with a foodless kitchen, ordering in to eat a lonely dinner with his video games?

CHAPTER TWELVE

Bryn

We headed inside. Josh settled on the couch and grabbed his game controller, either back to normal or making a valiant attempt to fake it. Probably faking—he was still occasionally rubbing his cheek with a deep scowl.

"I'm going to make a few phone calls." Best to do it while he was occupied. "Give a shout when the pizza gets here."

"Yeah, okay." Spaceships already filled the television screen.

I went into the kitchen, pulled one of the beers out of the fridge, and pressed the ice-cold metal can to my forehead for a long moment. Opened it and took a deep swallow. If Del had stocked any whiskey, I would have reached for that instead.

Carl. A hundred and fifty thousand dollars. We were totally, totally, totally screwed.

I dialed Steven and was fortunate enough to catch him still on duty and at his desk.

"Nothing new to report on Del, I'm afraid." Loud voices echoing in the background were overlaid with chewing sounds.

I could practically smell the Juicy Fruit. "Nothing has come back on either your sister or her car. Did you learn anything in Memphis?"

"No luck here, I'm afraid." I didn't want to say anything about drugs but didn't like the blatant lie. "Well, maybe a glimmer of something. I'm going to keep following up, and I'll let you know if I learn anything definite." There, that was a little better.

"Any information about your sister's activities can help, but remember, this is a police matter." There was a pause. "So . . . about Carl Griffith." His voice was much quieter, and I had to concentrate to make out his words. "I reached out to a buddy of mine on the Memphis force. The unofficial belief is that the reason Griffith hasn't been found guilty on his various charges is because of witness intimidation."

My nerves were so fried, I almost laughed out loud. Carl? Intimidating? Yeah, no kidding.

"Watch your step," Steven continued. "Stay clear of trouble. I'll keep working on tracking your sister. I'll let you know what we learn."

"Stay out of trouble." Good advice, but it felt like it was coming a little too late.

We traded another set of empty promises to connect at the lake someday, and I hung up.

I called Landon next and caught him as he was checking the goats. "Bryn, you wouldn't believe how fast these twins are growing. I'll send a video clip of them playing chase. Josh will love it. How's everything going? Is everything okay?"

No, everything was not okay. Del's troubles closed in around me, and hearing about the goats kicked my homesickness into high gear. "Today has been a mixed bag. We had a nice afternoon hiking and canoeing, but that already feels like ages ago."

I recounted Dave Bradford's story and walked Landon through my reasons for thinking Del had gone to Aspen. His listening powers were just as strong over the phone as they were in person, and I shared all the details.

"I'm sorry to hear that Del seems pretty far gone." Landon paused, and I could picture him by his barn, leaning against a fence post, thinking. "Do you believe her drug use is connected to why Carl is looking for her?"

"Yeah, that's the really bad news of the day. Carl was waiting for Josh and me when we got back here. It turns out Del stole two thousand tablets of some sort of opiate from him. That's what he wants back." I told him what Carl had said and done. When I got to the part where Carl stared at his lighter, I stumbled over my words. Just thinking about that scene tossed me back there, watching his disturbing fascination with the fire.

"Bryn, I don't like the sound of any of this. He hurt Josh and he could have hurt you. Do you really have to go all the way out to Colorado?"

The way he said it made it sound like Colorado was on the other side of the planet, but I wouldn't have expected anything different. I'd confessed my whitewater fears to him, and he'd shared the terror of being lost for hours on crowded city streets when he was five and on a family vacation. "I know it's not rational to hang on to those fears," he'd admitted, "but my brain won't let it go."

I knew plenty about irrational fears. "Yes, I need to go. She's my sister. I can't walk away and abandon her to Carl. And I can't leave Josh without a mother. Is there any way you can keep things going at home for a while longer? The way Carl was acting today, he's capable of anything. It will take two days to drive out to Aspen, and heaven knows how long to search."

Assuming I could even figure out exactly where to look. The hopelessness of what I was proposing hit me all over again, filling me with doubts.

"It's not a problem." Landon's calm voice made me believe it. "Everything's fine. Do what you have to, and I'll keep close watch here. If you don't give it your best shot, it's going to haunt you forever."

He was right. I had to keep going. By the time we finished, I almost believed I was on a reasonable path.

The next call I had to make wasn't going to be nearly so uplifting.

I punched the number on my phone. Tensed when, this time, it was answered right away. "Hi, Mom. It's Bryn."

I leaned against the tiny kitchen counter and braced myself for barbs. She was usually quick to tell me everything I was doing wrong. I generally responded with criticisms of my own, and we usually ended our phone chats with mutual sighs of relief.

I had hoped time would shift her attitude toward me—*look Mom, straight A's, a successful tech career, a life I love*—but none of those checkboxes mattered in the least. Her latest campaign was that she wanted me married. Preferably with children. Not out of any grandmotherly intention, but simply because in her mind, having children was a woman's destiny, and I wasn't toeing the line. She thought I should be working a standard nine-to-five job in a nice clean office, not spending my time in mud and manure, and she didn't hesitate to say so on a regular basis. I told myself to accept her chronic disappointment and move on, but every phone call rubbed ground glass into the raw patches.

Mom jumped right in, no *hello*, no *how-are-you*, no acknowledgment that she'd ignored my multiple voice mails. "Did you know Suzie Collin's daughter just got engaged? I talked to Beverly last week and . . ."

I could picture her surrounded by embroidered pillows on her ancient sofa, her feet propped on a hassock, a coffee mug and ashtray at her side. The curtains would be closed tight to block any glare on the television screen, and a low-wattage lamp in the corner would provide enough light to avoid tripping, but not enough to read by. I could hear some sort of talk show blaring in the background. Since Dad's death decades before, the TV never had a chance to cool down.

I zoned out. If she thought listing other people's successes hurt me, she was dead wrong. I tuned that shit out long ago. Or at least that's what I told myself.

It took about five minutes for the stream of pointless news to pause. When the break came—a break probably prompted by the fact she was reaching for a cigarette and fumbling for the lighter—I jumped in. "Mom, I need to ask you something. What do you know about the way Sawyer died?"

A normal person would have been surprised at my question. Asked why I was interested after so many years of silence. She asked nothing. I was certain she hadn't even blinked.

"Well, he was in that tiny plane—what do you expect? He flew way out over the Gulf, called for help, and disappeared. That was that."

I'd been surprised when I first heard Sawyer had taken up flying. His interests had always centered on the outdoors. But after a day in this stifling apartment, seeing how Del lived, I thought I understood. Alone in the sky. Able to travel hundreds of miles at a time. A bird's-eye view of a distant world below with no clutter, no traffic, nobody to hassle him. Each flight must have permitted a temporary escape from a life that trapped him.

"Did they find the plane?"

"Oh yes. Well, pieces of it. The Coast Guard found floating bits a few days later."

"And a body?"

"No. They didn't really expect to. Such a tragedy. So hard on your poor sister. She's had such a difficult life, losing her sweet husband in such an awful way, with a two-year-old to take care of and not even any life insurance money. I'm always telling that nice Mrs. Wilson next door how proud I am of the way she's carried forward."

I could feel an all-too-familiar tension knotting the back of my neck. "Have you heard from Del lately?"

"No. Not for several months. I sent her a check for her birthday in April, and she cashed it."

Of course, she did. How much of the money I sent Mom each month ended up passed along to Del for drug buys?

"Well, Mom, I'm actually in Memphis. Like I said in my message, Del has taken off, and I'm with Josh."

Again, any sort of normal reaction would at least involve some surprise that Del was missing and that I was in the same place as my nephew, but *normal* had never been the baseline state in my family. "Oh my. I'm sure everything is fine. You know Del has always been adventurous."

"Yes, well, I need to head out of state to look for her. I wondered if I could bring Josh to your place for a visit while I'm gone. Shouldn't be for too long, maybe a week or so."

I had thought Josh was thoroughly focused on his game, but there was an immediate squawk from the living room, and he materialized in the kitchen, his shoulders rigid, his fists clenched, and his face outraged. "No." He stage-whispered so Mom couldn't hear. "I'm not going to Grandma's. I'm coming with you. I won't go. I won't."

His insistence came in my right ear, and Mom's whine came in my left. "I don't think that will work, Bryn. I have women's club tomorrow, and I'm signed up for a potluck this weekend at church. There's nothing around here for a young boy to do. How old is he now? Eight? Ten? There isn't anyone his age in the neighborhood to play with. No, I don't think that will work at all."

I had thought maybe the fact Josh was the offspring of the amazing Del might give him special status, but apparently not. I'd get no help in this direction. "Yeah. All right, Mom. I understand."

"Well, thank you so much for calling, dear. Have Del get in touch to tell me about her travels. Such an interesting life. And I'm so glad you've left that awful farm and gone back to the city. I always knew that place was going to fail."

I said my goodbyes and hung up, shaking the stiffness out of my hand from clenching the phone so hard. I took another deep swallow of my beer.

As was true with all my calls home, there had been no inquiry about me or my life. Mom had stopped by my homestead once on her way to the Smokies. She looked around at my years of work—the barn resurrected from its original tumbled state, the organic garden built up from scratch, the Winesap trees in the orchard pruned to health and in full brilliant bloom—and she wrinkled her nose. *Rather far from the grocery store, isn't it?*

My throat tightened hard. Some things never changed. A storybook relationship with my mother was just as unlikely as a fairy-tale friendship with my sister.

I set my phone on the counter and turned to face a furious Josh.

"You want me to go stay at Grandma's? *Grandma's?*" His voice was half angry, half injured. "I trusted you. I thought you wanted my help."

He stormed back to the living room before I could reply, and at that moment the pizza arrived, so I let the argument lie. He wasn't safe with me, but even if I could convince him to stay with someone else, that might not improve the situation. Based on what Steven had said, Carl had a long reach. And if I left Josh against his wishes, who knows what he might try. Was it possible to Uber to Aspen?

We pulled slices of pizza onto plates in silence and sat on the couch with the TV off for a change. Josh's anger vibrated around him, and his pointed silence sucked all the energy out of the room, each passing second further underscoring my mistake. I should have talked to him before I called Mom. Should have treated him with respect. This temporary parenting gig was tougher than I expected.

"I'm sorry."

He grunted.

"I'll do a better job of including you from now on."

He took an angry bite of pizza, his face tense. "I'm not some little kid you need to ship out of the way or hide information from."

"You're right. It won't happen again."

He relaxed a bit. "Okay. Truce."

His distrust was still obvious, but at least the meal felt more companionable. I ate a slice of my pizza. "So. Colorado. Have you ever been that far west?"

"No."

"I went out for some whitewater trips when I was in college. You'll get to see the Rockies. I love the Appalachians, but the mountains out there are something else."

"They look huge in pictures." He sounded somewhat interested. Like his enthusiasm for the canoeing we'd done, it was a nice change from the constant video games.

"You'll be blown away. I'm sorry I didn't think to bring my camping gear. It never occurred to me we'd be heading out like this. Hotels are expensive, and sometimes it's hard to find ones that will take Tellico."

Josh swiveled to face me. "We've got camping stuff."

"You're kidding. Where is it?" Del was the last person on the planet who would ever sleep on the ground.

"There's a shed out back that was empty when we moved here. Mom put a bunch of stuff out there. She said she was going to sell it all one day, but I think she forgot."

"Let's check it out." We stashed the leftovers in the refrigerator, and Tellico and I followed Josh out the back door.

The shed stood in the far corner of the weedy backyard, a small wooden structure that looked even older than the house. The twisted wire holding the latch closed was rusted into a dense mass, and it took me a few minutes to pry the tangled strands apart, scraping my hands in the process. "After you." I followed Josh in, propping the door open to give us enough light.

Dusty heaps lined the edges of the room—a stack of empty boxes, a few full boxes that had never been unpacked. It smelled musty, closed tight for too many hot summer days in Tennessee humidity. It all looked as if it had been tossed in a hurry into random heaps and ignored. "When did you and your mom move in here?"

"Summer after I was in sixth grade." Three years ago. "They raised the rent where we were before."

I started working my way around the shed, checking box labels and looking into bags. Most of the things Del had stashed here were Sawyer's, and they brought strong memories. A box labeled *S's desk drawers*. He would have hated having all his stuff jumbled into a box. The dark blue winter coat he'd bought right after graduation, the one that made him look like an overripe blueberry. A pair of snowshoes from the time he went up to Michigan for a mid-December hiking trip.

There was a framed cross-stitched sampler commemorating Del and Sawyer's marriage—Mom's handiwork, I was sure—and a glass decanter that might have been a wedding gift. My jaw tensed, and I wondered how many of their wedding gifts had originally been intended as gifts for Sawyer and me. All Mom would have had to change was a single name on her cross-stitch—they'd been married on our planned wedding date.

And Josh was right, there was camping gear. Sawyer's and my camping gear. Every item—each reminder of what I'd lost—etched into me like acid. The tent Sawyer and I had bought together for our paddling trips. Our Coleman stove, blackened from steady use and smelling vaguely of propane. The dented cooking pots we'd assembled from yard sales. His sleeping bag, with a right-handed zipper. My sleeping bag, bought left-handed so we could zip them together, sleeping intertwined on cold mountain nights. All the things we'd treasured, callously discarded.

The photos in Del's apartment had triggered memories of her deceitfulness. These things of Sawyer's—of Sawyer's and mine when we were a couple—brought confusion.

He had kept the bright orange flashlight we'd bought in Virginia, the star chart we'd consulted on crystal nights when the Milky Way lit the sky, the battered cribbage board we'd used for countless games played on countless picnic tables. He'd kept them after his marriage. Did he ever look at them? Did he ever remember?

I flipped open a large flat box that looked vaguely familiar. My breath sucked in hard, and a low moan escaped before I could stop it. Josh gave me a sharp look. I forced my face into

order, or hoped I had, but I was gazing at a small framed painting, a mountain scene with a cascading set of rapids in the fore-
ground. Sawyer and I had bought this painting together. We'd
gone to West Virginia to run the Gauley, found a small café for
dinner, and put our name on their waiting list. With an hour to
kill, we'd wandered into an art gallery next door.

"Choose the one thing here you like best." His arm swept in
an arc to encompass the full gallery. "It's a game—don't worry
about price. I'll do the same, and we'll compare."

"All right. You go left, and I'll go right. No fair watching to
see where I stop the longest."

He laughed, and we separated.

It was a different way to browse, pretending I could actually
buy something. Most of the pieces were big, sized to form the
centerpiece of a wall, and they had big four-figure price tags to
match. Some were striking. Some were beautiful. But it was this
small painting that reached out to me. It was obvious the artist
knew and loved these mountains, and her brushstrokes had captured every nuance of the river's wildness.

Sawyer and I completed our inspection.

"Which one?" he asked.

"No way. You first."

He led me unerringly to the same painting I'd chosen. "This
one. This is the one with magic."

It felt like an omen.

Neither of us had money, both of us scraping by on student
loans, but Sawyer didn't hesitate. He lifted the frame from the
wall and carried it up front to pay. "I'll hold on to it," he promised. "We'll hang it together in our first apartment."

It was the first time he'd said anything that implied we had a future together—years before we became officially engaged. A shared painting. A shared life. It was a good memory, but it felt surreal, like recalling someone else's happiness, not my own.

Del would have thrown the painting out if she knew its history. Sold it if she knew its price. Seeing it this way—ignored in a box in a dusty shed—was like seeing an encapsulation of my whole relationship with Sawyer—something of beauty and value, cast aside as if it was worthless.

Del had no right to it, and she would never miss it. I set the painting aside to take with me. Maybe someday it would remind me of good days and not bad, and if that time ever came, I would hang it.

CHAPTER THIRTEEN

Josh

One thousand, two hundred and ninety miles. Arkansas. Oklahoma. Kansas. Colorado. It sure was a long way from Memphis to Aspen, two endless days that dragged on forever.

Bryn drove. I sat up front. Tellico was in the back seat, and the camping gear was in the truck bed. When we started out, Bryn rested her hand for a moment on that carving of her homestead in the truck, like she wished we were heading east. We weren't heading home, that was for sure.

"I can't believe you've never crossed the Mississippi River before." Bryn had traveled all over, but I'd never been out of Tennessee.

"Mom doesn't like to drive long distances. What of it? She said even the three hours to Grandma's was torture." Torture for me, too—she chain-smoked one cigarette after another the whole way and yelled at every semi that rumbled past.

Maybe Bryn and I were wrong about this whole Colorado thing. I couldn't imagine Mom sitting still in a car this long. But it was the only clue we had.

We went through the Ozarks, with signs for hot springs, which might have sounded like fun if I wasn't counting every mile. Passed a water park with giant slides. Saw billboards for caves that promised *beauty and amazement.* There was plenty of stuff I would have liked to see, but the only times we stopped were for gas and food. The good thing was that after we were a few hundred miles out of Memphis, Bryn quit checking the rearview mirror and stopped acting twitchy. Farther from home meant farther from Carl.

Bryn had gotten another text early that morning—*the clock is ticking*—but she shrugged this one off. "He'll never guess Colorado. I'm sure nobody's behind us, and we have the advantage now—he has to wait until we get in touch with him this time."

Well, maybe. He didn't have to wait to burn down Bryn's place. But I didn't say anything. If it made Bryn feel better to believe we were safer now, I'd let her.

In Kansas, we passed thousands and thousands of cows packed tight in one little fenced square after another, like a checkerboard stretching as far as I could see. Even with the windows rolled up and the vents closed, the stink seeped into the truck cab, burning my nose and throat and leaving a gross taste in my mouth.

"Where's their grass?" I asked.

"Nowhere." Bryn's face twitched. It was an answer that bothered her. "Why do you think I don't eat meat?"

I hadn't thought about it like that before.

I liked the camping part better than I expected. The first night, we stayed at a wildlife refuge with a big lake that had hundreds and hundreds of ducks, more than I'd ever imagined in one place. We took a hike with Tellico, then pitched the tent. There were still chores, but these were more fun than hauling mulch. I got to hammer the tent stakes in, and I was in charge of carrying water while Bryn lit the stove and fixed dinner.

That night, there was a rock under my back that dug into me no matter which way I twisted, worse even than sleeping on Bryn's floor. But I could lie there and hear owls talking back and forth, so I almost didn't mind. Mom would have hated every minute of it.

The next day, we were stuck back in the truck, watching the road move by, the seats hot and sticky, even with the air conditioning on. Bryn was quiet if I left her alone, but if I thought of questions, that would get her talking. She must have read a lot of books, because she knew an awful lot about animals and birds and trees.

"Why do hawks perch on fences by the roadside?"

"Because mice and voles like the grassy edges. It's like lining up to be served at a café."

"Why are there so many signs for tornado shelters?"

"This part of the country is called Tornado Alley because they're so common here."

She made things more interesting than in school.

I asked her about when she and Mom were little, because Mom had never talked about it. After all, they were sisters, right? She would know.

Bryn frowned, but after a bit, she came up with a story. "One time when your mom was three or four, we decided to have a tea party on our back porch. We lined up our dolls and stuffed animals along the edge of the porch—fifteen or twenty by the time we collected them all.

"We wanted the party to be very fancy, so we emptied your grandma's china cabinet, which was strictly off-limits. We took out all the fragile cups and saucers, and since there weren't enough for that number of guests, we took out dessert plates and dinner plates and wine glasses and crystal water goblets. Mind you, these were never used, ever, even on holidays—they were far too precious to eat off and were only to look at."

I tried to imagine a house with all that. Mom and I usually just ate off paper plates.

Bryn was smiling as she talked. "We set the whole thing up. Filled each cup with iced tea from the fridge. But a proper tea party needs food, so we took the special cookies Grandma had baked that morning for bridge club and shared them out between the dolls and stuffed animals."

"So, what happened?" The two of them probably got grounded for life. Or worse. I rubbed my sore cheek.

"Well, Grandma had been in her bedroom all that time, getting dressed for bridge club. When she came out and saw what we'd done, her face got red and she sort of grabbed onto the edge of the doorway like she was light-headed and trying not to fall. It hadn't occurred to me that we'd get in trouble—we were having such fun—but in that moment, I got really scared. I was the oldest, so I knew it would be me that got it."

She stopped and she had a funny look on her face.

"And then? You can't stop there."

She shook her head real slow like she couldn't believe what she was going to say next. "And then, after a minute, she sat

146

down beside us on the porch floor, not even worrying about the dirt getting on her clean dress. She drank tea and ate cookies and told us how a real tea party would be. She added a lock on the china cupboard the next day, but she never said another thing about it." She glanced my way. "I haven't thought about that day in years. But when your mom and I were little, we were close. We played together and there were some happy times. It all feels like a lifetime ago."

She sounded tired and very sad, and she didn't tell me any other stories about Mom.

Later that day, I tried to find out more about Landon, but she wouldn't say much. She had called him again before we left Memphis. He and Bryn talked for a long time, and afterward she was restless again. Looking through all the camping gear. Picking up her phone a few times like she wanted to call him back. But she didn't.

I had a little better luck asking about Dad.

"Do you think Dave was right about maybe Dad having a twin in Colorado?"

"No, I don't think so." She sounded certain. Real certain. "He wasn't adopted, and he didn't have any brothers."

"Tell me more about how you met my dad."

There was a long wait, and I thought maybe I'd have to go back to talking about hawks and tornadoes, but she finally answered. "We met when we were in college at Memphis State." She talked slow, like she was picking out what to say. "I was a freshman. He was a junior. I joined a backpacking club because I'd never been to the mountains before, and I figured that was a good way to get there. They would hire buses for big trips because

147

so many students didn't have cars. That's how I learned to love hiking. Camping. Spending a lot of time outdoors." She looked my way. "Just like you're figuring out now."

Yeah, okay. "But what about Dad?"

"He was a member of the same group, and he liked the camping and hiking, but what he really loved was kayaking. He used to organize whitewater trips, and he was always trying to talk people into trying it. He'd reserve the swimming pool at the school gym, haul in a few boats, and teach basic paddle strokes. How to roll. That sort of thing. It was like he'd discovered the Promised Land and was on a mission to lead everyone to it."

"Dad taught you how to kayak?"

"He did." Bryn's mouth closed, with her lips all skinny, and I thought for a minute that was it, but then she kept on. "When he graduated, he got a job in Memphis, and we kept dating. Traveled a lot together for paddling trips. When I graduated, I got a job in Nashville." Her hands tightened up hard on the steering wheel. "And that's pretty much it."

Okay, so Mom used to laugh at me sometimes, telling me I have to be a whole lot older before I understand women, but I'm not an idiot. Bryn was hiding plenty. "So, where all did you go to kayak?"

"Different places." Her face was stiff, but this time I wasn't going to back off.

"And you did this all through college?"

"Sort of."

"You said Dad was good?"

She relaxed at that one. Smiled a little. "He was amazing. He came alive when he was out on the water. It wasn't Sawyer and a boat, two separate things. The kayak acted as if it knew his every thought before he'd done a thing. Like a centaur, but half boat, half human. He was fearless. Class V rapids, flood-stage water, long-distance races—he'd tackle anything. The harder it was, the happier he got."

Fearless. I liked the idea of a fearless dad. I wished I knew that trick, because every day that went by, I got more worried about Mom, thinking about Carl and drugs and disappearance and death. *Fearless* was a long way out of reach.

Bryn was on a roll now, so I stayed quiet and still, hoping she would forget I was listening.

"He was a perfectionist. He spent one whole summer testing out different kayak paddles. Narrowed it down to the top three, then had me video him going down the same rapid with each one. He ended up picking this short, stubby, composite one people laughed at, but he didn't care about the laughter as long as that ugly paddle gave him an edge. One time we . . ."

She broke off, and the smile that had been getting bigger turned off fast, like someone had jerked an electric plug out of its socket and cut the current. She cleared her throat. Looked away. "There's a rest stop a mile ahead. Let's stop and let Tellico out."

The way she said it, like an order, told me I wasn't going to hear anything else about my dad, but I figured I could sneak in one more question. "If you did all that whitewater stuff back then, could you teach me like Dad taught you?"

Bryn's tense frown gave me the answer before she said anything. "Sorry, kid. I've sworn off whitewater. Nothing could get me back out there again."

And that really did shut down any more questions.

It wasn't until we got past Denver that I could see mountains ahead—a wall of them, stretching right and left as far as I could see. I glanced down at Landon's carving on the glove box, but those mountains of Bryn's looked nothing like these. Some of these had snow on top, even though it was June. I tried to pretend I was a pioneer ready to cross them, like in the Oregon Trail game, but if I were in a wagon instead of a truck and spotted those mountains ahead, I would have turned around and headed back home.

We started up into them, the road still a highway, but twisty. The truck roared like it was angry on the steep stretches, and a bunch of cars zoomed past us. When we turned off on the road to Aspen, mountains closed in on all sides.

Huge mountains. Jagged and gray. Rocky, like their name. They were a little spooky, not at all like the curvy green mountains at Bryn's homestead. Looking at them made me feel cold, even though it was warm out.

I started seeing big open paths carved down the mountainsides, with towers along the edge and chairlifts. "Ski slopes," Bryn said. If those paths were covered in snow, there'd be people flying down them on skis and snowboards. I'd watched that stuff on TV, but seeing how steep it was for real was a whole lot different.

"Can we start looking for Mom now?"

Bryn didn't answer. We were passing huge houses, and when we got into Aspen itself, there were stores and hotels and ski shops and more stores. Everything looked very clean and very fancy. Narrow streets zigzagged every which way. Clumps of people waited outside restaurants and wandered the sidewalks. How could we ever find Mom in the middle of all this?

Bryn slowed the truck way down, and she looked right and left and then right and left again, like she was wondering the same thing.

I rolled down the window. The air was a mix of green smell like at Christmas and the smell of pizza from a Domino's we were passing. "Have you been here before?" I asked.

"Long time ago." She looked around again, frowning. "We were just passing through. I don't remember all these stores and bars and restaurants."

"So, can we start looking for Mom now or not?"

She made a don't-bug-me face. "Not. It'll get dark soon. Let's find a grocery, get some supplies for dinner, and figure out a campground. Tomorrow we'll get started."

I started to argue, but she cut me off.

"It's late, we're tired, and we have to figure out how to tackle this. Tomorrow we'll get started for real, and I even promise a hamburger lunch. It's cool enough here that Tellico can hang out in the truck while we go in places."

"Yeah. Okay." I didn't like it, but I didn't have any better ideas. This town didn't look very Mom-like. Too clean, too dressed-up, and too expensive. What if we'd come all this way for nothing?

So it ended up the only place I searched that day was the inside of City Market while Bryn picked through the produce. I looked hard for Mom there, but I didn't see anyone like her.

We drove on a little farther, and we got the last campsite at a campground that was part of the National Forest. No showers, which Mom would have fussed about, and pit toilets, which would have sent her stratospheric. I had to hold my nose to even get close. A huge creek roared right by our campsite, with a big metal bridge crossing it and lots of hiking trails. We took Tellico for a long walk and then set up the tent.

We had scrambled eggs and pan toast and apple slices for dinner, the hot food tasting good because the air got a whole lot colder once the sun went down. A few other campers had camp-fires going, and everything smelled smoky. A big motor home a few spaces down had a satellite dish and a row of colored lanterns hanging from its awning, making our tent look small and fragile.

I waited until after we'd eaten before I started asking questions again. "How are we going to find Mom?" I hoped Bryn had had the chance to think about it and come up with one of her plans.

But she looked puzzled. "I'm not sure." She drummed her fingers on the picnic table for a few minutes. "I guess what we need to do is think like her. If she came here to look for the man Dave saw, what would she do first?"

I tried to think like Mom. She'd need a place to sleep. She'd need food. She'd need a drink, after all that driving. "She'd look for the bar Dave told us about. The one with the baseball stuff on the walls." I pulled out my phone. "What was it, the Red Sox?"

"That's what Dave said."

I typed it in. "No hits under *Aspen Red Sox Bar*. But there are sports bars. I'll start looking through photos."

"Great. And we can ask around. Based on the bank statements, she didn't have much cash with her, so she'd need to do something to get money."

She didn't have much cash. My stomach turned into a hard, heavy lump the way it did nowadays whenever I thought about how long she'd been gone, and I was sorry I'd eaten that third piece of toast and honey. She didn't have cash, but she had the pills. Carl had said so.

I opened a new tab and looked up hotel prices. Most were hundreds of dollars, and there was no way Mom could have even paid for one night after buying gas and stuff to get here. She'd have to sell some of the pills, which meant we'd never be able to get them all back for Carl. There were way too many ways for that to go wrong. "Maybe she met someone."

I knew how that sounded, and I felt like a traitor for saying it. But that was better than picturing her out there selling drugs.

Bryn frowned like she wasn't all that convinced. "Maybe." She stood up. Started a pot of water heating on the stove for washing dishes. I scooted closer because the warmth felt good. "See if you find any clues to the right bar in the photos. Tomorrow, we'll go for an early hike while we wait for things to open. Then we'll start with the sports bars and go from there."

"Okay." I'd thought getting to Bryn's would solve everything, then I thought going back to Memphis would work. Now we had to find Mom in Colorado, and Bryn didn't sound too sure we could do it. "The sign in front says there's a five-day limit to camp here."

"There are other campgrounds. But you're right—we can't waste time. I need to get back home sometime. I need to get back to work."

She didn't look at me, and I could tell she was being careful not to say anything about Carl and his countdown. It was nice she'd quit looking around for him everywhere, but even with him back in Memphis, we needed to hurry. He'd said one week when he first came to Bryn's place. We'd spent one day getting to Memphis, one day there, and two days getting to Aspen. Today's text message had said *Today is Wednesday. Deadline Saturday.* Three days left to search. The heavy stone in my stomach grew into a giant boulder.

No matter how I looked at it, we didn't have enough time.

CHAPTER FOURTEEN

Bryn

It had been years since I dreamed about drowning, but that first night in Colorado my nightmare returned, familiar and frightening. Maybe it came back because Del and Sawyer were so present in my thoughts again, or because the sleeping bag I was using still carried a vague scent that made me think of Sawyer. Maybe the sound of the rushing stream by our campsite dragged the dream out of hiding, or perhaps my subconscious chose this way to warn me of danger.

Whatever the reason, the nightmare returned, a vivid Technicolor replay of things I didn't want to remember.

The accident happened a week after I'd discovered the truth about Sawyer and Del. Five of us met on a chilly spring Sunday at the Chattooga River in northern Georgia. Its fearsome reputation had been forged by the movie *Deliverance*, but to me it meant distraction and escape. I was the odd woman out, our three-couple weekend skewered by the minor little detail that my former fiancé wasn't with us. I tried not to picture him tucked in bed with my sister.

The trip had been planned weeks earlier, and I didn't even consider cancelling, bizarrely convinced that if I acted as if nothing was wrong, the pain of Sawyer's betrayal would ease. *Stay busy, forge ahead, forget what happened.* That was my mantra.

I wasn't sleeping. I wasn't eating. I wasn't thinking clearly. But the water, the river, the intense adrenaline rush of successfully running a major rapid, had always been my escape valve. Pressures at school? Layoffs at work? A worrisome bank balance? Head to the water as soon as possible, and all my problems became inconsequential. It had worked for everything else, so why wouldn't it work for a shattered heart?

Sawyer and I had met the others in Asheville at a kayaking competition the previous fall. We'd connected and quickly made plans. Their real names were somewhere in my jotted-down contact list, but in private Sawyer and I had nicknamed the photo-worthy pair Barbie and Ken and the super-fit outdoorsy couple, Jane and Tarzan. We met as arranged at the put-in point and unloaded the boats amid laughter and high energy. Theirs was real. Mine was a meticulous fake.

"Sawyer came down with a bug," I explained. "He's so sorry he can't be with us." The last thing I could face from these not-quite-friends was pity, and they accepted my easy lie.

"No worries." Jane distributed power bars and energy gel, the mother figure of the group. "We'll stay together. We'll watch out for you."

Tarzan nodded dutifully. He was the one most familiar with

this stretch of the Chattooga. I'd never paddled it before. "The river's not all that high. It'll be an easy run."

Easy wasn't what I was looking for. I wanted danger and diversion. I wanted oblivion.

Ken was focused on a gadget that was new at the time—a GoPro camera he wore on his forehead.

Sawyer would love one of those. The thought came unbidden and left a stale taste in my mouth. I choked it down and tried to act normal. "Can you send me the video later?"

"Absolutely. Once we're done, I'll post it online and send you a link."

His confident statement had the effect of further minimizing the river's risks. *An easy run. Once we're done.* A successful conclusion was preordained.

We zipped into life vests, double-checked safety supplies, and launched the five kayaks into the current. My tired muscles protested, my foggy brain fumbled, but I shrugged it off, telling myself I just hadn't warmed up yet. Once I got moving, all would be well.

The river and the surrounding wilderness brought a harsh beauty to the day. Rock formations rose on both sides of the water, framed by the emerald green of a dense growth of conifers. A kingfisher swooped overhead, his strident rattle warning us to get lost. A startled doe darted from the water's edge at our approach. The clean, fresh air almost sparkled in the sunlight.

I hung back at first, taking last place as Sawyer had taught me, seizing the opportunity to evaluate the skills of these paddlers I didn't know well. *Identify the weak link so you can keep an extra eye out.*

I pushed his voice out of my head, but I followed his advice and watched the others. Ken and Tarzan knew their shit. Jane was damn good. Barbie was the novice of the group, the most likely to get into trouble, but she stuck close to Ken and followed his lead. He checked on her often, acting responsible. There was no reason to expect trouble from that direction.

The four of them twisted around every few minutes, looking back to make sure I was following, and after half an hour, I decided to save them the neck strain. At the first opportunity, I passed into the lead. Easier for them to watch me that way, plus, when I was first, I didn't have to see them behaving like well-established couples. Pointing out the best route. Cheering a particularly good run. Chatting in quiet moments about earlier trips. The things Sawyer and I would be doing now if he were here.

I focused on the river. A long chain of Class II and III rapids, a short calm, then a zigzagged Class IV that burned off the day's chill. My body hummed with contentment, my adrenaline ensuring deep, efficient breathing and fast responses. I would never be as good as Sawyer, but I was a reasonable second best.

I'd been right to come. To hell with grief and pain and betrayal. This was what I needed; this was what I craved. The roar of the water, the bite of the paddle, the scream of arm, shoulder, back, and stomach muscles as I placed my kayak in exactly the right place, run after run. Sawyer couldn't take this from me. He could take everything else, but not this.

Sawyer.

I pulled farther ahead, trying to outrace my own unhappiness.

A spot of bright red waved in the breeze along the left bank, positioned just before the river twisted into a narrow rock-bound chute. A red bandanna, maybe a piece of a red T-shirt. A warning. A warning I should have taken seriously.

Sawyer would have paid attention and eddied up at once. He would have gathered the group, told them to hold steady. He would have put into shore, forced his way forward on foot to assess. Was there a problem ahead? Was it safe to go forward?

But Sawyer wasn't there, and my head was back in Memphis. I whipped past the warning flag with barely a glance and executed a nicely timed pivot to head through the narrow gap in the rocks. The river, compressed in this cleft, surged forward with added power, and I bit hard with my paddle, exultant in my supercharged haze.

Too late, I saw the blockage ahead.

"Strainer!" I screamed the last-minute warning to the others. A tangle of downed trees formed a wall just past the outflow of the chute, and I had no way to go around, no way to eddy up, no way to stop. It was a major obstruction, and I was in serious, heart-stopping trouble.

I tried to angle toward the edge that looked less dense, digging my paddle in deep to minimize the impact, but there were only seconds between recognizing the danger and the nauseating crunch of fiberglass smashing against wood. I slammed into the massive trunk, bounced off the rock wall, and flipped upside down.

The shocking cold of the water. The pummeling churn of the current. My hair ripped from my ponytail and wrapped around my submerged face, making it impossible to see.

The tremendous force of the plunging water wedged my kayak into the angle between tree trunk and solid rock and forced me forward, my chest pressed tight against the front edge of the cockpit. A boulder at my back kept me from moving.

I'd practiced recovery rolls in swimming pools, lakes, and rivers of all sorts. On whitewater trips, I'd rolled so many times, my body's response had become pure reflex. Arms, paddle, stomach muscles, shoulder power. Flip the boat upright. Or, if in a serious mess, rip off the spray skirt and scramble out of the boat. I was no amateur. I knew how to save myself in a crisis.

But not this time. I was firmly pinned, my paddle useless, my legs locked into the kayak, with no way to extricate myself and no way to take in oxygen. My chest clamped painfully, its command insistent—breathe, breathe, *breathe*. Every fiber of my being wanted to inhale, but all I would suck into my lungs was river water. Every instinct told me to move, but I couldn't.

Panic exploded.

My head pounded with every heartbeat. My useless arms twitched. My vision narrowed. One minute. One and a half. Two. Two minutes and fifteen seconds. Thirty seconds. I was so oxygen deprived, the world spun, and I started hearing voices.

The kayak jerked. Jerked again. Its bow lifted a few amazing inches and then lifted more, creating a narrow gap, and oh my god, there was suddenly air. I twisted my head sideways out of the water's churn and took huge gasping breaths, desperate to fill my lungs before I found myself drowning again.

"Hang on!" The voices weren't imaginary. Ken and Tarzan, Jane and Barbie. They were out of their boats, perched on and in the downed tree. They hauled the bow of my boat up by brute force, creating just enough of an air-filled space to save me.

I concentrated on pulling in oxygen. Fear still swamped me. What if they let me slip under again?

"Is she breathing? She's breathing! Oh my god, she's alive."

"Shit, Bryn, are you okay?"

"We're getting ropes in place. Sit tight."

Sit tight. As if I could do anything else.

I watched the video later, posted on YouTube, out there for the entire world to see my helplessness. *Rescue on the Chattooga.* Fifty thousand views.

The others had seen the warning flag, heard my shout, rammed their boats to shore. A path through the underbrush, beaten down by previous paddlers more cautious than I, let them race around the blockage, the camera view jiggling as they stumbled over rough ground. The four of them, these people I barely knew, whose real names I couldn't even remember, hadn't hesitated. They'd risked their lives, organized fast, clambered out on the downed tree, and dragged me into air.

Then, with the situation stable, there was time for safety lines and sensible decisions. I vaguely listened to animated discussion about angles and fulcrums, how best to use the ropes we each carried to fight the tremendous water force that kept me pinned, but it all felt irrelevant, a standardized test question that didn't apply to me. I could breathe. That was the only thing that mattered.

It took a half hour to drag the boat far enough so I could creep out, my body cold and stiff, every inch a battle. It took another half hour to get my empty kayak to shore, and for the others to portage their boats around the blockage. The day had warmed, but I couldn't stop shaking. I ate chocolate. Coughed up river water. Talked little.

Then, of course, we all loaded up again and headed down-river, because downriver was the only way to go. It was a sub-dued group this time, me in the middle, my thinking blurred and my confidence badly shaken.

The nightmares that followed me those next few years were choppy and varied, often including the super-charged adrenaline rush of the early part of the trip before flipping into those moments of sheer panic underwater, ice-cold, blinded, and unable to breathe. Even during the day, the sound of rushing water at exactly the right pitch plunged me back into those moments of drowning, my hard-wired reptilian brain screaming danger despite the fact I was safe on dry land.

I tried two or three times to go back out on whitewater. I committed to a group trip, showed up on time, had the right gear. I was fiercely determined to get past my fear. Once, I got as far as loading the boat. Another time, I got into the boat and almost launched. But each time panic took hold, the memories flooded back with burning intensity, and I abandoned the mis-guided attempt.

I gave myself pep talks. Called myself a wimp. I tried to con-vince myself that one day I'd find enough backbone to reclaim the joy. Nothing worked. Since that day of near-drowning, I confined myself to calm, quiet lakes and left the rivers to others.

The nightmare I had that first night in Colorado was a new version, with Sawyer safe on shore with his arm around Del, laughing as I swept downriver. I woke, soaked in sweat, the unrestrained roar of the creek that bounded the campground pounding in my ears, and the bitter taste of fear and failure coating my throat.

I waited for my heart to slow. For reality to return.

I wanted to go home. I wanted to go out and work in my garden. I wanted to see how Python and Java were growing. I needed to gather eggs, check the orchard, start on my next coding project.

Del had hijacked my life once again.

I sat up in the tent, pulling the sleeping bag—Sawyer's sleeping bag—tight around me for warmth. Tellico lifted his head but didn't get up. Josh slept on, undisturbed, in that dead-to-the-world sleep I vaguely remembered from my teenage years, one arm wrapped around the shaggy dog.

Based on all I'd learned, he might be better off without his mother, but that wasn't my call. We'd look. I'd do my best. If we didn't turn anything up by the time we needed to head home, I'd go to the Aspen police and dump the whole thing in their laps—Carl, drugs, and all—regardless of whether that got Del in trouble.

The light shifted, brightening. I unzipped the tent flap as quietly as I could and stepped into the cool morning, stretching and rubbing my lower back. The ground had gotten harder over the past decade. Or perhaps I'd just gotten older.

Tellico followed me. I fed him, heated water for tea, enjoyed the calm. I'd told Josh we would start with the bars, and that was logical enough. But then what? I was no detective. Drive up and down streets, looking randomly for Del? Or for Sawyer's mysterious doppelganger?

I should call Landon. He would stay calm and sensible. We could brainstorm ideas together, and that would give me new avenues to explore. The idea of reaching out surprised me. I'd spent plenty of energy keeping Landon at arm's length, but now I wanted to talk, and in that moment of need he was the only one who'd do.

I pulled out my phone. My finger hovered over the icon to dial. But I couldn't call. If I ever said *yes* to Landon, I'd be handing him my heart, and that was even scarier than my whitewater nightmares.

I slipped the phone back in my pocket and forced my thoughts back to the search. By the time Josh got up, I'd twisted myself into knots, convinced our trip was doomed to failure.

We walked Tellico. We finished breakfast.

"*Now* can we start looking?" Josh was right to sound so impatient. I was just piddling around the campsite, avoiding the inevitable, dreading the day.

"Yep. Come on. Hop in the truck." I pulled out of the campground and headed back into town. "Did you have any luck later on, finding photos of a bar with baseball stuff on the wall?"

Josh was scrolling through his phone again. "No. But I found a list of sports bars. I can give you directions."

"Great."

So, we were off. At least I didn't have to constantly search the streets here for a lurking Carl.

The first bar was still closed, but the guy sweeping up let us in to look at the walls. There was a heavy smell of stale beer, but no Red Sox stuff, and he didn't know where we might find what we were looking for. No luck at the second bar either. By the time we got to the fifth one, we had it down to a science: find a parking place, make sure the windows were down for Tellico, go in and look, ask for the employee who had been there the longest, see if he or she knew where to go next. We worked down the whole list of sports bars. Nothing.

"Now what?" Josh sounded just as discouraged as I was.

"Now, that burger I promised you. Then we start down the list of non-sports bars."

A cheeseburger and fries improved Josh's mood, and at least vegetarian options were plentiful here. My pasta was excellent, and my optimism went up in sync with my recovering blood sugar. "We'll have better luck this afternoon." I hoped.

We started on the new list. At the second place we checked, Josh and I walked from outdoor sunshine into the gloom of the interior, and it took a moment for my eyes to adjust. I could smell fresh popcorn and hot butter, a good omen.

A young woman with green hair and a bar T-shirt stepped forward. "I'm sorry, but we don't permit underage children here."

I nodded—some of the other bars had fussed as well—but I stood my ground and looked around. It was a rabbit-warren bar, with a small entry room and a half-dozen doors leading off into separate spaces, extending behind the adjacent retail stores. It was the sort of place you'd book for a private party. Or the sort of place you'd go to stay out of the public eye.

The room we stood in had photos of the Golden Gate Bridge and Lombard Street. The side panel of a San Francesco cable car was mounted on one long wall. There were posters for the Giants and the Golden State Warriors.

Not a sports bar. A bar with a city theme. "Do you have a room dedicated to Boston?"

The woman raised an eyebrow, a bit startled, but she nodded.

"Could we see it, please? We're not here to drink, and Josh here won't give you any trouble. We're trying to find someone."

This all sounded lame, even to me, but Josh stepped up. "Please?" The helpless-orphan expression on his face would have melted granite.

The woman visibly softened. "I guess it's okay if you just want to look. It's this way."

We followed her, leaving San Francesco behind, and passing through New York City and New Orleans. The Boston room was in the far back corner of the building. Photos showed the city skyline, the harbor, and crew teams rowing on the Charles. One entire wall was filled with Red Sox memorabilia.

"This is it." I glanced at Josh, who was grinning, but then I slammed up against the *what-next* question and turned back to the waitress. "We think the person we're looking for has been here. Could we show you a photo? And maybe show it to other people who work here?"

She started a reflexive headshake, but once again Josh saved us. "Please? It's my mom we're looking for. It will just take a minute." He pulled up the photo of Del we'd given to the police. "This is her. Have you seen her?"

She shook her head but took the phone. "Give me a minute. I'll go check with the other waitresses."

Josh and I waited.

166

After a few minutes she came back, but she was frowning in failure. "Sorry. No one recognized her."

Josh took the phone with downcast eyes and turned for the exit.

"Wait a minute." I touched his arm to stop him. "Turn this way, Josh." He turned, and I shifted him to one side so the light from a wall sconce fell on his face. "Have you seen a man who looks sort of like this?"

The *no* head shake started before she'd even looked properly, but then she caught herself. "Hang on. Yeah. There's a guy who comes in here every once in a while, and he looks a lot like him. Come to think of it, he usually asks if there's a table back here in this room."

Interesting. Sawyer's doppelganger liked to hide in the back. "Do you know his name? Or how we could get in touch with him?" If Del had been successful in finding him, maybe he knew where she was.

"No. Sorry. I've waited on him before, but he's not very chatty. Usually here by himself. He orders tequila shots and always pays cash."

It sounded like the same guy Dave had spotted. "Thanks very much." I pulled a grocery receipt from my pocket and borrowed her pen to scribble down my cell number. "If he comes in over the next few days, could you give me a call? I just want to talk to him. See if he knows anything that would help."

She looked doubtful, but she slid the paper into the back of her order pad.

"There's a reward," Josh chimed in.

My dismay at this bit of initiative must have shown on my face because Josh gave me an I'll-do-what-I-want look, as if he was delighted to irritate me. But the girl perked up. "Sure. I'll call if he comes in on a day I'm working."

"Thanks." It was a long shot—she'd probably forget the whole conversation as soon as we left—but worth a try.

Josh and I headed back out to the sidewalk.

"We did it!" His enthusiasm was infectious, and my pessimism shifted off to one side. Maybe, just maybe, we were on the right path.

But we walked back to the truck, and the remaining challenges slammed home. Yes, we'd found the right bar. We'd confirmed a man existed who looked a lot like Sawyer. But even if we found this guy, there was no guarantee he would lead us to Del.

"Now what?" Josh was still looking happy, and he turned around in his seat to scratch Tellico behind the ears.

Great question. "I guess now we keep looking."

"Yeah, but we found the right bar. So, what are we looking for now?"

"We found the bar Dave had been to. But we're trying to find your mother, not this lookalike stranger. We need to pretend we're Del and look for other places we think she would have gone."

I now knew every street in the Aspen business district, the location of every public parking lot, and the best green spots to walk Tellico. Other than that, nothing.

My phone chimed, and I wasn't surprised to see yet another countdown reminder from Carl or one of his minions. I clicked "Delete," blocked the number—he must toss his phone after a single day, because the numbers were always different—and got back out of the truck. "Come on. Maybe sugar will help us think."

We got ice cream cones and sat on a bench. "How do detectives do this?" We were trying to sift through a fair-sized town one millimeter at a time. "Any suggestions from your video games?"

Josh gave a dispirited laugh. "Yeah, we should go on a quest, earn extra life energy, and kill an alien. That wins the game."

"Wrong game." But my question had jostled a memory that put my thoughts on a different track. "I read a mystery a long time ago where the detective found the missing woman because he knew she raised heirloom vegetables. He tracked her down because she kept her subscription to a special seed catalog."

Josh took a lick of his rocky road. "Mom hates vegetables."

"I know, I know. But your mom isn't stupid." Underneath the thick layer of crap she wrapped around her life, she had plenty of brain cells. Or at least she did before she started taking pills. "I think she believed—really believed—the man Dave saw was your father. So, she wasn't looking for a twin, she was looking for the real Sawyer."

I was so intent on thinking my way forward into an action plan that the words spilled out. I didn't realize what I'd done until Josh's ice cream cone landed on the sidewalk in front of us, slipping unnoticed from his slack fingers. Tellico leaned down to lap up the unexpected treat.

"My dad is alive? He's not dead?"

Shit. I'd screwed up yet again. "I'm sorry. No. He's not alive. He died in a plane crash, just like you've always been told." Josh looked at me, wide-eyed, his face a jumbled mix of hope and anger and disbelief. I squeezed his hand. "He's dead, Josh. I didn't mean to suggest otherwise."

He nodded slowly.

"I'm sorry I didn't make myself clear. I was thinking *your mother* believed it was really Sawyer." And she chased out here to find him. She'd been working at the bank when the safety deposit box was emptied—maybe she thought there'd be money involved if she found him. "At any rate, if that's what she believed, and she came here to find him, maybe she would think the way the detective in the story did."

"My dad liked vegetable seeds?"

I would have laughed except for the fact that he was deadly serious. "No. At least not when I knew him. The question is, what *did* he like?"

"And then that's where we look, because that's where we think Mom looked."

"Exactly." More than a few brain cells in this kid's head, no question.

Josh looked like he was thinking hard, so I held back from spitting out the things that popped to mind.

After a minute, he came out with his own list. "Flying. He took lessons. Had his license. Mom said a bunch of times that she hated how much he liked flying, so maybe she would believe he'd keep doing it." He gave me a fast look. "If he were alive. Which he isn't."

"We passed a sign for the county airport on our way in. We'll check there."

"Camping. He had all that camping equipment."

We had all that camping equipment. But it was a good point. "Yes. Maybe your mom would have checked with the outdoor stores."

"Kayaking."

That one hit me closer to home, but of course he was right. "Absolutely. We'll check with places that sell boats or organize whitewater trips."

"But what if he's changed? What if he does different stuff now?" He sounded genuinely concerned that his father could be different now.

I reached over and gave him a gentle one-armed hug to try to soften what I had to say. "He's dead, Josh. I'm sorry to keep repeating it, but it's true. The Coast Guard investigated. They issued a death certificate. We're not looking for your actual father. We're thinking of places that might lead us to your mom."

I'd been startled by Josh's offer of a reward, but I was starting to hope Del had done the same in her search for Sawyer. It would make her more memorable. Her cell phone was still off— Josh tried it every morning—but maybe Del had left her own scraps of scribbled contact information scattered around town. Maybe that would lead us to her.

Josh pulled out of my hug, and it took him a minute before he said anything else. "So, can you think of anywhere else?"

Bars, of course, but we'd already done that. "I think you've hit the top three. Good job. I'll keep thinking."

Thinking about Sawyer was exactly what I'd trained myself to avoid. What else had Sawyer loved? Campfires. Classic rock. Thrills, no matter how they came packaged. Waffles and creamy-smooth mashed potatoes and chocolate-chunk brownies warm from the oven.

He loved quiet hikes and noisy parties. His lucky flannel shirt from high school. Holding hands in private, but not in public. Making slow delicious love in the early morning, when the sunlight was just beginning to filter through the east window of his bedroom.

What else had Sawyer loved? Me.

Or so I'd believed. I'd been dead wrong about that. And maybe that meant I was wrong about everything else.

CHAPTER FIFTEEN

Josh

"He's dead, Josh."

Bryn and I drove to the airport without talking, but I kept hearing that one sentence in my head, repeated over and over. Bryn believed it. Before today, I believed it too. Even when we talked to Dave, I'd thought about crazy stuff like twins, but I hadn't thought about the simpler thing. Maybe Dad was still alive.

Was that possible?

I'd seen it on TV lots of times, especially in the soap operas Mom liked to watch. Crooks on the run. Witness protection. People with amnesia. They made it look easy—you go somewhere new, pick a different name, start again. You leave your old life behind and never look back.

But really, was that possible? And if it was possible, then what kind of dad would do something like that?

Bryn had shot the idea down right off. And maybe she was right. But if there was any chance, any chance at all, that Dad was out here, then we were looking for two people now, not one.

I called out the last turn to the airport from my phone map. It turned out to be a tiny place, nothing like the big airport in Memphis where Mom and I had gone to pick up one of her boy-friends. That one had all kinds of traffic and roads and signs, and we sat in a parking lot and watched the airplanes come in and land. Here, small planes were parked in a long row beside a single landing strip, and only two bigger jets were lined up by the terminal. Mountains rose up tall on all sides, making the airport feel hidden.

Bryn found a parking spot away from the terminal. "Do you want to wait in the truck with Tellico? You could play your game. It shouldn't take long."

It was nice to have a stronger cell signal here so close to town, but I stuffed my phone into my pocket. "No. I'm coming." Bryn thought Dad was dead, so she wouldn't ask the right questions. I needed to be there to do it.

The terminal wasn't all that big, but it was hard to find some-one to talk to—people busy at counters, busy with luggage, busy with a short line through an area labeled "Security." People lined up who had their family right there with them, moms and dads both, on vacation, going somewhere fun.

Bryn walked up to a woman at a check-in counter. Her nametag said "Suzie," and she had picked up her purse and was stepping away like she was done for the day.

"Excuse me." Bryn stopped in front of her so she couldn't leave. "We're looking for someone who might have been here a few weeks ago." She held out her phone with Mom's picture on it.

The woman acted like she wanted to be somewhere else, but Bryn just stood there and waited. When Suzie finally looked, she took her time, then frowned and waved at us to follow her. She walked over to a counter that said "Information," where a lady with gray hair sat behind racks of maps and brochures. "Hey, Martha. Were you here a while back when that crazy lady tried to talk her way out onto the tarmac without a ticket?"

Martha looked at the picture. "Yeah, I was here. She's the one. High as Mt. Elbert. Yelling that her husband's plane was parked out there, and she needed to get to it so she could talk to him."

Bryn gave me a quick look, like she thought I'd be upset to hear Mom acted that way. All I cared about was the fact she had been here. We were in the right place.

"When was this?" Bryn asked. "I'm her sister, and we're trying to find her."

The two consulted. "A week or ten days ago."

"What happened to her?"

Martha made a nothing-good face. "The TSA guys called for additional security, but I don't think they called the cops. I mean, she made a lot of noise, but once they pulled her away, she just sort of sat over there on a bench and rocked herself back and forth. Talked things that didn't make sense. It wasn't like she was making threats or trying to hurt anyone."

I'd seen that rocking thing before on Mom's worst days. I would try and get her to eat ice cream when it happened or watch a favorite show. Try and make her rest. But now she was out there with nobody taking care of her. My teeth ground together so hard my jaw hurt.

Bryn gave me another worried glance. "What did security end up doing?"

"I'm not sure. They talked with her for a while, then led her away."

Suzie gave a nod and walked on. Bryn started to turn away, as if she was done asking things, so I jumped in. "Did her husband really have a plane here?"

That earned me a frown from Bryn, but Martha just shrugged. "Who knows? She said his plane was here, but then she said it crashed and he died a long time back. Just mixed up, I guess."

"Thanks so much. Appreciate it." Bryn turned to leave.

"Hey. Wait a sec. Did you say you were this woman's sister?" Martha leaned across the counter.

Bryn nodded.

"And you?" Martha looked at me.

"She's my mom. We're trying to find her."

Her face softened, and she seemed to come to a decision. "Come with me."

She pulled a set of keys out of a drawer, put a "Back in Five Minutes" sign on the desk, and led us to a tall metal cupboard that sat to one side of the security line. She unlocked it. The shelves inside were stacked with all kinds of stuff, each item in a clear plastic bag, each bag with a tag and writing on it. Hats, coats, sweaters. Glasses. A stuffed turtle. An iPad, a few cell phones, a laptop. She rummaged through a box of small things.

"I wouldn't have remembered except I did Lost and Found inventory yesterday, and I was looking at it." She flipped through a few more bags. "Here you go."

She held it out to me. "Is this your mom's? It showed up on the floor over there by where she was sitting, after the security people led her off." She looked at me like she felt sorry for me. "My kids made them like this for me when they were at camp."

I took the bag, and it was all at once hard to breathe, like a giant was sitting on my chest. It was Mom's lanyard bracelet. Blue and green and purple stripes. It didn't look right, seeing the bracelet in a bag instead of on Mom's wrist. The knot was untied, with one end short like it had given way when the bracelet got jerked.

"Yeah, it's hers." I turned to Bryn. "I made it in third grade, back when I still had after-school care. They had us do stupid art projects sometimes, and for Mother's Day we were supposed to braid a bracelet."

I hadn't wanted to make one, but I picked strips in her favorite colors, and even though it turned out lumpy, it ended up kind of pretty. I figured Mom would say thank you and then lose it, but no. She cried when I gave it to her and put it on right away. *I'm never taking it off. I'll think of you every time I look at it.*

"She tied it on with a tight knot and said since it was plastic, it would last forever. It was one of those times when she threw out all the beer in the fridge and said she was done with bars and parties and late nights out." Her promise didn't last, but the bracelet did.

Bryn gave my shoulder a squeeze.

"Can I keep it?" I tightened my grip on the plastic bag. There was no way I was giving it back.

"I'm not supposed to sign things over except to the original owner, but something like this . . ." Martha pulled out a clipboard, scribbled something, and handed it to Bryn to sign.

I vaguely heard Bryn thanking her again. Then we were back at the truck. Without her bracelet, Mom was more lost than ever. Without her bracelet, maybe she wouldn't even think of me. I swallowed hard and it tasted all salty, but I scrunched my eyes closed a few times and stuffed the tears back inside.

"You okay?" Bryn asked. She didn't start the engine back up.

"Yeah."

"Here. Let me see the bracelet a minute."

I made my fingers let go, and she took the bag and looked at the writing. "They were right about the date. She must have come here to the airport right after she got to Colorado."

"Uh-huh."

"I know all this is hard, but this is good news. Seriously. Now we know she came to Aspen. We know she was looking for Sawyer. That means our plan for tomorrow still makes sense— we can ask at the outdoor shops. And for sure they didn't end up arresting her, because an arrest would have shown up in the search Steven did."

"Uh-huh." She was forgetting the part about Mom acting crazy and then sitting and rocking. I wouldn't call that good news.

She slid the bracelet out of its bag and held it out to me. "Here. Which wrist?"

I didn't understand what she meant to do, but I held out my left hand, and Bryn tied the bracelet on. She had to work at it because of the torn part, but my wrist was skinnier than Mom's, so it worked.

"There. Now you can think of her when you look at it."

She sounded so much like Mom when she said it, I had to look away. I didn't need a bracelet to remind me. I thought about Mom all the time anyway. But its weight on my wrist was a presence, like Mom reaching out to hold my hand.

* * *

Next morning, we stuck to the plan and visited outdoor stores, showing Mom's picture to one clerk after another. Lots of walking and no news at all. Same at the kayak sale and rental places, and it didn't take long to run through them 'cause there weren't that many. We stopped at a café in town for lunch, and they had racks of free magazines out front. Bryn picked up one for tourists, and she flipped through it after we ordered lunch. Burger and fries again for me. Something weird, as usual, for her.

"I'm not sure where else to look." She sounded more hopeless than I'd ever heard her, and I wasn't sure how to make sure she'd keep going. "We haven't even figured out where she was staying. We're assuming she's still here, but it's been more than a week. She could have moved on."

I figured she was looking at the magazine so she wouldn't have to look at me, which was for sure a bad sign. Next, she was going to tell me we had to stop looking and go home. I could tell.

Easy for her to quit, but I couldn't give up. "We just need to look harder. She's here somewhere."

"She *used* to be here. Who knows where she is now? With Carl so desperate, I hate to think what will happen if we can't find her." She glanced up at me for a second, but she must not have liked what she saw in my face, because she went back fast to the magazine. "Maybe I should just call Steven and let him know what we learned here. Leave it up to the police."

"Do you think they could find her?"

Bryn sighed one of those from-the-toes sighs, still turning the pages of her stupid magazine. "I don't know. I'm just frustrated. Running out of ideas."

I'd thought plenty about finding Mom, but with Bryn talking about quitting, I started thinking about what if we failed. "What happens to me if we can't find her?"

She scrunched down in her chair and avoided my eyes. "After we get back to Memphis . . ." She stopped. I thought it was because she didn't know what would happen to me when we got back, and I opened my mouth to argue—shit, I had a right to know. But she was staring hard at the magazine like she'd found something important.

I stayed quiet.

Our food came, smelling hot and greasy. The fries were the super-skinny kind I liked best, but I hardly noticed, watching Bryn. My stomach growled its hunger, which didn't seem right since the rest of me was too mixed up to want to eat.

I couldn't stand the silence any longer. "If you can't tell me what's going to happen to me, could you at least pass the ketchup?"

She shook herself as if she were coming out of a trance. "You want the truth? At the moment, I don't know for sure what happens to you if we can't find your mom. But in the short run, I'll make sure you get back to Memphis, and we'll figure it out from there."

Such a vague statement didn't make me feel all that cheerful, but it was better than hearing a bunch of talk about foster homes.

She passed the ketchup, but instead of starting to eat her bowl of chopped-up vegetables, she nodded like she'd made up her mind. She slid the magazine in my direction. "Take a look at this." She tapped a half-page advertisement.

Mountain Games. Starting the next day. Some place called Vail. Food, beer, vendors, family entertainment. Yoga. A fun run. Lots and lots of paddling competitions: flatwater races, whitewater races, canoe, solo kayak, tandem. A freestyle kayak rodeo, whatever that was.

"So?"

She took a bite of her food. "So. Maybe there's one more thing we can try."

I looked again at the ad. "This? Mountain Games?"

"Exactly. See the line that says they have a kayak rodeo? Well, if your mother saw that listing, and if she's still around here look- ing for Sawyer, this is where she would go. Because your father would never miss something like that. Not in a million years."

"You mean Dad could be there?" Maybe Bryn was starting to believe.

"No." She said it fierce and sharp, and she glared at me like she was trying to hammer the word in. "Your dad will *not* be there, because he's dead, got it?"

I got it. Pretty harsh, but I got it.

She pointed her fork at me. "If your mom thinks he could be alive, then *she* could be there."

In other words, it was a great place for me to look for both of them. "Where's Vail?"

Bryn was smiling now, liking this idea. "We passed it on our way here. A couple of hours away. We can pack up, find a campground closer to the Games, check out the area. Then we go to the kayak rodeo tomorrow, and we do some serious looking." She gave me a narrow-eyed stare that would have looked good on a Klingon commander. "And then, Josh, we will have tried everything. Everything. No options left. If we don't find your mom there, we'll have to leave the search to people who know what they're doing and figure out how to deal with Carl. Okay?"

"Yeah, I get it." I tried to sound like I meant it. Letting her think she'd convinced me.

I ran my finger along Mom's bracelet for luck. No matter what Bryn said, I wasn't going home to Memphis without Mom. This plan gave me the rest of that day and all of the next to think of something, and I intended to do exactly that. The next day was Carl's deadline, but with any luck maybe we'd be with Mom by then, and she would know what to tell him.

I took a huge bite of my burger, suddenly hungry again.

CHAPTER SIXTEEN

Bryn

I had definitely lost my mind, promising Josh we'd go to the Mountain Games. Going to this festival was the longest of long shots, and I fully expected it to be a bust. But if we didn't give it a chance, I would always wonder. What if, against all odds, Del did show up, and we weren't there to find her?

The next day was also day seven of Carl's one-week countdown, which was another reason it had to be the final day of our search. I would have to call him, convince him we were closing in, and buy enough time to get the police involved. His daily texts were a steady reminder of his threats, but I clung to the reassuring belief that he was halfway across the country. The homestead was still at risk, but here in Colorado, Josh and I were safe.

Damn Del and her drugs and deceptions. This entire mess was her fault. If she wanted to live a drug-addled life, that was her call, but she had *a kid*. A nice kid. I'd tried to offer him some on-the-fly reassurance, but the chances were good he was going to end up in foster care again, and this time it wouldn't be temporary. Sister or not, anyone who left Josh adrift that way got little sympathy from me. If it wasn't for him, I would let Del sink.

And yet, in the middle of the Del tirade that played steadily in my head, I remembered that long-ago tea party—the sun warming my skin, the feel of delicate porcelain and crystal in my hands, Del's delighted laughter as she served cookies to her favorite stuffed bear. Josh had stirred up more than thoughts of Sawyer. After years of living comfortably with a black-and-white story—me, victim; Del and Sawyer, evil traitors—I found myself confused by these multicolored memories.

* * *

Josh and I broke camp, piled all the gear into the truck, and drove east. Just before dinner, we reached another national forest campground near Vail. I'd exceeded my maximum-tolerated dose of expensive ski villages, but after we set up the tent, we went into town to pick up some food for dinner.

Work crews scurried everywhere, putting up canopies, posting signs, and setting up temporary bleachers at event sites. There would be thousands of people here the next day, packed into a small space. Music and noise. Junk food and souvenir stands. All in all, a claustrophobic crunch.

Crowds made me jumpy. To make matters worse, at the Games, I wouldn't be able to escape watching the whitewater competition because that's where Del would be if she came here. Being here would thrust me straight back into the whitewater crowd, into the middle of avid paddlers reporting water levels, exaggerating exploits, talking shop. Debating equipment and tricks and judges' scores. It was the last thing I needed when my head was so anchored in the past and my nightmares were keeping me so off balance.

In contrast, the frenzied preparations in town had Josh bubbling with enthusiasm about the next day's events. "We'll find her here. I know it. I can't wait to see the kayakers. Can you teach me more once we're back in Tennessee? You said no whitewater, but what about teaching me on the lakes you like to visit?"

The question sideswiped me, and I bent to tie a shoelace to give myself a moment. Josh was assuming a lasting connection—assuming his mother would set aside past differences and allow such a thing. This was such a leap, I couldn't quite process it.

He was so excited about the festival, I didn't want to say anything pessimistic about finding his mother, and I didn't want to dash his hopes of staying in touch. Somewhat to my surprise, I could indeed imagine Josh coming for a weekend now and then, or maybe even a whole week in the summer. I was usually ready to poison houseguests after a day or two, but this nephew thing was growing on me. "We'll see. Maybe your mom will let you come visit. There are quite a few spots you'd like that are an easy drive from the cabin. I could borrow a second boat."

The answer seemed to satisfy him. At the very least, it promised a vision of a more normal future.

We grabbed our groceries and chatted about paddling and the next day's schedule on the way back to the campground, but all talk stopped when we reached our campsite. Our bright orange tent, the camp stove, and the full water jug on the picnic table made it obvious the site was occupied, but a car with Colorado plates was parked squarely in our pull-in space. Two men, dressed in jeans and short-sleeved shirts, sat on the table with their feet on the bench. Waiting.

Josh noticed them an instant after I did. "Oh no." His face lost all color.

"Do you know them?"

He nodded with a sharp jerk. "I saw them one time talking to Carl. Back home when he and Mom were dating. He was telling them something, and they were listening like he was the boss."

Shit. Both men looked tough and ready for trouble, characters straight out of central casting. Far more threatening at first glance than Carl had initially seemed in his fancy clothes. I debated simply driving away, but where would that leave us? I pulled off the road and parked, careful not to block their car in. I wanted them gone, not trapped.

"Stay here. I'm taking Tellico."

Josh caught his upper lip in his teeth, his eyes darting from me to the men and back again, but he nodded.

I stepped out of the truck, letting Tellico out and locking Josh in. The dog stuck close to my side. If this turned out to be a confrontation, I wasn't at all sure what he would do to defend me, but I felt better having him there.

I filed away the license plate number of the parked car. Looked around at the adjacent campsites. A family with two small children was fixing dinner at the next site, paying no attention to whatever was going on here. No practical help from that direction if trouble started, but I hoped their presence as witnesses would keep these men on good behavior.

I slipped Landon's knife out of my pocket and cupped it in my palm, my thumb resting close to the release button.

"Can I help you? We've registered for this campsite. There are a few empty ones farther along the loop." They looked nothing like campers, but an unrealistic part of me held on to the feeble hope their presence was all just a mistake.

The man on the left—stocky with dark hair, a flashing signet ring, and a machine-gun tattoo along his arm—snorted. The smell of alcohol came off him in waves. "Carl asked us to check on you. Remind you of priorities. Your time runs out tomorrow."

My comforting belief that Carl's influence was confined to Memphis, the belief that we'd left him far behind, punctured and deflated like an ill-conceived party balloon. Carl might still be in Memphis, but apparently Colorado was part of his domain. I stuffed my empty hand into my pocket to hide the fact it was shaking, and I clenched the knife hard with the other.

The second man—younger, thinner, but with a harshness in his eyes that chilled me to the core—took a slow drag on his cigarette. "He wants to know the status of his missing investment."

My heart skipped a few beats and my thoughts raced. I had nothing to offer them. "How'd you know we were here?" I was constantly checking behind us. There was no way they'd followed.

"Magic powers." He took another slow drag, and our eyes locked. "Where's your sister? Where's Carl's stuff?"

"We're still looking." I tried to sound tough, but my voice came out squeaky. I didn't want to admit we'd confirmed Del had been in Aspen. I didn't want Carl or these guys finding her before we did. "We're following up on some rumors."

"Look faster."

Tellico growled, the rumble deep in his throat, and I put a restraining hand on his collar. "We're trying. What if we find her and she's sold it? Lost it? Used it?"

The stocky man leaned forward, and his face tightened. "You'd better hope that's not the case."

The menace in his tone sent me back a few feet.

They both stood and stepped forward, and my whole body tensed. I thought for a moment they intended to hit me, and I tightened my grip on the knife, but seriously? Could I ever use it? Just thinking about stabbing someone turned my stomach.

But the two men shouldered past, the one tossing his lit cigarette butt to the ground, heedless of whether it landed on dirt or dry leaves. It was an uncomfortable reminder of Carl's fascination with flames.

"Stay in touch." The thin one tossed the words behind him. They got into their car and drove off in a rattle of gravel without glancing back.

I sank onto the picnic bench, ill and shaking. Tellico licked my hand, either seeking reassurance or offering it, I couldn't tell which.

I'd been in shouting matches before, arguments with fiery anger kicking up adrenaline on both sides. I'd been in creepy alleys late at night, expecting every shadow to attack. I'd been deep in the woods, following bobcat tracks at home, and I'd felt the weight of watching eyes on the small of my back, my heart racing because I knew I wasn't hunter, but prey. None of that frightened me the way Carl and his cronies did.

Carl, with his calm voice and his manicured hands and his perfectly polished shoes. These two, with their thinly veiled air of violence. All three were lethal.

Josh tumbled out of the truck and raced over to me. "Are you okay? What did they say? How'd they find us? I haven't posted a single picture. Honest." His voice was high and tight and tinged with fear.

I shook my head. "You were right—they're with Carl. Sent to remind us we're out of time. I don't know how they found us. Maybe my phone?" It was possible, but it would be a tricky hack. Far more sophisticated than following a kid on Instagram and checking out his photos.

"So, what do we do?"

Crawl into a hole somewhere. That sounded about right. I was outmatched. Outmaneuvered. An ant trying to fight a bulldozer.

Despair seeped into every cell, my body heavy and my brain fogged.

My eyes fell on my truck, and a thought managed to find a clear path. When he was at the homestead, Carl had been out of sight for several minutes. Maybe he'd been busy doing something other than killing my pet chicken.

"There's something we should check. Grab the flashlights from the tent." I moved the truck into its proper parking spot and took one of the lights from Josh. "You take that side, I'll take this one, then we'll switch. It would be simplest if he put something on the outside of the truck, but if we don't find anything, we can search inside too."

Josh tossed his flashlight from one hand to the other, his brow furrowed. "You think some kind of tracker?"

"I don't know. Just look for anything out of place."

I started inspecting every inch of the truck, squatting to look underneath, but it took Josh less than a minute. "Found it. Come look."

He'd found a small box made of thick black plastic, about the size of a deck of playing cards, with a short, fat antenna and a red on/off switch. A strong magnet on its underside held it securely inside the rear wheel well. It was inconspicuous, designed for secrecy, and we would never have noticed it if we weren't looking.

"Is this gadget how they found us?" Josh looked more intrigued than worried.

"I would guess it's a GPS tracker. I think it sends a signal to an app. All Carl had to do was pull it up on his phone, and he could see where we were and where we'd been."

Josh nodded. "So, he could see we drove this way today and spent time here setting up camp."

"Exactly." This little gadget pissed me off even more than the Instagram trick. Carl—or his men—were following us after all. Watching what we did. The idea of them watching an electronic dot on a map, knowing our every zigzag, creeped me out. I ripped the tracker from its magnetic mooring, dropped it onto the asphalt and picked up a sizable rock, ready to smash it.

"Wait, Bryn. Don't." Josh grabbed my arm, pulling it down to my side. "Maybe there's a way we can use it later." He let my arm go and picked up the tracker, turning it over to find the power button. He switched it off. "Now he can't find us until we want him to."

I should have thought of that. "Thanks. You're right. Maybe, if we end up going to the police, they can follow that signal in some way. Maybe this gadget could help find him." Josh stuffed the inactivated tracker into the glove compartment. "We're going to pay Carl back for all this. For Annabelle, for scaring us, for following us. I don't know how yet, but we're going to find a way."

Tough talk, and it was a pleasant change to think about fighting back, but even as I spoke, I knew the words were hollow. Pay him back how? And what was going to happen when our deadline passed?

"Tomorrow, we do exactly what we'd planned. Go to the Games. See if we can find your mom." I tried to sound hopeful for Josh's sake. "We'll see what tomorrow brings. Then we'll figure out what to do next."

I checked the neighboring campsites again. The family with their kids, and a bunch of college students, newly arrived, unpacking their tent. This visit from Carl's thugs had propelled me back into a state of watchful fear, looking for hazards even in a peaceful campground. It was one more thing I needed to pay Carl back for.

CHAPTER SEVENTEEN

Bryn

The next morning brought cloudless skies and short-sleeve weather, an odd feeling when snow was so visible on the adjacent peaks. Josh and I shared a quick breakfast of fruit and granola, both of us lost in our own thoughts, then we headed to town for the festival.

Vail was a stretched-out spaghetti noodle of a town, running along the length of its narrow valley, a place where you could swoosh down a manicured ski slope and practically walk straight into a bar on Main Street. The annual Mountain Games, an attempt to promote summer activities to counterbalance the winter ski season, were scattered across multiple venues in town.

I'd heard about the Games before, and I'd seen the preparations going on the previous night, but it turned out to be an even bigger deal than I expected. Bewildering signs hung at every intersection—this way to the climbing venue, that way to the music amphitheater. PortaJohns hulked everywhere, with lines already forming. The only good thing about the crush of people was that Carl's men would have a hard time finding us in such a crowd.

We parked in a rapidly filling town lot. An endless stream of cars and SUVs flowed in behind us, and I was glad we'd come early. Everywhere we walked, there were souvenir booths and food trucks, open-air bars and outdoor gear for sale. The smell of grilling bacon mingled with the smell of fresh coffee, and crowds already clustered, waiting for food.

All around us, people were laughing, talking, drinking. They were living ordinary lives without a care in the world, not searching for a missing sister and dodging threatening creeps. I scanned the crowd, looking for Del, looking for Carl's men, looking for anything suspicious.

The crowd's standard costume was sunglasses, sun visor, quick-dry clothing, and water shoes. Josh and I looked dowdy by comparison in our ordinary T-shirts and shorts. It was barely mid-morning, but once we left the food trucks behind, the musky smell of marijuana permeated the air, a reminder that, unlike in Tennessee, it was a legal indulgence here in Colorado. This was a festival, and people were here to be festive.

We paused on a street corner and downloaded the Games app, which gave a detailed map and a searchable schedule. I scanned the lengthy list. "Looks like freestyle isn't happening until late this afternoon, although with this crowd, we'll want to get there early. What do you want to do in the meantime? Your choice."

Josh grinned a joyous, uncomplicated grin. He'd had more highs than lows ever since the report of his mother at the airport, and the previous night's visit by Carl's men had caused only a temporary dampening effect. He frequently ran one finger over his lanyard bracelet, as if it inspired his confidence. "We'll find her. She'll be at the kayak contest. I know it."

I dreaded the moment when I'd have to let him down.

"Let's start at the climbing wall." He pointed.

We headed that way, both of us watching the crowd for Del.

For much of the day, he led, and I followed. He enjoyed every second, and I tried hard to fake it, not wanting to spoil his fun. Tellico stuck close, pausing only to greet the dozens of other dogs we encountered.

We cheered the competitive climbers, who swarmed up sheer walls with the ease of spiders.

We marveled at the goggle-wearing DockDogs, who leaped from high platforms into water to retrieve thrown toys. Compared to them, even Tellico was underdressed.

We wandered past the amphitheater and listened to some good bluegrass while Josh downed four hot dogs and I ate an ultra-spicy falafel pita.

The buoyant energy of the place was infectious, but the crowds hemmed me in, and I couldn't enjoy myself. I wasn't here for pleasure. I needed space. I needed quiet. I needed home.

Josh's unrestrained delight at each new activity reminded me how young he was. By the time we headed toward the whitewater park for the men's freestyle kayak competition, I was nursing a headache, and he was acting like he could do this forever.

The whitewater venue was filling fast. The park funneled water from a nearby creek into the whitewater stadium, the twisting channel designed to create the sort of large standing waves kayakers liked to play in. Josh wiggled past a clump of laughing women and found us a few square feet of empty bleacher bench to perch on. Tellico sat between his knees, patient in the crush. It was a good location, and I could see the crowd on both sides of the water. If Del was here, I should be able to spot her.

The crowd was noisy, but not noisy enough to drown out the roar of tumultuous water. The sound burrowed into my nerves, echoing my nightmares and flooding me with memories. The joy of all the good times with Sawyer; the terror of my near drowning. It all tumbled endlessly through my head, leaving me even more unsettled and restless. A few more hours. I only had to face all this for a few more hours.

"So, what's freestyle kayaking like?" Josh asked. He, too, was searching the crowd, but that didn't stop his fascination with the event.

"It used to be called rodeo, which gives you a rough idea. The playboats they use aren't standard kayaks like mine. They're shorter, almost tiny, to let them do flips and stuff."

"Flips? You mean like in the air?"

I laughed at his amazement, relieved to set my fears aside for a few moments and focus on the technical aspects of the sport I used to love. "Exactly. Some of the tricks are phenomenal. Since the water flow and the design of the park are controlled, the paddlers are competing on a consistent background, and the judges are trained specifically for this event. Each trick carries a certain number of points for difficulty, with extra points for doing it extra well and bonuses for added flare. I can tell you what's happening once they get started."

More and more people crammed into the stadium, and we got squeezed in from both sides. Freestyle was always a popular event.

The first set of five competitors in the men's division were upstream, warming up. "Each paddler will do two forty-five-second runs, and the goal is to pack as many strong tricks into that time as possible, to score the most points. The paddlers with the best total score in the first round go on to the second round, and so on."

The waterpark's huge standing wave churned right in front of us. The starting signal sounded, and the first paddler swept in and began his routine, his tiny boat whipping through the air in flips, twists, and turns that defied both gravity and common sense. I called out the tricks as they happened—Space Godzilla, Phonics Monkey—surprised the crazy names came back to me after so many years. It was a mesmerizing display of balance and raw muscle power, but I watched with one eye while I focused the other on the people swirling around me.

The first three competitors had runs packed with successful tricks, and the rowdy crowd cheered its enthusiasm. The fourth paddler tried a trophy move I'd never seen before—an impossible combination of flip, roll, and spin—and it didn't work, the paddler scrambling hard to get back into the wave and sneak in a half-hearted finale.

"What happened? Why is everyone still clapping?" Josh tossed the questions my way without taking his eyes off the action.

"They're clapping because he tried something difficult. Did you see what he did wrong? The angle of his paddle . . ." My attention shifted to the fifth paddler, still in the warm-up pool, and whatever I was going to say faded into nothingness.

The fifth man looked like all the others. Multicolored long-sleeved jacket. Streamlined life vest. A black helmet, shadowing his face. What caught my attention and froze me to my hard bleacher seat was the paddle he held.

A short, stubby, composite paddle. The sort of paddle any sensible kayaker would laugh at. The sort of paddle I hadn't seen in more than fourteen years.

I dragged my racing thoughts back onto rational ground. I was reading too much into such a minor detail. Sawyer had commissioned his paddle for specific reasons. He chose it as his favorite because it gave him a competitive edge. That could be equally true for someone else.

But despite my logical pep talk, my mouth grew pasty, and it was suddenly hard to swallow.

The fifth man got the signal to start his run, and an instant later he was directly in front of us, playing in the huge standing wave.

Josh watched the man's routine with the same fixity he'd shown with the previous competitors. I watched with my breath locked in my chest and my heart racing so fast I could feel the throb of each beat in my neck.

The slight twist of his body as he leaned into his flips. The angle of shoulder and arm as he stretched to place his ugly little paddle in precisely the right place for a pivot. The little head nod of self-acknowledgment when he pulled off a flawless series. The hands-over-head paddle wave at the end of his run, acknowledging the thunderous applause surrounding him, embracing the public acclaim that gave a buzz like no other.

Sawyer. It was Sawyer.

It couldn't be.

It had to be.

Something nameless spasmed hard in the center of my chest, then released with an audible whoosh, leaving me hollow and empty. I'd come here a whole person. Now I was only a human shape with nothing solid inside.

I grabbed Josh by the hand and heaved him to his feet with a harsh jerk. "Come on."

I dragged him behind me, forcing my way through the endless mass of people, heading for the takeout point, my eyes never leaving that impossibly familiar fifth man. Tellico scurried to follow in our wake.

"Stop, Bryn, stop. I was looking—Mom isn't here. Where are we going?" Josh pulled back hard, but I yanked him onward. "We're going to lose our seats. I want to watch!"

I ignored the stream of protest, my fingers steel clamps on his wrist.

The fifth man was pulling his blue freestyle kayak out on this side of the water. Unbuckling his helmet. Loosening his jacket.

I doubled my pace, shouldering people aside without apology, stumbling down bleacher steps, barely hearing the roar of noise that greeted the next set of competitors.

The man reached down to grab his boat, and I was afraid I would lose him, but he stopped before he had his hands on it and stepped aside to talk to another paddler.

Yes, yes. Keep talking. Keep talking.

Thirty feet to go. Twenty. Ten. I turned loose of Josh, abandoning him behind me. I seized the arm of the fifth man and spun him toward me.

Sawyer.

I was screaming the name in my head, but I didn't scream it out loud because the man who now faced me looked at me without a hint of recognition or acknowledgment. Startled, yes, but who wouldn't be if confronted by a frenzied woman with a death grip on your arm. Startled, but with no fear, no oh-my-god-I've-been-discovered anguish, just a mildly curious puzzlement.

It threw me for a moment. Made me doubt what I'd seen on the water.

It was easy to see why Dave had thought this man might be Sawyer's brother, because he was both Sawyer and not-Sawyer. Older, of course. He had long hair, swept back into a dripping ponytail instead of cropped in a short professional cut. That change made more of a difference than I would have expected. This man had the same facial build, same etched cheekbones, same dimple as Sawyer, but even so, his face wasn't quite right. This face was heavily lined and subtly softened. Sad, that was it. A face of failure and regret, not the confident take-on-the-world face I'd known and loved.

If this was Sawyer, he was a different man than the one I remembered.

Or perhaps I was wrong, and this wasn't Sawyer at all.

He gave a pointed glance at his arm, as if I needed to be reminded I was hanging on for dear life. "Can I help you?"

Four words.

Four words, spoken in the flat tone of complete indifference, but those four words dispelled any doubt. This was Sawyer's voice. The voice of countless lazy mornings in bed, the voice of whispered love, the voice of a future I'd been promised and then denied.

"Sawyer." Not a scream, a statement. I choked out the word, the air devoid of oxygen. My head spun, and the festival around me grew fuzzy, the noise fading. Sawyer, alive and standing in front of me, was my only anchor point.

"I'm sorry." His expression still betrayed no trace of recognition. "I think you've mistaken me for someone else. My name is James, not Sawyer." He grasped my wrist and pulled gently but steadily until my fingers loosened their clawed hold. "Excuse me. I need to get ready for my second run."

I stood and stared. I wasn't wrong. I couldn't be wrong. I'd been confident Del was chasing a mirage, convinced Sawyer was dead and gone. I'd been wrong to doubt her then. I was right now. Sawyer Whitman, the man I loved, the man I hated, was standing there in front of me.

"Why? Why would you do this? Abandon your family? Leave it all behind?"

He ignored my questions, his face sympathetic but his attitude dismissive, the way I'd ignore the pleas of a panhandler who wasn't quite grounded in reality.

The performance was so perfect, I started doubting what I knew. Could this actually be a stranger?

He gave a last little nod of farewell and turned as if to reach for his kayak.

His eyes slid off my face. He looked slightly behind me and froze. His eyes widened, shocked and terrified, the reaction I'd expected but hadn't seen when I confronted him. Every last bit of blood drained from his face, and he sucked in a single sharp breath.

I turned to see what had prompted such an extreme reaction.

Josh stood a few feet behind me, tense, unmoving, and just as pale as his father. I looked from one face to the other, mirror images of stunned disbelief.

Sawyer gave a choking gasp, a startled half sob that ripped into my chest and seized my heart. All pretense had disappeared. His face was distorted, the face of a man fighting to cling to fragile shreds of composure. "Josh."

The single strangled word acknowledged I was right in recognizing him, and it sucked all the air out of my lungs.

He ran a trembling hand over his forehead and turned back to face me as if he couldn't bear to look at his son. "You. I was ready for you. I thought I could convince you. But Josh . . ." His voice broke. "I never expected . . ." His voice faded.

"Sawyer. Please. Tell me why you've done all this."

A flicker of profound sadness passed over his face. "I left to protect Josh. And to protect you. I never intended to hurt you the way I did."

The words scrabbled to find a foothold in my stunned brain, and I stood there, frozen, trying to understand.

In a single swift motion, Sawyer grabbed his kayak, whipped it onto his shoulder and disappeared upstream into the crowd.

Before I could take a step to follow, Josh raced past me, trying to catch up with his father, but the surging crowd blocked him. In only seconds, Sawyer disappeared. Josh turned back and stumbled into my arms. He clutched me with the fierceness of a drowning victim, sobbing uncontrollably—his entire world destroyed. I hung on to him with equal strength, too staggered and too dismayed to stand unsupported.

CHAPTER EIGHTEEN

Josh

I'd wondered about my father my whole life, this man who lived in a handful of photographs but nowhere in my memories. A name on my birth certificate, a name rarely spoken, a name with no connection to anything solid.

And then there he was in front of me, in a waterpark in Colorado, alive for two short minutes, facing off with Bryn.

I just stood there, staring like an idiot and unable to move, my heart beating so hard it bounced off my ribs and made my chest hurt. There were so many things I wanted to do and say, but they cancelled each other out and I did nothing.

An actual dad. Someone I'd just watched do flips and turns in a kayak in front of all these cheering people. I'd be able to point him out to my friends. *See, that's him. Not bad, huh?* I wouldn't have to pretend any longer that having no dad was no big deal.

And then he abandoned me. Again. He ran away. He saw me and recognized me and still ran away.

He disappeared into the crowd without saying hello or good-bye or anything at all. I lost sight of him almost at once, too many people in my way to even move. I turned and stumbled into Bryn without even realizing my legs were moving. Her arms wrapped tight around me, a rib-bruising Mom hug, and when she turned loose, she rubbed my back.

"It's all right. We'll figure things out." Her voice was shaking so bad, it was hard to understand her.

And I knew for sure not to believe her. Nothing was all right. I'd forgotten the most important thing about dads. The thing I'd known my whole life. Dads leave.

I lifted my face off Bryn's shoulder, the sun too bright, my cheeks too wet. People around us were laughing and cheering, and for a second I thought they were making fun of me, but it was only another kayaker doing tricks. Maybe nobody noticed the fact I'd fallen apart. I pulled up the edge of my T-shirt and wiped my face. Tellico was squished tight against my legs like he knew I needed hugs from everybody.

"That was him. Dad." It felt unreal to say it.

"That was him." Bryn's face was tightened up and frozen hard, like she was trying not to cry or maybe trying not to scream. "I can't believe it."

I'd been right; we did need to look for Dad. I was going to say *told you so*, but I bent down and patted Tellico instead, my voice stuck deep inside. We had needed to look for him—but this wasn't at all what I'd expected once we'd found him.

Bryn gave a gulping sort of swallow. "We'll never find him in this mass of people if he doesn't want to be found. Let's see if we can figure out who he's pretending to be."

I nodded, on autopilot. Dad dead. Dad alive. Dad gone. It was a chant in my head. I breathed in the smell of too many people too close together, and the hot dogs in my stomach lurched like they wanted out. I had to swallow hard and fast to keep them down.

Bryn was already moving, shouldering her way upstream, mumbling some serious profanity when people got in her way. Tellico and I hurried to keep up. She reached the roped-off area where the four judges sat, positioned close to the standing wave for the best view. They were talking to each other, pens and pencils down, waiting for the next round to start again. She ducked under the rope and stormed up to their table.

"Hey! You can't be in here." A young guy, all blond hair and muscles, tried to grab her arm. Bryn brushed him off.

"The fifth kayaker in that first set. Where'd he go? Who was he?"

Three of the judges turned their faces away to ignore her, but one guy with a beard, sitting closest to Bryn, looked up at her. "He didn't show up for his second run. No notice. Maybe he got sick or something."

Bryn took a breath so deep it shook her whole body, and her jaw got tight like she was trying not to yell. "What's his name? James, but James what?" Her voice had a frantic edge, and I worried she was starting to lose it. I didn't feel very pulled together myself. My insides launched into another flip.

The guy shook his head. "We don't get names, just entry numbers."

Bryn's shoulders slumped. The muscle guy waved her away, and she came back to the rope and ducked to my side. One of the other judges chuckled. "Sort of old for a groupie."

Bryn's neck turned pink, and her face got blotchy. "Come on. Let's get out of here." She led the way to the grandstand exit, the crowd shouting and cheering as the next group of paddlers started their runs. I hustled, trying not to lose her.

We stopped when we got to some open space, and she pulled up the Games map on her phone. "There must be a registration place somewhere. Names. Addresses. E-mails." She scrolled through, her teeth biting down on her bottom lip so hard I thought she'd tear all the way through.

I tried to sort things out while she looked. We weren't searching for Mom right now; we were searching for Dad, and I wasn't sure how I felt about it. If he didn't care about me, care about us, he should just stay lost. No dad was better than a rotten dad. Fuck him if all he wanted to do was run away.

Then again, we had found him, so maybe Mom had too. Maybe he knew where she was. I kept quiet and waited. I'd let Bryn decide.

After a long few minutes, she nodded. "Here's a central office. Lost children, security, first aid. Maybe they have access to the names of competitors. It's over this way."

Once again, she led, and I followed. Tellico ignored the other dogs we passed, his eyes glued to Bryn as if he knew how upset she was. I kept looking around, thinking maybe I'd see Dad again or maybe Mom, but no.

We hurried past the area with the food trucks and past the LL Bean tent and past the climbing wall. It was too crowded, too loud, and too pointless. *I found my dad and then I lost him.* The sentence looped through my head like it was stuck.

We came at last to a small building with all sorts of tables out front. A Red Cross tent on one side. A pickup table for registration packets on the other. Stacks of brochures advertised next year's Games. Bryn talked to a woman, who pointed toward the door of the building. Bryn led Tellico to a quiet spot and told him to stay. I thought I'd hang with him and catch my breath, but Bryn waved at me to come in with her, so I went.

Inside, lots of desks, lots of noise, and lots of people running around. Bryn stepped up to a desk on the left where a woman with a butterfly tattoo on her neck was typing fast at a computer. She had a name tag that said "Cheryl," and she was looking back and forth between a stack of handwritten forms and her computer screen without slowing her typing at all.

"Excuse me." Bryn sounded ultra-polite. "I need to find out some information about one of the competitors in the kayak freestyle competition."

The woman barely gave her a glance. She flipped to the next form and kept going. "Confidential. Sorry."

Bryn leaned forward, as if trying to slow the woman down by casting a shadow over her work. "It's important. And it will only take a minute."

This time, the woman didn't even look up. "Send an e-mail to the director. Go away." She flipped to another form and continued her quick typing. We were out of luck.

Bryn and I stepped to one side. "Maybe it's worth checking with someone else." But she didn't sound too sure.

"Hey, Cheryl, can you detangle this for me?" It was a man at a computer at the far side of the room calling. "I've gotten stuck in a loop with this pivot table."

"Coming." Cheryl punched a final flurry on her keyboard and then hustled out of her chair. She didn't even look our way. Maybe she'd already forgotten we were standing there.

Bryn glanced around at the chaos surrounding us—people zipping in and out, talking on cell phones, nobody paying attention to anyone else. "Josh." It was an urgent whisper. "She didn't lock her screen. Can you look?"

I didn't want to—what if I got caught?—but maybe it was our only chance. I went around Cheryl's desk and sat in her chair. A half-eaten slice of pizza was in her trash can, and the smell didn't help my stomach any. Bryn picked up a flyer from the desk and stood where she blocked the view of most of the people in the room. She pretended to read it like she was waiting for someone.

An Excel spreadsheet titled "Competitors" was open on the screen where Cheryl had been entering data. She'd been working on line 1300, which was way too many entries for me to remember. The columns in front of me were names and contact information, and it looked like the spreadsheet went on and on to the right, off-screen, maybe with event information or other stuff.

My mouth was so dry I couldn't work up enough spit to swallow, and when I glanced at Bryn, she looked nervous too. If I had the time, I could probably figure out how to filter down to kayakers or even freestyle kayakers, but I didn't think I could risk it. *Keep it simple.* I did an alphabetical sort on first names and scrolled to the J's. "There's eight Jameses."

"Can you remember them all?" No whisper this time, just an ordinary voice. "If we get caught, I'd rather not have pictures on the phone."

Eight was easy. I nodded, scrolled so I could see addresses and telephone numbers lined up and took a snapshot in my head. Then I did it again to make sure I had it. I turned and looked across the room at Cheryl. She was starting toward us, talking to someone beside her, and my hands got so sweaty my fingers slipped on the keys.

"Check under Jim too."

Shit. I wanted to leave, but I scrolled down. "Three more." I memorized them as well, then I hit "Undo" a few times until the screen looked the way Cheryl had left it. I scooted out of her chair, Bryn set down the flyer, and Cheryl closed in, but not in any hurry, checking her cell phone now and smiling at whatever she saw. We kept our heads down and walked out the door with one of the other busy people.

Bryn collected Tellico and walked toward the truck, moving super-fast like she wanted to escape. I practically had to run to keep up. We passed a side street that had a grocery store, and she stopped at the corner and waited for me.

"We're staying in Colorado. We're tracking him down." Her voice was an icicle, cold and sharp. "Let's pick up the groceries we need for the next few days. If we don't find him, I'll hire a detective. Whatever it takes."

This was good. I wanted to talk to him. It was bad. He didn't want to talk to me. More importantly, Bryn was missing the main point. I hadn't come all this way for a father who didn't give a shit. "We still have to find Mom."

"Yeah. We do. And we have to get Carl off our backs." She stared down the street with one of those looks where you don't really see anything. "Your father. I can't believe it. Why did he do it? Leave? Hide? Run after he saw you?"

All I could do was shrug and stare at the sidewalk. They were the same things I'd been wondering, the things that were eating away at my insides with needle-sharp teeth.

CHAPTER NINETEEN

Bryn

Sawyer was alive. The truth of it burned its way into my brain with such intensity I could smell smoke.

I told myself it shouldn't matter. Alive. Dead. Whatever. He had been out of my life for years. What difference should it make to me now?

Well, it did make a difference. Anger, that old familiar friend, surged through my body like a toxin and radiated from my skin to taint the air around me. Sawyer had cheated on me. He had abandoned Josh with no explanation. He deserved my fury.

But if I looked deep enough, I was also angry at myself. Here was even more proof that my judgment sucked. The man I had loved and planned to marry had faked his death, and that probably meant he had robbed that safe deposit box as well.

If he had done all this, what else was he capable of? Del had been right in coming to Colorado to search. If she'd found him, what had he done to her? I'd spent the last week believing Del's disappearance was all her own fault, but what if it wasn't? What if Sawyer held the key?

Maybe I was just trying to justify my reasons for finding Sawyer. For setting out on yet another ridiculous search. It was stupid. It was pointless. But I didn't care. I wanted to face him down and find out what the hell was going on, whether that led me to Del or not.

Josh and I got back to the tent. Time for dinner, and most evenings that meant a quiet bustle around us, with people cooking, talking, tending to fires. This night, everyone was still in town at the Games, and we had the campground to ourselves. I was relieved. At least no one from Carl's group was waiting for us this time. I couldn't face them. Not now.

We'd reached the end of Carl's seven-day countdown, and I needed to call him, try each of the numbers I'd blocked until I reached him in Memphis. I needed to negotiate more time, but first, I had to get my thoughts straight and figure out the next steps in finding Sawyer.

I rummaged through my stuff, pulled out a pad of paper and a pen, handed them to Josh. "Do you think you can write down the information on the people you saw?"

"Sure. But I don't need to write it down. I'll remember."

"It will help me to look at it. We need to decide how to tackle this. How to find him." *How to find your father.* I'd been so immersed in my own reaction to our discovery I hadn't given much thought to Josh. After his initial breakdown at the Games, he'd been all business, but inside, he must be reeling. The magnitude of Sawyer's deception was too much for anyone to deal with. I wanted to help him but didn't know how.

Josh nodded, picked up the pen, and started writing.

I'd bought some ready-made mac and cheese at the grocery. I warmed it on the Coleman stove and sliced a few apples while he worked.

"Here's the list." Josh slid it my way.

I read through it while I ate, but everything tasted like cardboard. Too much going on—my taste buds were in hiding. I pushed the food aside and gave the list my full attention. Eleven names and addresses. Josh had even written down zip codes.

"We need to decide how to prioritize this. Figure out which one is him." I picked up the pen. "One of these men is from California and one from Arizona. It's possible they could have been in Aspen in January, but that waitress said he was a regular at the bar. Let's put them lower on the list. That leaves nine."

Josh pulled out his phone. He typed for a minute and then showed me his screen.

He'd entered the first name and address into a general White Pages search, and he read the result aloud. "James Manchester, age twenty-two. Same address as Helen and Howard Manchester, both in their fifties, so he's probably living with his parents."

"Brilliant. Not Sawyer. We'll scratch him off for now."

We worked our way through the rest of the list using the same approach. Too young. Too old. Too distant. Nobody was an exact match for Sawyer's age, but if he'd reinvented himself this thoroughly, why not make up a new birthdate as well? We kept everyone in a ten-year range.

We ended up with three possibilities that seemed most likely. James Willoughby lived in Colorado Springs. Jim Princeton lived on a remote road halfway between Vail and Aspen. And James Staunton lived just west of Aspen. Amazing what you could learn on the internet.

"We can try Princeton first. He's closest. Then move on to this Staunton guy. If that doesn't pan out, we can head for Colorado Springs."

"Okay." Neutral tone. Blank face.

"Hey. Are you all right? If you want to talk . . ."

Josh's lips tightened, but not before I detected a suppressed quiver. He straightened. Stiffened his shoulders. Swung his legs over the picnic bench, stood up, and stalked off. Tellico followed at his heels, his head lifted, nosing gently for a pat, but Josh pushed him away.

My grade as a substitute parent? F minus. Admittedly, this father-rising-from-the-dead scenario probably wasn't a chapter in any parenting book, but I needed to do better.

I sighed and started in on the dishes, the campground still silent and suddenly lonely.

*   *   *

We broke camp the next morning in silence. I hadn't slept well, waking each time my dreams plunged me into another rapid. Sawyer was there in my dreams, alive; he was there in my dreams, dead. I was moving in a daze, numb and exhausted.

We loaded the last bit of gear into the truck. Josh's face was gray with fatigue, and dark circles sagged under his eyes. Every time I'd wakened in the night, he'd been awake as well, staring silently at the tent roof.

"All set?" I tried to sound enthusiastic.

Josh gave me a tired nod in response.

"Let me do a final check." I circled the campsite, looking for stray tent stakes or other overlooked odds and ends. Josh leaned against the truck, waiting with Tellico beside him. And in that moment of calm, a large SUV rolled to a stop on the campground drive, blocking our exit.

I froze for a fatal instant. Josh whirled, too late, but faster reflexes probably wouldn't have made any difference. Three of the SUV doors swung open simultaneously, and three men leaped out, moving fast.

Two of them were the thugs who'd showed up at the campground Friday night. The stocky guy carried a long metal pole with a wire loop at the end, and he headed straight for Tellico. In one quick motion, he dropped the loop over Tellico's head and tightened it with a jerk. The dog yelped and then gave a strangled whine, the snare choking him.

The thin guy zeroed in on me, grabbed me by the shoulders, and threw me hard onto the picnic table.

The third man was Carl—here, in Colorado, not safely distant in Memphis—and the sight of him launched an instant surge of adrenaline that sent my heartrate soaring toward a panic-driven extreme. He seized Josh, twisted his arm behind his back, and pushed him my way.

It all happened incredibly fast. They were organized, efficient, and domineering. Except for Tellico's yelp, the attack had been totally silent.

The three men clustered tight around me. I was breathing fast, almost gasping, and it took a massive effort to sit still instead of trying to break loose and run. I should never have

believed I could win a battle with Carl. The hard lump of the
knife in my pocket only underscored how powerless I was. What
good would a knife be against these three?

Josh was immobilized by his twisted arm, but Carl also held
a small revolver in his hand, its muzzle pressed against Josh's
side. I couldn't stop staring at that gun, so compact but so lethal.
The sight jolted me back to that icy scene in Memphis so long
ago, when the horrors of the accident were replaced by the shock
of imminent danger. Carl had aimed his gun at Sawyer then,
and my fear had been tinged with incredulous disbelief. But I
didn't have the luxury of disbelief this time. We were in a public
campground with other people around us, but I didn't doubt
Carl would shoot if it gave him an advantage.

I tore my eyes away from the gun and looked at Josh. "You okay?"
My voice shook so hard, the words were barely intelligible.

A stupid question, but Josh gave me a curt nod, looking
more angry than scared.

"He's okay now, but whether he stays that way is up to you."
Carl shoved Josh forward, letting go of his arm, and I caught
him as he stumbled. He sat beside me on the picnic table bench,
rubbing his shoulder and glaring at Carl.

Tellico growled and tugged against the snare that trapped him,
but his struggles were futile. I'd seen such a device used long ago to
catch a rabid raccoon—a way to capture a crazed animal while
keeping the handler safe from attack at the other end of the pole. I'd
never imagined seeing it used on my own dog.

"Tellico, sit. Stay." He gave one final jerk but obeyed. The
man holding the pole relaxed slightly, but he continued to hang

on with both hands. He eyed the dog as if he expected him to attack at any moment despite the restraint.

"Everything okay over there?" The voice came from the campsite next door. The young family there was eating breakfast, and the father had taken a step in our direction, peering through the saplings and undergrowth that separated us, his face concerned. Carl and his men had been careful to block any view of the gun and the snare, but their abrupt arrival must have attracted notice.

"Wave to them," Carl ordered quietly. "Tell them everything is fine. This is a private discussion."

I gave the family what might have passed as a smile and waved as directed. "Everything's fine. No worries." My voice creaked, but I got the words out. I felt like a total coward, obeying Carl that way, but it worked. The man turned back to his family, and his wife went back to doling out cereal and juice.

Carl looked far too smug at this evidence of my obedience. "Now then." His voice was hard, and its menace dropped the air temperature by at least ten degrees. "I gave you a week. You've brought me nothing. Give me one good reason I shouldn't put a bullet in Josh's leg here." He glanced at Josh. "It's your mother's fault you're in this mess. What a useless bitch."

Josh drew in a sharp breath and leaned forward as if preparing to leap, and I put a restraining hand on his knee. "Carl, wait. Don't hurt him. He's just a kid." That brought Carl's focus back to me, the look in his eyes so intimidating I broke out in a sweat. "I'll do what you ask. I'll do anything." I choked down a tight swallow and tried to control the shaking in my arms and legs.

There had been moments at the homestead and in Memphis when I'd faced Carl in anger and held onto my self-respect, but the risk was too great for that kind of bravado now. "We've been trying. Honest. You've been tracking us, so you know we've been here in Colorado looking. We have a lead—someone who may know where Del is. Give us a few more days." I hated the pleading tone in my voice, but that gun never wavered from Josh.

Carl frowned, and a muscle in his forehead twitched. "Give me the name. I'll honor them with a personal visit. Find out what they know."

"It's not one name; it's thirteen." I wasn't about to admit we'd narrowed the list down. I tried to find the right words to convince him. "You don't want to waste your time zigzagging around half the state, do you? We'll do it. We'll find her."

Carl leaned toward me, and waves of poorly restrained anger pushed against my face. "This had better be straight." He looked at Josh, and his hand tightened on the gun. I tensed, wondering if I had the nerve to jump in the way if he decided to shoot.

Carl considered it. I could see it on his face. He wanted more than fear; he wanted to maim. He wanted to prove he was in charge. But he glanced at the family in the next campsite, and I think it was their presence, not anything I promised, that tipped the balance.

He straightened and took a step back. "Today is Sunday. You have until Wednesday, but I need those pills by noon. I'll text you Wednesday morning, and you will call me back at that number within five minutes of my text. I'll tell you where to bring the pills." He was issuing orders as if my compliance was guaranteed.

And he was right—I would do as he said. There was no way I could stand up to this man, not with Josh at risk. I nodded. "Wednesday. I'll call when you text. We'll have the pills."

"Don't think for a moment you've got a way out. You're still working for me. I'll give you these few more days, but you'd better come through."

He gestured to his men. The gun disappeared. The man holding Tellico waved me toward him. "Come grab his collar."

I did so, and he loosened the snare and slipped the loop off Tellico's neck. Tellico lunged toward his captor with a snarl, but I held him back.

The three men stalked back to their SUV and drove off without a backward glance. I sank onto the bench beside Josh. Tellico rested his head on Josh's knee, and Josh rubbed the ruffled fur where the snare had tightened down. Neither of us had the energy to say a word.

"Hey, is everything really okay over there?"

I looked up. It was the father from the site next door, who had ventured again in our direction.

I fought down a wave of hysterical laughter. *Okay? You've got to be kidding.* But I lifted a reassuring hand. "We're fine. Just a minor family issue. Thanks for checking."

He nodded, still not looking fully convinced, but he returned to his kids. He had no idea that he was the one who had saved us.

CHAPTER TWENTY

Bryn

It took ten more minutes before I stopped shaking. It was my fault Carl had found us—I should have packed up and moved as soon as we disabled that tracker. I'd been so sure he was miles away; I'd dropped my guard. Finding Sawyer had been a further distraction.

I kept replaying the scene, wishing I'd stood up to him, wishing I was a warrior instead of a wimp. But just thinking about the look on his face when he considered hurting Josh swamped me with fear all over again.

"He wouldn't have shot." Josh paced in front of me. "He wouldn't have dared."

He was on an adrenaline high, acting tough, and I didn't try to argue. The fact that we'd gotten out of the confrontation without major damage was nothing short of a miracle. And now we had to follow through and find Sawyer, which was still the best path to finding Del.

"Come on." I forced my legs to support me and hauled myself off the bench. "Let's get going."

We climbed into the truck, and I pulled back onto I-70, heading west toward Aspen. My thoughts were ricocheting so violently I could hear them pinging off the inside of my skull.

Avoid Carl. Find Del. Find Sawyer to find Del. Find Sawyer to vent my anger. Find a way to walk away from the whole damn mess and leave Sawyer to his personal hell.

From one instant to the next, I changed my priorities, the after-effects of the altercation with Carl making my head spin. But eventually I calmed a bit. Find Sawyer. That was step one.

Josh stared out the window, calmer now and no doubt lost in his own struggling thoughts. He'd gone straight to bed after his walk the previous night, ignoring my attempts to get him to talk. Now, in addition to seeing his long-dead father, he had Carl to worry about.

"How are you doing?"

He shrugged.

Maybe the best way to help him was to focus on the task at hand. "Pull that Jim Princeton address up on your phone, will you? Tell me where I'm supposed to turn."

He grunted but did as I asked. We wound our way from the freeway to a twisting local road, then turned onto a rutted, gravel track that zigzagged straight up a mountain. Stands of aspen were scattered at intervals, their leaves dancing in the breeze, and broad swaths of wildflowers tinted the undergrowth with blue and pink and yellow. It would have been pretty if I were in any sort of mood to notice beauty.

Houses were scattered out here, perched on stilts to counter-act the steep ground and positioned for the best views. Many looked empty, maybe vacation homes used only in the winter for skiing. I slowed, dodging potholes and washboard stretches of bumps.

We finally reached a dirt driveway beside a blue mailbox.

"Turn here." Josh closed his phone screen. "This is it." His jaw was locked tight, his voice shrill. He plucked at the hem of his T-shirt, more nervous than I'd ever seen him.

I was in no better shape, every muscle taut. This could be where Sawyer lived. This could be another confrontation.

We bounced our way up the drive, with trees so close on both sides their branches threatened to scrape the truck. A few hundred feet up, a small house stood tucked in a miniature clearing with a dented pickup parked to one side. A German shepherd bounded off the porch as soon as we were in sight, barking like crazy, and Tellico gave a deep growl from the seat behind me.

"Just sit here and wait," I said to Josh. "Whoever's here knows we've arrived."

To the left, a weedy garden plot struggled for sunlight. On the right, a sandbox stood beside a child's swing. This, I hadn't considered. Sawyer with a new family?

Josh stared at the swing, his teeth grinding so loud I could hear it.

A woman stepped onto the porch and peered out at us. She looked like she was in her early thirties, pretty, with long black hair pulled into a single thick braid.

I lifted one hand in what I hoped was a reassuring greeting.

She said something to the dog, and he stopped barking and trotted back to join her on the porch, alert and panting hard. Josh and I climbed out of the truck, and I took a few steps forward to talk. I could smell bread baking, and the homey scent seemed out of place in the house of a fugitive.

"Can I help you?" The woman sounded nice enough, but she was understandably wary. This wasn't a location that saw many drop-in visitors. I flashed back to Carl's visit to my homestead, with its horrifying result, and tried to look harmless.

"Sorry to bother you. I'm trying to track down a distant cousin of mine, James Princeton. We last heard from him when he was living in Denver years ago." The lie rolled easily off my tongue. Josh gave me a quick glance, and I hoped he could keep his face neutral. "We were out this way on vacation and saw a Jim Princeton listed online at this address . . ." I wrapped up with what I hoped was an ingratiating smile.

The woman pursed her lips, her head tipped to one side. Behind her, a small boy, perhaps three or four years old, peered through the open door. I inspected his face but couldn't detect any echo of Sawyer.

"I'm not sure you've got the right Princeton." The woman sounded genuinely regretful. "Jim is an only child, as are both his parents, so he doesn't have much in the way of extended family. I think I met all of them at our wedding."

"It's a distant connection. Is your husband here? I've seen old photos, so just seeing him would reassure me this is a dead end."

She looked skeptical, as well she might. It sounded pretty thin.

"He's not here . . . but I expect him back any minute. You should leave. If you meet him on the drive, one or the other of you is going to have to back up."

She wasn't skilled at lying, her eyes dropping to her shoes as soon as she claimed he'd return shortly. He was probably still at the Games. Or, if he were Sawyer, perhaps he was headed for Outer Mongolia.

I wasn't sure what to do next, but Josh jumped in and saved me. "Mom, you should tell this lady the whole story."

I hoped my look of pure astonishment at being called Mom was brief enough that the woman wouldn't notice. Startling, but at the same time, kind of nice.

Josh forged ahead without missing a beat. "I mean, if this is the right man, all that money would be theirs."

The woman straightened and gave me a sharp look. "What money?"

I fumbled for an answer that might not sound too idiotic. "It's an estate from my great-uncle. None of it can be distributed until we either find James or prove he's dead. So, you see, we're eager to figure it out." *Was this how estates worked?* I didn't have a clue. Fortunately, neither did she.

"Wait here. I'll get a picture." She disappeared into the house, returning in a moment holding a framed photograph. She stepped off the porch and handed it to me. The shepherd flopped onto his belly, reassured all was well, and the boy, dark-haired and dumpy, plopped down beside him.

I held the picture so Josh could see. The man in the photo had a rugged handsomeness, but he absolutely, positively wasn't Sawyer. "I'm sorry. I'm afraid this looks nothing like my cousin."

The woman shrugged, unsurprised. "Figures. Well, worth a shot."

We returned to the truck, and I inched around in a twelve-point turn to head downhill. "Good job," I said to Josh. "I didn't know what to say next." I was still recovering from that *Mom* reference.

He rolled his eyes. "Same as offering that reward. Money does it every time."

He was right, of course. Money was at the root of all of this—Sawyer's disappearance, Carl's interest, all of it.

"So, we're headed for this Staunton guy next?" Josh tapped the address into his phone. "Head back to the highway and keep going west. We should be there in an hour and a half."

We arrived at James Staunton's house without any trouble—paved roads with neat street signs every step of the way, with no bouncing down narrow gravel tracks. I rolled down my window and inhaled the smell of the firs. The final miles of our drive paralleled a narrow tumbling river I could glimpse occasionally through the trees. Most of the houses we passed had canoe or kayak racks out front. The river was probably the reason they'd built here.

Staunton's house was small and simple, perched on the steep pitch of the mountainside, with an entire wall of glass overlooking the river. Despite the fact there were neighbors down the way, this house felt just as isolated as our previous stop. Trees closed in on all sides except the one facing the water. No yard. No flower beds. No children's play equipment.

Also, no sign of life. There was no car or truck, and the house looked locked tight. I parked and got out. Josh and Tellico followed. Nothing happened when I knocked on the front door, so we walked around back. A deck there held a grill, a small table, and one chair. I pressed my face to the sliding glass door and cupped my hands so I could see through the glare. Josh came up beside me and did the same.

The house was a single room—living, dining, kitchen—sparsely furnished with comfortable-looking sofas and chairs. An alcove held a bed, and a door nearby probably led to a bathroom. The kitchen counters were clean. A glass coffee pot was upside down on the drainboard. Whoever lived here could have left ten minutes ago or ten days ago.

"No one around." Disappointment echoed in my voice. I could easily picture Sawyer living in this house.

"Nope."

"Let's go look at the river."

We followed steep steps down to the riverbank. We were trespassing, but I wasn't leaving without learning who lived here. Tellico lapped thirstily from the water's edge and sniffed along the base of several large spruce trees. There was no one in sight.

The river was calm here, but I suspected that was deceptive. The road had been steep. There was no doubt whitewater lay below us as the river plunged downhill.

That was confirmed by the paddling gear that lined the bank. A long wooden rack, homemade, stood at the base of the path. It held a canoe, three river kayaks, and a short freestyle playboat, with a gap wide enough for an additional boat. Whoever lived here was a paddler.

A small shed stood at the far end of the rack. Inside were paddles, vests, helmets, and boat maintenance gear, all hanging from pegboard in neat rows. I ran my hand down the line of paddles and found an ultra-short one. I hefted it. Composite. Custom-designed. It had to be Sawyer's. We were in the right place.

Josh stepped closer to look over my shoulder. "Why are you staring at a paddle?"

"It's the kind your father used at the Games. He always liked this kind for tricks."

I vividly recalled a high-water weekend on the Nantahala, Sawyer practicing the rapids over and over with a paddle like this one, repeating the run until he was satisfied he'd got it right. We spent that night in a small cabin on the riverbank, the windows open to the mountain air and the sound of the water. We snuggled in bed and itemized all the things we liked and didn't like about the cabin, refining our image of how our own house would look one day. That night, I couldn't conceive of anything that would tear us apart.

I felt Josh's eyes on me and put the paddle back in its clip, worried he had seen more on my face than I would have liked. "It's his. Your father's. He's using the James Staunton name."

Josh cleared his throat. "It bothers you. Being around his stuff. I was the reason you two never got married."

I gave him an emphatic headshake. "Not you. Not your fault. It was about your father and me. And it was a long time ago." It felt like yesterday.

"So, just because it was a long time ago, does that mean it doesn't matter?"

I busied myself latching the shed and didn't try to come up with an answer. Of course it mattered. Anything with the power to shred my heart this way mattered.

Josh persisted. "Doesn't it make you mad that he ran away again yesterday? I mean, at first he didn't even admit who he was."

I headed for the stairs. "Mad? Yes, of course, I'm mad. Aren't you?"

"Yeah. Big time."

"So, we'll both tell him that when we see him." I took the first two stairs in a single stride, then stopped and twisted to look at Josh. "But the main thing we need to do is find your mom. That's why we're here, remember? That's what we have to do to get rid of Carl. Let's go back up and wait a while. See if he comes home."

That sounded good, and I did hope Sawyer knew something about Del, but the truth was, I had barely given her a single thought since the moment I first glimpsed Sawyer. It was him I was after now, and at last we were getting closer.

We climbed toward the house in silence and settled ourselves on the front steps. Tellico explored the edge of the clearing, then sprawled at Josh's feet.

"Do you want anything to eat?" We had plenty of food in the truck.

"No."

"It could be a while."

"Don't care."

I expected Josh to pull out his phone and start in on one of his games, but he sat still and stared down the driveway, his hands in his lap. He sat still and simply waited. Waited to meet a father he didn't know. A father who was far too skilled at running away.

CHAPTER TWENTY-ONE

Josh

Bryn and I sat on the front steps of James's house for a long time. At least a few hours, but it felt a lot longer. Tellico took a nap. Bryn checked some stuff on her phone. I just sat, the sun warm on my face, the wooden stair numbing my butt. The only noise was from big black-and-white jaybirds hopping from branch to branch in the nearby trees, screeching at each other. That, and the sound of the river below us.

My arm still hurt from where Carl's guy had twisted it, and when I thought about Carl saying he would hurt me, I got mad and sick to my stomach. But scary as Carl was, I wasn't thinking much about him. He wasn't the one coming home to this house.

My father's house.

I liked this house, all neat and precise inside. I'd liked watching James—Sawyer—Dad—do kayak tricks before I knew who he was. Did that make me a traitor? Would Mom be angry if she knew I was sitting here, waiting for him to come home? I halfway hoped he would hurry up and halfway hoped he would never show.

The rumble of a truck coming closer filtered through the trees at last, and my insides gave a jerking twist. It might not be him. It might be a package delivery truck. Or somebody lost. Someone, anyone but my dad.

An old black SUV came into view, dented and rusty in big odd-shaped patches. A short blue kayak was tied to the roof, exactly like the one I'd seen Dad use at the Games. The SUV pulled partway into the clearing and stopped, as if the driver had just seen Bryn's truck and couldn't decide what to do. I could see pale yellow hair and a man's blurred white face through the windshield, but I couldn't tell for sure who it was.

He just sat there. Not moving forward to park. Not backing up to leave. I waited for Bryn to do something, but she sat perfectly still, neither of them willing to budge. I'm not sure Bryn was even breathing. This was the guy she'd wanted to marry, so maybe she was feeling as mixed up as I was.

A long few minutes passed, then the SUV rolled forward. Slowly, like even the tires and the engine didn't want to come any closer. It parked beside Bryn's truck. The door opened. There was another long pause, then the driver got out.

Dad.

He came right up to the stairs, but he didn't look straight at either one of us, just bent for a quick second to give Tellico a pat. "I figured you'd find me." From his voice, he didn't sound very happy about it. "Come inside. We need to talk."

He tried to slide his key into the door lock, but his hand shook so hard it took him three tries to line it up. He got it in at last, swung the door open, and stumbled a little as he stepped in.

He left the door open, and we followed. He went straight to a bar that was built in on one side of the big room and grabbed three glasses. He still didn't look at her. He still didn't look at me. "Bryn, you want your usual?"

"Just water." Impatient. Fierce. As pissed off as when she talked about Carl.

He filled the glasses. Water, water, and straight tequila. He held out the water glasses to Bryn and me and gestured toward the bar stools at the kitchen island. "Sit down. I'll fix some sandwiches."

Sandwiches? Like we'd come by just to eat and say hello? I hadn't been sure what to expect, but not this. I mean, yeah, it was way past lunch, but shouldn't people be yelling at each other?

Dad grabbed his glass and the half-full tequila bottle, went into the kitchen, and set them on his side of the island. Bryn gave my shoulder a squeeze, nodded, and moved over to sit on one of the stools. She was pale and unsteady, which was pretty much how I felt too. I went and sat beside her. The air in the room pressed down hard, and I wanted to be outside again, where I could breathe. I wanted to be anywhere but here.

"Where's Del? Did she find you? Is she okay?" At least Bryn wasn't buying the everything's-normal-let's-have-lunch game. Her face was stiff like a mask, and her voice was pretend calm and faking nice.

Dad lined up plates, a package of brown bread, sliced turkey, mayo, and tomato along the counter in front of us, an excuse to take his time answering, an excuse to keep his attention anywhere but on us. "I found her. A buddy called and told me she was going around to the bars in town, looking for me. She's at a rehab center, and I just came from there. Visiting her. She's . . ." He stumbled to a halt. "They're trying to help her."

He knows where Mom is. She's not dead on the street somewhere. Relief hit me so hard I rocked backward a little. A whole long list of horrible possibilities disappeared as soon as he said she was alive.

But then Dad gave Bryn one of those not-in-front-of-the-kid looks I was way too good at recognizing, maybe the first time he'd looked straight at her. That kind of look meant I'd need to dig for more, but right at that moment it was enough just to know she was here. Someone was taking care of her. When Michael's dad went to rehab, he was a whole lot better for a real long time after, so maybe it would work for Mom too.

"Can I see her?" I squeaked it out.

"Yes. I can take you." But the answer was slow in coming, and Dad gave Bryn another sharp don't-ask-more look that made me wonder again what he wasn't saying.

Silence settled in. A silence so thick you could spoon it up and taste it. A silence that wrapped around me and squeezed, getting tighter and tighter. I set my water glass on the counter, and the clunk it made sounded too loud in the quiet.

The noise made Dad jump. He pulled out six slices of bread, then paused, looking at Bryn. "Are you still vegetarian?"

She nodded. She looked like she was still thinking hard about what he'd said about Mom. The way he'd said it. All he didn't say.

Dad put two bread slices back, got some hummus and carrots out of the fridge and crackers from a cupboard and made a plate for Bryn. He set it in front of her, but she didn't even glance at it. He went back to making sandwiches for him and me. "I figured someone would come looking for her. Wasn't sure it would be you." He glanced at Bryn. "And it never occurred to me it might be you, Josh."

He turned and stared straight at me. It was the first time he'd looked at me and the first time he'd said my name, and some of the twist in my stomach eased off. He searched my face inch by inch, and I examined him the same way. *This was my dad.* Maybe if I repeated that sentence a few times, it would feel real.

He cleared his throat, the noise a harsh rattle, and it looked like now he was the one having trouble pulling in air. I wanted to be mad at him, but he looked so sad it was hard for me to hang on to it.

"Josh, I'm sorry I ran. At the Games. When I saw you . . ." He blinked hard, swallowed, and downed the rest of his drink, way more than a shot.

The smell of alcohol came at me in waves, like when Mom came home from a bar. He set his glass down and turned back to the stupid sandwiches. He stared at them for a minute, and his face sort of crumpled into itself, like he didn't know what to do next. "You used to hate crusts. Do I still cut them off?"

That pissed me off, like the anger had been lying there after all, waiting for an excuse. It flared up fast and spewed out in a rush. "I'm not a baby anymore. If you'd stuck around, you'd know that."

He flinched. He cut one of the sandwiches in half—crusts on—and slid it in front of me. He poured another drink. Took another huge gulp.

Bryn's hands grabbed hold of the edge of the counter in front of her. "What happened, Sawyer? Why did you leave? Pretend to be dead? How did you end up here?"

"Yeah, Dad. Why?" I meant to hurl the question at him like a spear, but it came out sounding sad.

He emptied his glass, set it down on the counter with a shaking hand. He picked up the bottle and turned it around and around in his hands, staring out the window toward the river. "I screwed up, Bryn. Well, you already know I screwed up . . ." He gave her a quick glance, like explaining only to her was all that mattered. "But this was even worse than the stuff you know about." He shook his head, drank straight from the bottle this time. He wobbled a little on his feet. "Do you remember Carl Griffith? That jerk who was with Del the night we found that wreck?"

Bryn snorted. "He's part of the reason we're here. Del stole drugs from him. He followed Josh to my place, followed us here. He's making all sorts of threats. Insists that we find her."

"That explains a few things. Sounds like Carl hasn't changed. Well, that night of the wreck, he stole a bunch of money from that car."

"He told me."

"It set him up in style, but after a few years, he was low on cash, and he started wondering about a safe deposit key he found with the money. The bank name was on the key, and he tracked the box number to the specific branch and discovered I was the manager there."

Bryn nodded like this wasn't news to her, but I hadn't heard anything about a bank before. I stayed quiet, listening hard. I pushed my plate away. Bryn hadn't touched her food, and Dad was ignoring his sandwich and just drinking.

"Carl cornered me after work one day. Wanted me to open the deposit box and give him whatever was in it. He didn't want to step into the bank himself and get on camera. He argued it wasn't really robbery since the owner was that dead guy, and if nobody had emptied the box by then, they probably wouldn't. Claimed if I didn't do it, he'd tell the cops I'd left that accident. I laughed at him—it wouldn't help me at work if something like that came out, but I didn't think there would be real consequences. The guy was dead when we found him. I certainly wasn't about to rob a deposit box just to keep that quiet."

A robbery? Dad and a robbery? I wasn't sure what he meant about a box. I glanced at Bryn. She was frowning but still not looking surprised.

Dad sighed. Took another swig of tequila and made a face like it burned. "Laughing at him was a mistake. He got dead serious and started making all sorts of threats. Against Del. Against Josh. Against you, Bryn. Describing what he'd have his men do to you. In detail. Him and his men." He closed his eyes. "I believed him. I believed he'd do it. It shook me up bad. I hadn't decided what to do, but I took the key."

He set down the bottle. Picked up his sandwich. Set it down. Picked the bottle back up. Bryn waited. I tried to stay invisible.

"The box had been paid up in advance for five years, but the rental had only a few months to go. No one had accessed it since before the wreck more than two years earlier. I wasn't thinking straight, I admit it—I started thinking maybe it was better to just do it and get rid of Carl than to refuse and risk letting him hurt people."

He looked at Bryn as if he hoped for some sign of understanding, but she was made of concrete. No sympathy there.

Dad's jaw locked tight for a minute. "Bottom line, I opened the box one night when everyone else was gone. No cameras in the vault itself, and I had every right to go in and out. Carl kept saying he needed fifty thousand dollars to kick off some new scheme, and I figured I could at least check and see whether it was even possible that much was in there."

He paused. Bryn shifted on her stool. Leaned forward. She must not have heard this part before. "And?" she asked. "What did you find?"

Dad took a deep-down breath. "It was the largest size box, and it was packed solid with cash. Hundred dollar bills. When I eventually counted it all, more than two million dollars. I'd never seen so much money in one place before. The sight of that much cash, right there, just waiting for me to take it, sucked something right out of me. It made me hungry. It made me crave everything that money could buy. Del would quit whining about cash and give me some peace. I could buy my own plane. College for Josh would be a snap."

Money? Dad left us because of money? I stared at Bryn. I thought I was the one who understood money was what made things happen, but she just shook her head sadly, still not looking all that surprised.

Two million dollars. I tried to imagine that much cash. All the credit card bills paid. A new computer. Summer camp. Mom wouldn't even have to keep her job at the Kroger.

"So, you decided to grab all that money and disappear? Abandon your wife and son?" Bryn snapped it, not cutting him any slack.

"No. No, that's not it. At least not at first. I thought, okay, maybe if I gave Carl what he expected, the fifty thousand, maybe even a little more, and I didn't tell him about the rest, then that would leave the extra for us. I wasn't planning on leaving." Another gulp finished the bottle. "But when I gave Carl his share, he started laughing at me. He said now I was a thief, and we'd be partners. He started talking about all sorts of other wild schemes. Crazy stuff. Robbing the Brink's truck, breaking into the vault—things that could have gotten me killed. If I had stayed, I would have been trapped. And none of you would ever have been safe."

Finally, he turned to face me, apparently recalling the inconvenient little detail that he had a son. "I didn't want to leave you, Josh. It killed me to do it—it's been killing me every day, all these years—but I had to run. I had to protect you all. I had no other choice."

"Nice try, Sawyer." Bryn's voice had a vicious edge that made her sound like someone I'd never met. "Act like you've been out here pining away for your son, lonely and deprived. Bullshit. You were the one who screwed up. You were the one who left. You were the one who ended up rich."

Dad looked at me like he wanted me to understand, but by then I didn't know what to believe. He'd left with all that money? He'd tried to protect us? He was a thief? He was my dad? It all swirled around in my head, mushing together into a brown mess that didn't make sense.

He flinched, like whatever he saw in my face was a hard slap.

Bryn shook her head. "So you crashed the plane. You let the world think you were dead."

Dad dropped his head into his hands. "I was screwed. I had to leave. And once I left, I couldn't do anything that would let anyone know I was alive."

Bryn looked at him the way I'd look at something gross and slimy, and she didn't say anything.

But some of my garbled thinking straightened itself out, and all at once I had plenty to say. "So you took millions of dollars and left Mom working at a grocery? You took millions of dollars and left me juggling her credit card bills and begging for used computers and worrying about whether I could ever even go to college?"

I heard the anger in my voice, and yes, I was angry about every one of those things. But I was angry about plenty more than the money. This whole *I-was-protecting-you* thing was bullshit. If he'd wanted to let us know he was alive, he could have done it. Instead, he just stayed gone. Not there for homework or video games. Not there to teach me how to kayak or camp. Not there while Mom drank and took pills and hung out with guys like Carl.

If Carl was evil, how much worse was what my own father had done? He'd left in order to save his own skin. Hatred boiled up inside me, red and hot and scary.

238

I was on my feet with my fists clenched. He just sat there, hunched and staring at the floor, not even giving me any sort of answer. "Where's Mom? What have you done to her?"

Bryn reached toward me like she was going to try to calm me down, but I sidestepped out of range. I didn't want to calm down. Not then. Not ever.

Sawyer—I couldn't think of him as Dad anymore—gave me an anguished look. It might have been enough to make me regret how pissed off I was if I still gave a shit. "I haven't hurt her. Honest. I've been trying to help."

"Yeah. Right." It was hard for me to force the words out.

"What's happened to her? Tell us." Bryn's voice was so quiet I could hardly hear her.

Dad looked at her and then down at his hands. "When I went to town and scouted around to find whoever it was who was looking for me, I figured maybe I could pay her off . . . make her promise not to say anything. Del had been hanging out in one of the bars, but I missed her—the bartender told me she'd just left."

He ran a hand over his forehead like he was trying to sop up the sweat that dribbled there. "When I stepped out of the bar, I heard a bunch of people yelling for help, and I ran over to see what was going on. Somehow, I knew. And sure enough, it was Del. Right there. On the ground. Unconscious. The others were freaking out, making noise but not doing anything, so I did what I could. She wasn't breathing. No heartbeat. I did CPR until the ambulance came."

"And?"

His face twitched with a flicker of guilt, and I waited for him to tell me something awful. Maybe he was lying about rehab and my mother was really dead. I braced myself for it. Told myself I could take it. I'd wondered for weeks if she was gone forever, and now that was what I expected to hear.

He turned his empty bottle around and around in his hands, as if he didn't even realize he was doing it. "She's alive. But the combination of alcohol and whatever kind of pills she was taking stopped her breathing for a long time. There's serious damage. They don't know if she'll ever get better."

I rocked onto my feet, the room spinning. All I could see was red. Pulsing red. Flowing red. Red that was alive. Red hatred for Sawyer and Bryn and Tellico and even for Mom.

I staggered toward the door, retching as I went, desperate for space, desperate for air. Most of all, I was desperate to believe none of this was real.

CHAPTER TWENTY-TWO

Bryn

I was glad Josh had left. Sawyer's words about Del's condition hung in the air, the sort of news that cuts through skin and muscle and bone to slice deep and leave a scar. "What do you mean? *Serious damage?* Where is she?"

"Like I said, it's a rehab facility just outside of town. They're good, Bryn. Addiction patients. Long-term care. If anyone can help her, they can."

"And what? You paid them off to not let us know what had happened?"

He jerked back like I'd punched him, and all I felt was deep satisfaction. I wanted to do more. I wanted to hurt him like he'd hurt me. Like he'd hurt Josh.

"No. I told them I was her husband. I used identification with my old name. I told them there wasn't any other family. Just me."

"And Del's too out of it to even try and call Josh?"

He gave me a look of such pity, I dreaded whatever came next. "You don't get it, Bryn. She barely speaks. She can't dress or feed herself. She walks, sits, sleeps, but it's a body with no person inside."

He paused, which was good because it took a moment for those words to burn their way in.

Sawyer watched my face, and after a moment he went on. "I've taken photos of Josh in to show her, photos off his online accounts, and I'm not sure she even knows who he is."

"And you never even tried to let anyone know where she was?"

He looked away. "I needed time. Needed to put some things in place. You would have been notified in the end."

His phrasing was odd, but I was too upset to try to figure out what he meant. "So, let me get this straight. You just go on your merry way—head out to a kayak competition, do some rodeo flips, have a good old time while Del is on her own? Talk about *needing time* is just bullshit. You're still just trying to hide. You're still just trying to protect yourself."

He was shaking his head, trying to deny it, but I wasn't buying any protest.

I walked to the windows that looked over the surrounding woods. Josh sat huddled on the front steps, out of hearing, his face buried in Tellico's neck. I needed to go out, see how he was dealing with this, but I had to pull myself together first.

I'd hated Del for so many years. Blamed her for so many of the things that hadn't gone right in my own life. No husband. No child. Turning Landon down for fear of yet another betrayal. Josh's arrival had stirred it all up again. His presence had tempered my anger as I worried on his behalf, but anger and resentment had been the anchors that kept me stable for more than a decade.

Even with those years of anger behind me, I would never wish something like this on Del. My sister. My poor sister. *Brain damaged.* It was the only way to label Sawyer's description. The words exploded in my head, destroying my carefully rehearsed speeches, all the words I had planned to throw at her. I had envisioned ways to humiliate her, ways to get under that obnoxious *I-won-and-you-lost* surface that she loved to face me with. But this horror Sawyer was describing was too much.

Then I caught myself. Sawyer had lied before. Had been lying for years. Maybe this, too, was a lie. Another way to hurt and deceive.

I turned back to him. "You need to take us there. I want to see her. Now."

"Of course."

He straightened, as though bracing himself for what came next. "I know it doesn't seem like it—ducking you at the freestyle like I did—but I'm glad you're here. I'm glad I got to see Josh, even if just for a short while. He has every reason to hate me—I get that—but there are a few things I want to tell him."

"Why? To spin more lies? To try and get him on your side? You've had more than a decade to tell him things, but you've hidden out here instead."

"You're right not to trust me. But these last few weeks since Del showed up, I've taken a step back to look at things. Everything I told you and Josh was true. I left with the money because I didn't think I had a choice. But marriage to Del was hell, and I admit that was a factor. And I hoped getting away would make me miss you less. Hate myself less." He gulped. "It didn't work. None of it worked."

I said nothing. Sawyer had dug his own pit of hell. I wasn't about to reach in and pull him out. And I wasn't about to force Josh to listen to a lot of crap.

But being here, talking to Sawyer, hearing him say he missed me, brought back so much. I took a deep breath and tried to set aside my fury. Maybe there were things I needed to say too. "Remember that painting? The one we bought together in West Virginia?"

He nodded.

"Del had it stashed in a storage shed. When I looked at it, all the good times we'd had came rushing back. The love. The travel. The plans we'd made for the future. We bought a painting that neither of us could afford, imagining ourselves together when we hung it. You destroyed all of that. You destroyed all of that long before you opened a deposit box."

"I'm sorry, Bryn. I can't undo any of it."

He waited for me to say something more, but I just shook my head, suddenly bone tired.

Sawyer turned away and leaned against the refrigerator, staring down at the floor. "I'm not looking for sympathy, but hiding like this, jumpy all the time, waiting to be found out . . . it's no way to live. I've tried these last few weeks to set a few things right. I can't keep on like this, not now."

He said he wasn't looking for sympathy, but part of me hated to see him this tortured. When I thought about what he'd left behind, what he'd missed in Josh's life, all that money didn't seem a fair trade-off.

I stiffened my backbone. If I was going to feel sorry for someone, it should be Del or Josh. And I couldn't lose sight of Carl and his threats. "Enough. We need to go now. Take us to Del."

I opened the door to let Josh know, but he wasn't there on the steps any longer. Went out onto the porch, but he still wasn't in sight. Walked out to the truck to check the cab, curious but not yet worried. He wasn't there either.

"Josh!" Silence. "Josh! We're going to go see your mom!" Nothing.

Sawyer came out on the porch. He was weaving slightly, but I would have been unconscious after downing the amount of alcohol he'd just consumed. "Not here?" He looked around as if he expected Josh to pop out of hiding.

I shook my head. "Tellico!" Odds were good they were together. "Tellico!" That second time was louder, and a faint bark came in response. "They must be down by the river."

Sawyer grunted some sort of acknowledgment, and we headed in that direction. Josh had been forced to absorb far too much in the past few days. We would no doubt find him sitting on the bank, staring out over the moving water, sorting through his turmoil with Tellico beside him. I would give Josh a hug. Let him know we'd figure it all out. See if I could be a proper aunt for a change.

Despite such reassuring self-talk, I was anxious by the time I reached the top of the long flight of stairs that led down to the river.

"Josh!" I still couldn't see him, but Tellico stood below, looking downriver and whining. *Looking downriver.* Fear seized me by the throat, shaking me off balance, and I had to lean on the handrail for a second to keep from falling. I raced down the stairs, my heart jolting in my chest with every tread. Sawyer's feet thudded hard behind me.

The staging area by the river was small, a narrow clearing carved out of the woods, and it took only a single glance to confirm Josh wasn't there. The door of the storage shed stood open, and I hurried to look inside, illogically hoping he might be hiding there.

"Oh my god." Sawyer's voice was panicked, and I spun around. He stared at the boat rack, his face bleached white. "One of the kayaks is gone."

The rack had held three full-size kayaks. Now there were two.

What had Josh done? My fear converted into a full-fledged adrenaline storm, my heart pounding high in my throat, my arms and legs trembling.

I raced to the edge of the water and looked down the mountainside, Tellico anxiously nosing at my leg. The river was deceptively calm here, and Josh may not have realized that was temporary. Maybe he had run aground at once. Or realized his mistake and turned toward shore. But all I could see from that vantage point was churning white froth that disappeared around a sharp bend twenty yards away.

"What's downriver?"

"This is the top of the Silver Run. Two chains of Class IIIs just down from here, then a tricky fifteen-foot waterfall. If he makes it through that, the river calms for a while, but lower down it's completely impassable—a genuine deathtrap." He snapped the words, moving fast, already flipping the second kayak over, grabbing paddle, rope bag, helmet, gloves, and vest from the shed.

His own adrenaline must have been overriding the vast quantity of tequila he'd consumed, because he moved with the same efficiency I remembered from so many years before.

"How much experience does Josh have?" He zipped into his flotation vest and crammed his helmet in place.

"None. We went canoeing one afternoon. That's it. Nothing on whitewater." I'd told him he was a natural. Heaped praise on his beginner efforts. He probably thought he was ready for anything.

"I've got to stop him before he hits the falls. Bring the other boat. I need your help."

In an instant, he was in his kayak, digging in hard with his paddle. He disappeared downriver in only seconds. Tellico danced along the bank, barking.

I stood still for a moment, unable to force my legs forward through the fear that paralyzed me. For fourteen years, I'd stuck to calm placid lakes. Water that didn't attack, didn't fight back, didn't try to kill me.

But Josh needed me. I had to go.

I ran toward the shed. Grabbed helmet, vest, and paddle. Searched for a second rope bag. Not there.

I wasted precious seconds looking in a storage chest. Found nothing.

No time.

I slid into vest and helmet, flipped the remaining full-size kayak off the rack, pushed it into the water. Grabbed the paddle and waded in, heedless of my soaking wet tennis shoes. The water, recent snow-melt, was bitterly cold. Tellico whined from the shore.

"Stay, boy. Stay with the truck. I'll be back."

I straddled the boat, ready to get in and launch, and that's when the full force of what I was about to do hit me. Whitewater. Class III rapids and a fifteen-foot waterfall. For an instant, I was back in the Chattooga, trapped and crushed by hundreds of pounds of river, unable to move. I was back in every nightmare I'd had since that day.

The river tugged at the kayak, and I was shaking so hard, I almost lost hold.

I couldn't do this.

My stomach clenched, my lungs seized, and my heart tried to climb out of my ribcage.

I had to do this. I had no choice.

Ten minutes earlier, I would have sworn I would never again battle a river. Now, I had to fight. I had to win.

I took a deep breath, hoping for comfort, but it did nothing to steady me. *Landon would help if he were here.* I thrust the out-of-place thought aside, but the idea he'd be in my corner gave me enough strength to move.

I swung my feet into the cockpit, slid my butt into the seat and my legs into the thigh hooks. The boat slipped into the frothy current. I took a few tentative strokes, the awkward strokes of a total amateur. *Come on, woman, you know how to read a river. Get your shit together.*

My paddling settled into a more confident rhythm. In only a few minutes, I reached the first set of real rapids, whitecaps and a loud rumble, but easy to read. I stayed to the left, did a hard-right pivot, then took a straight shot between a pair of huge boulders and rode a long washboard of whitewater downhill. One set down.

My old paddling patterns started to return. My breathing slowed. My timing was still off, but I hadn't screwed up yet. I was doing better than I had any right to expect.

I scanned both riverbanks, looking for Josh, for Sawyer, for an overturned boat.

Nothing.

Josh must have made it through this first set, and now there was no easy way for him to change his mind. The river had narrowed, with high, steep banks. It would have been impossible to pull in to shore even if he knew he was in trouble and wanted to escape.

I gained speed over a short stretch of flatwater, then hit the second set of rapids Sawyer had mentioned. *Plan. Think ahead. Don't screw up.*

This one was trickier. I mistimed one of my turns and scraped hard against a boulder, fiberglass scraping across stone, the screech broadcasting my incompetence. The small bit of confidence I'd scraped together vaporized instantly. I couldn't do this. Everything around me tossed me back to the day of the accident—the roar of the water, the harsh pull of the paddle against the current, even the freshwater smell of the churning river. Panic blindsided me once again. I tried to force my terror to one side, but it refused to be confined.

The river narrowed even more, entering a canyon with sheer walls on either side. A heavy rumble of falling water came from up ahead—the waterfall—and a suffocating new wave of fear swept in. I was going to die. I was going to lose everyone and everything I'd been trying to save—Landon, Josh, Del, my homestead. It wasn't Carl who would destroy me. I was taking care of that on my own.

I back-paddled hard, slowing my forward momentum. I wanted out. I wanted dry land. But there wasn't even a place to eddy up to give myself a moment to prepare.

I'd done plenty of falls like this before the accident, and the memory was etched in my core. That final moment of balance at the top. The backward lean as the bow dropped forward. The kayak tipping, becoming vertical, time slowing as I kept my paddle poised and ready. A freefall, then an impact at the base, the boat spiking deep into the water. Every muscle had to work in synchrony to keep balanced. I had to flatten the kayak out at the bottom, dig my paddle in hard, keep my head in the game.

I knew that adrenaline rush. The buoyancy of success. The addictive feeling of being ultra-alive, victorious over a powerful opponent.

But that was then.

I also knew what could happen when the river won the fight—boats overturned, paddlers dumped, broken bones, bodies smashed against rocks.

My fingers dug like claws into the paddle, my pulse pounded my head like a battering ram, my stomach knotted so hard it made it difficult to draw a full breath.

Despite my backward strokes, the river pushed me forward. If Josh or Sawyer were in trouble directly below, my arrival could make things worse, but it was too late to change course now.

Enough. I stopped backpaddling. Angled left to line up with the falls. With my heart lodged tight in the back of my throat and an absolute conviction I was facing catastrophe, I let the river sweep me toward the edge of the drop.

CHAPTER TWENTY-THREE

Bryn

There was a moment at the top of the waterfall when the kayak's bow embraced only air, not yet tipping downward. A moment when I could glimpse what lay ahead.

Below the falls, a huge flat-topped boulder on the left. It created a narrow channel, forcing the current through a passage on the right.

Beyond, Josh's red kayak. And a dark head in the water, unmoving.

Josh was here, I'd found him—but the instant's relief that let me breathe was swamped at once by the horrified recognition of the danger he was in. He wasn't moving. He must be trapped.

The next instant my kayak slipped forward, dropping down the cascade.

Some dim scrap of muscle memory took over, and I leaned backward to balance, part of my brain screaming in terror, the rest analyzing what I'd seen from the top.

I suffered a few wild seconds of additional panic during free fall, then my kayak plunged underwater at the waterfall's base. My paddle thrusts and backward lean finally brought the bow back to the surface. Abysmal form, but at least I didn't flip.

I muscled the boat forward and shot through the narrow channel between the boulder on the left and the canyon wall on the right. Then I pivoted hard left, spinning my kayak into the calm eddy that lay tucked on the downriver side of the massive granite boulder, a space protected from the current. I was shaking, but maybe I wasn't going to die quite yet.

Sawyer stood there on the slab, his kayak pulled onto the rock beside him, his throw bag in his hand. "Hang on." He hurried toward me, seized the grab loop on my kayak's bow, and hauled the boat up by brute force, dragging it beside his kayak on the huge rock.

I scrambled out.

"Rope bag!" He didn't even look at me, never doubting I'd brought the right supplies. His attention was focused on his hands—tying a carabiner to the end of his rope with a guaranteed-to-hold bowline.

"Couldn't find it."

He whirled toward me, his frustration instantaneous, but then he shivered. "We'll have to make do with this one." He ripped the bag away from the long coil of rope it enclosed.

I stepped to the edge of the boulder to see Josh.

The waterfall had ratcheted my level of fear up to what I'd foolishly believed was a maximum level, but all the moisture in my mouth disappeared when I understood the details of his situation. Josh was trapped mid-current, facing upstream. He must have flipped at the base of the falls, fallen out of his boat. He'd smashed into the rock, and the boat had slammed into him. His capsized kayak was in front of him, pinning him in place against the tall thin rock at his back.

It was one of the worst kinds of entrapments. One of the easiest ways to drown.

"Josh! We're coming!"

The waterfall pounded so loud it made my head throb, but he heard and looked my way. He nodded. No attempt to cry out or yell, but at least he was conscious. The water was frigid, and hypothermia would hit fast. He wasn't wearing a helmet, but he'd had sense enough to put on a flotation vest before taking the kayak.

The speed of the water as it shot through this narrow canyon was incredible. The kayak was on its side, its cockpit facing upriver, and the water's force bent the fiberglass boat into a curve, wrapping it around the trapped boy. The boat's pillars kept it from collapsing flat, but the pressure on his chest had to be enormous. Josh's arms were pinned to his sides, trapped by the boat, so there wasn't even a way for him to grab a rescue line.

All of this took only seconds to comprehend. Sawyer clipped his rope to a D-ring on his own vest. "Can't snag his boat from this angle and current's too fast to do anything from my kayak. I'll have to swim for it. I should be able to get enough leverage to shift the boat off him."

Wrestling a boat in this torrent was crazy, but it was the only chance Josh had.

"What can I do?" I had to shout over the noise of the waterfall.

"Belay me." He gestured toward a small fir tree that was anchored in the crack between our boulder and the left-hand canyon wall, and we shifted that way. "Once I've freed Josh, you'll need to swing us back into this eddy."

I nodded like that was no big deal, but desperation weighted my arms.

I tugged on the tree. Not all that big, but it felt solid. I sat down on the spray-soaked boulder and wedged my back against its trunk. Sawyer passed the rope around me and the tree trunk. The tree would keep me from being dragged into the water, and it would act as a rough pulley, letting me use both hands to manage the rope.

"Okay." My mouth was lined with sandpaper. I couldn't even swallow. Cold spray soaked my hair and face.

Sawyer dropped the long coils of rope at my side, ripped his gloves off, and handed them to me. "Give me plenty of slack to start."

"Okay." I slipped the gloves onto my shaking hands. Too big and saggy, but without them I'd never be able to hang on.

These preparations took less than a minute, our motions quick, each decision urgent. Sawyer and I were working together in the same seamless rhythm we'd developed so many years ago, as if the decade apart had never happened.

Now, my job was to simply sit still. *Sit still, belay the rope, don't let anyone wash downriver, don't let anyone drown.* Sitting still was the hard part. I wanted to fling myself into action. Do something, anything, to save Josh. I couldn't just sit here and watch him die.

My hands double-checked the coil of rope, the necessary movements coming without thought. Untangled with plenty of slack. *Ready.*

Sawyer stepped to the edge of the slab. "Josh, I'm coming!" One last look at the current, then he gave a springing leap into the water. He landed in the center of the chute and was swept downstream, the rope playing out smoothly, floating loose behind him.

But he hadn't jumped far enough. He needed to head straight toward Josh and the wedged kayak, but instead I watched, horrified, as the current pushed him sharply to the left. Sawyer swam hard, trying to correct his course, but the river was too strong, and it forced him downriver and toward the left-hand wall of the canyon.

I tightened the rope, stopping his progress, the cord burning my hands through the gloves, my muscles screaming from the strain.

Behind me, the tree creaked but held.

There was no way for Sawyer to swim across that current to reach Josh. The force of the water was too strong, and my safety rope was at an angle that would swing him toward me and away from his son. Sawyer came to the same conclusion, and he kicked hard to the side to reach the rock wall.

The current wasn't as fast there, and he could grip an occasional outcropping to pull himself toward me, his bare fingers scrabbling for purchase on the rough rock. I hauled the rope in with all my strength, inching him upstream.

When he reached the eddy, he was strong enough to make progress on his own. He swam to the slab I was sitting on and pulled himself up.

"That current is fierce. I've got to line up exactly, because once I'm downriver from Josh, I can't get back up." His words came in quick gasps, his fight with the water taking a toll. His lips were blue. He was shivering. His fingers were scraped and bloody from clinging to the rock wall.

I flexed my aching hands. Coiled the wet, heavy rope, ready for the next attempt. I glanced toward Josh. His eyes looked unfocused. His head drooped forward. If Sawyer wasn't successful this time . . .

I swallowed hard. "Sawyer, you can do this. You have to."

He didn't seem to hear me. He struggled to his feet. "I'll try again."

"Sawyer." I raised my voice this time, and he turned. "Be careful."

For a flashing instant, he gave me a wry grin that acknowledged the ridiculous. Me telling him to be careful, after all we'd been through. Then his look of concentration returned, and he turned away.

He walked to the edge of the slab and gave Josh a nod and a thumbs-up that belied the risks. This time he gave a galvanic leap, landing in the water on the far right-hand edge of the chute. Once again, the current caught him and tossed him downstream, but this time the angled flow pushed him directly toward Josh.

I couldn't put tension on the rope to slow him down because it would drag him off course, so Sawyer was going full speed when he slammed into Josh's kayak. The hard thud echoed off the rock walls, and Josh threw his head back, his mouth open as if yelling in pain, but his voice was too weak to carry.

Sawyer clung to the edge of the open cockpit. It looked like he was saying something to Josh, but I couldn't hear, and Josh's head sagged to the side.

Sawyer swung his legs over the submerged bow of the boat, which put him on the downstream side of the curved kayak, and I tightened the safety rope. He braced his back against the narrow rock, brought both feet up against the boat with his legs bent, and pushed. Pushed hard. His muscles bulged, and I could see the strain on his face.

If he could shift the boat even a few inches, the force of the water would no longer be balanced on bow and stern. The boat should break free, and Sawyer could grab Josh.

Nothing happened. The boat didn't budge.

Sawyer stopped trying, and he grabbed the cockpit again to keep himself stable. He lifted one hand in a *give-me-slack* gesture.

I let out a few feet of line.

Sawyer unclipped the rope from his vest and attached it to the grab handle on the bow, the end of the boat farthest from me. This gave me leverage against the bow, but it left Sawyer without a safety line. If he lost his grip, he'd be swept away. I bit down so hard on my lip I tasted blood. If that happened, Josh was doomed.

Sawyer maneuvered himself to the downstream side of the rock that trapped Josh, wrapped one arm around its narrow top, and seized the stern grab handle of the boat with his other hand. He looked my way, his face desperate. "Pull!"

I pulled with every ounce of strength I had.

If I could haul the bow toward me, while Sawyer dragged the stern toward him, we could dislodge the boat.

If Sawyer could hang on to the boat and grab Josh fast enough to keep him from being swept away, I would have

Sawyer, Josh, and the boat, all three, on the end of my single safety line.

Two very big *ifs*. Impossible odds, but there was no other option.

The wet line hummed, taut and vibrating above the water. Sawyer pulled on the stern. No effect. No change. Then suddenly, without warning, the boat shifted an inch. Another inch. Almost. We almost had it.

Loud cracking sounds echoed off the canyon walls as the fiberglass splintered under the strain. A third inch, and suddenly, too quickly to be believed, the balance of pressure shifted. The water's force on the boat was no longer evenly distributed, and the river now helped instead of fighting us. The kayak sprang free. It whipped across the current, its stern pivoting straight toward Sawyer.

I screamed.

The kayak jerked to a halt; its bow still clipped to the end of my safety line, Sawyer still clinging to the stern.

The sudden stop broke Sawyer's hold. A heartbeat later, the current caught him. He was gone.

Shit, shit, shit. I dropped my rope, Josh's battered kayak spun away, and I lunged for my kayak, my eyes never leaving Josh. He remained where he was for a long moment, unmoving, the pressure of the water holding him pinned against his rock.

Too cold. Too little air. Too much time in the water.

I couldn't tell if he was even still breathing.

I launched my kayak, but I was too late. Josh's slack body tipped sideways, and the current caught him at once. He disappeared downriver, his vest keeping him barely on the surface.

I dug in hard with my paddle, and the river surged beneath my boat. Sawyer had said a stretch of flatwater lay ahead before the river got worse, and I forced myself to focus. Watching for rocks and unexpected holes. Watching for Sawyer and Josh, floating or struggling in the water. Watching for bodies, swept onto shore.

I was on autopilot, fueled by fear and paddling harder than I'd ever paddled in my life. My arms ached. My chest struggled for air. My heart pounded hard in my ears, drowning the sound of the water.

One more set of Class III chop, and I was out of the canyon. Thankfully, the river fanned out to triple its former width here, calming its violent course as it hit more gentle slopes. Dense forests lined both banks again, replacing the vertical rock walls.

Where the hell were Josh and Sawyer? My shoulders and arms screamed in protest, but I kept up my frantic pace, far outstripping the water's more sedate flow.

A gentle turn to the right had built up a sandy spit on the left-hand bank, a spot where debris had washed to the side. A weather-beaten log lay half in, half out of the water and pressed tight against the log was a small patch of red. I drew closer. It was Josh's life vest. Hope propelled me forward. The vest was still on him. I could see his hair. An arm. "Josh! I'm coming!"

I strained to hear an answer and looked for at least a raised hand in response.

I heard nothing. Josh didn't move.

I angled toward shore, beached the kayak, leaped out. The current was slow enough here that I could stand, and I forced my way through the icy flow to where Josh floated. He was face up, but he was frighteningly still.

With my last bit of strength, I dragged him onto the edge of the sand spit. I pressed my cold fingers to his wrist. His neck. No pulse. Bent my ear to his mouth. No breath.

I dropped to my knees. Unzipped his vest and shoved it out of the way, rehearsing the steps in my head. Tip his head. Give two rescue breaths. Heel of my left hand two fingers above the end of his breastbone. Right hand on top. Shoulders aligned. Elbows locked. *Go.*

Thirty compressions. Two rescue breaths. At least two inches of movement needed in each compression. I chanted the cadence in my head, working hard, sweat warming my face. Thirty again. Another two.

Even this, I owed to Sawyer, who had demanded I take advanced first aid classes before spending time on whitewater. His insistence back then might be what saved his son now.

Josh's chest was thin and fragile. It felt as if my hands would crush him like an eggshell, drive straight into the sand below him. But I kept going. My arms ached. Every breathe burned.

Nothing got better.

Come on, Josh, Come on.

Still nothing.

Damn it, Josh, come on. Breathe.

"Josh. Don't die. You can't die. You can't." My voice choked, swamped by tears. My insides shriveled into a shaking mass.

Maybe the CPR made a difference. Maybe it was my voice. Maybe his own determination pulled him back toward life. Whatever the cause, after I made that desperate plea, Josh gave a gasping heave. I rolled him onto his side, and he vomited a froth of river water, his abdomen spasming hard. His eyes opened, but I'm not sure he saw me.

"You're all right, Josh. You're okay."

I felt for a pulse and found it now, pounding away in a reassuring rhythm. I pulled his shirt aside. His chest was a horrible network of bruises, already purple and swollen from the boat's pressure when he was trapped. The pummeling I'd just given him was only going to make things worse.

I ran my hands down his arms and legs. His left wrist was swollen to double normal size, at least sprained, possibly broken. I worked my fingers through his hair to check his skull. There was a sizable lump on the back of his head, but he was in better shape than I'd expected.

"What happened?" His voice was a feeble croak, but his eyes were more alert and focused now. He struggled to lift his head but gave up fast.

"Just rest. Don't try to move. You'll be all right in a bit." Not the full truth, but that sounded more reassuring than saying *you drowned and then came back to life.* We were both shivering, and Josh's skin was ice, but I didn't have anything dry to use to warm him.

"You came." He sounded astonished.

"Of course, I came. Why wouldn't I?"

"Whitewater." Josh croaked out the word.

The promise I'd given—*No whitewater. Ever.* I squeezed his hand. There was more to be said, but my voice wouldn't work right. Josh was family. And Sawyer had been right all those years ago—life was not a spectator sport.

I sat back on my heels, my wet clothes heavy and clammy. Sawyer was still out there somewhere. I stood up and looked downstream, but I couldn't see him.

The river was slow here. If he were conscious, he should have been able to swim ashore. This sand spit reached toward the current in a long arc, and even a weak swimmer should have been able to detour to reach it.

But he wasn't here—wasn't anywhere in sight. I looked back upriver. Could I have passed him somehow without noticing? I didn't think so, but my doubts cascaded. After all that tequila. After battling the river. He could be in real trouble. He had said the river was impassable farther down.

The irony struck me—worried about Sawyer after so many years of hate and anger. But regardless of all he'd done in the past, he'd just risked his life to save his son. He'd taken charge, and I'd fallen automatically into the habit of trusting his judgment. Part of me resented my obedience, but when it came to situations like this one, there was no one better. By myself, I could never have rescued Josh.

I wanted to search for Sawyer, but I couldn't leave Josh in the shape he was in. "How are you feeling?"

"It hurts to breathe." He licked his lips and reached toward the back of his head with a trembling hand. "My head hurts."

"You've got a nasty bump. Must have slammed into something along the way."

He looked around. "Where's Dad? I was stuck . . . he swam up to me . . ." His voice was returning. Much closer to normal.

"I don't know where he is. He got swept downstream when the boat came free."

"Is he okay? He said . . ." Josh stopped. Looked away. "When he was hanging on to the boat, out there in the water. He said he was sorry. He told me he loved me." His voice broke, and he cleared his throat. He closed his eyes.

Sawyer had said he wanted to say a few things to Josh. Maybe he'd seized his final chance to say what mattered most.

We sat for another minute, Josh's color improving, and I heard a truck shifting gear, its engine straining uphill somewhere in the woods behind us. "Are you okay for a bit? It sounds like the road is close here. I need to find someone. Call for help. Get you dry and warmed up, and get people looking for your father."

He looked frightened at the idea of being left alone, and his fear confirmed my decision to focus on him and let others lead the hunt for Sawyer. I hated to leave him for even a few minutes, but I didn't have much choice. "Rest. Don't move. I'll be back. I promise."

His slow nod of agreement held no enthusiasm.

I took off my vest and slid it under his head as a pillow, and I started toward the trees to look for help. At the edge of the forest, I stopped one more time and looked along both riverbanks, hoping, but the river was the only thing alive. It roared its way downhill, relentlessly carving its path, confident that, in the end, it would always be victorious.

CHAPTER TWENTY-FOUR

Josh

They gave Bryn and me two of those orange blankets like you see on TV, the kind they give to people on the news who've survived burning houses or exploding bombs. I wrapped mine tight around me and tried to ignore its moldy smell. It was good to have something to hang on to. My head hurt. My wrist hurt. Pretty much everywhere hurt. No burning houses here and no exploding bombs, but now I knew how those people felt.

We sat on a huge rock a little downstream from where Bryn had flagged down a FedEx driver who called 911. It was people who lived nearby who came, first volunteers bringing blankets and dry clothes, concerned voices and kind eyes. An ambulance with EMTs was on its way, but they said it would take a while for it to get here.

Then more people kept arriving and getting organized. Volunteer firefighters. Wilderness searchers.

They were going to search for Dad.

The guy in charge came over to Bryn. "One of us can drive you toward town, meet the ambulance coming up." He said it like maybe he'd be happier if we were somewhere else, not watching his every move.

He wasn't talking to me, but I jumped in fast. "No, we need to stay here." I couldn't leave without knowing about Dad. I looked at Bryn for her support, and even though she shook her head at first, she finally sighed.

"Any harm in letting us wait here for the medics? His father's the one who's missing."

The guy frowned like he was going to push it, but he looked at me and relented. "Stay out from underfoot. The ambulance should be here soon."

So, we sat there, doing nothing, watching everyone else be super busy.

A bunch of people arrived all at once with kayaks and canoes on the roofs of their cars. Bright colors, bandannas, handshakes, and quiet hellos. They looked serious. They loaded a lot of extra gear into the canoes. Radios and ropes. A big box with a red cross on it. A folded-up bundle that could be a stretcher. People kept glancing our way and whispering.

"What do you think happened to him?" I didn't want to hear what Bryn would say, but I had to ask anyway. That river was so cold. I'd never been that cold before, my skin numb but my bones freezing, so cold it was hard to think. I hated thinking about Dad freezing somewhere like that.

Bryn reached over and squeezed my hand. A bad sign. "He's probably just onshore somewhere. Pulled himself out of the river at a spot where he can't hike out. He's sensible. He'll wait. Hell, he'll probably just wave hello when the boats get there and then start bossing everyone around."

She said it like she meant it, but I didn't believe her. She kept glancing downriver, twisting her blanket in her hands and looking worried.

Another truck pulled in, parking behind the line of vehicles already there. Bryn's truck. The next minute, Tellico raced up to us, pausing at Bryn to get a pat and a "good dog" but then coming to me. I gave him a hug. I rested my head against him for a minute, his fur warm and soft. He sat right next to my legs so I'd know he was there, and I moved the blanket so he was underneath with just his head sticking out, watching and waiting like I was.

A woman in jeans and a Bronco T-shirt came down from the road. She carried a big thermos and handed Bryn her truck keys. "Found your truck with no trouble. And you were right—the dog was waiting right there."

"Thanks so much for bringing it over, Diane." Bryn must have gotten introduced when she told about the truck.

Diane handed Bryn the thermos and two plastic cups. "I stopped by my place on the way back. Fixed you some hot chocolate."

"Thanks. Sounds good."

Diane looked at all the people who had gathered. "They'll find him." She sounded certain. "They won't stop searching until they do." It was what I wanted to hear, but she looked worried too.

"Thank you. Everyone has been great."

The rescuers finished getting ready, and the boats took off downstream in a long straggling line, leaving a half-dozen people clustered around a guy in a red cap who held a walkie-talkie.

"This is all my fault." The words had been there the whole time. Waiting. I hadn't meant to say them out loud, but once those first words were out, I couldn't stop. "If I hadn't taken the kayak and Dad hadn't followed me, he wouldn't be out there now. He could be hurt. He could maybe be dead."

Bryn gave me a quick hug. "You were upset. I shouldn't have let you walk out on your own after you'd heard bad news about your mom." She looked just as miserable as I felt. "They'll find him. It will all be okay." But this time she didn't sound convinced.

I wiped my nose on my damp sleeve. For practically my whole life, I'd been used to the idea of my dad being dead. I missed him sometimes, and other times I was mad he was gone, but I didn't get teary-eyed over him. So why was I crying now? I'd only learned he was alive the day before, but it felt like part of me had been ripped out and thrown away.

I'd wanted to cry when I went over that waterfall. The drop. The icy water. Sliding out of the boat even though I was trying to hang on. Slamming into that rock, hitting so hard the world got fuzzy. The boat trapping me so I couldn't move. Could barely breathe.

I was certain I was going to die. I was going to die and I wasn't going to see Mom again. I wasn't going to go home again. And it was all my fault.

But then Dad shot over the falls like it was easy, like he did it every day, and the next minute he was out of the water, yelling he was going to come get me. Telling me he was sorry. That he loved me. Even though the water was freezing, his words made me feel warm, like when Mom gave me a hug or Tellico snuggled up close.

They had to find Dad. He had to be safe. He just had to.

Bryn and I waited another half hour or so. Drank the hot chocolate, which warmed up my insides but coated my mouth in sugar and made me more thirsty, not less. Then Red Cap held his walkie-talkie to his mouth and talked back and forth a few times. The crackling sound of voices came through from the other end, but not the words.

The people who'd waited on shore got tight around him to listen. Several of them glanced at us but then turned away fast, like they were embarrassed to see I'd noticed. No smiles. No high fives. My stomach dropped like I was in a too-fast elevator.

Red Cap finished talking, looked at Bryn, and came slowly our way.

Bryn tossed her blanket off and stood up. My legs were stone, locked tight to the ground, and I hung on to Tellico with both hands.

"The search team has covered the next stretch of river with no luck. They can't go any farther. Once you get past the final take-out point, the river's a nasty mess of rocks. Impassable." He was using his hands, pointing downriver, shaking his head. "They found the kayak you described—the one with the safety line attached. Or rather, they found what's left of it. But they haven't found anything else."

They hadn't found Dad.

Bryn listened, and her whole body shrank up small. "What next?"

"We'll send people in on foot. Call in a helicopter. But it doesn't look good. If he were conscious, there are a handful of spots where he could have pulled himself to shore, but there's no sign he did so. If not . . ." His voice trailed away. He gave her an awkward pat and turned away.

Bryn was crying big silent tears like they'd never stop, but she didn't even try to wipe them off. "They . . ." She stopped, her voice not working right. "They'll keep looking."

I nodded, freezing cold all at once despite the blanket. They would keep looking, but now they were looking for a body.

My dad was dead. He'd always been dead, but this time it felt harsh and real, not a story from long ago. I wiped my face on my sleeve again. My stomach and throat were twisted up so tight, words couldn't work their way out.

A bright shiny ambulance rumbled in to join the cluster of trucks and SUVs, its lights flashing but no sirens, no fuss. Two medics climbed out, looking my way. I wanted to stay where I was, but I couldn't think why.

"Let's get you to the hospital. They need to check you out." Bryn put a shaking arm around my shoulders and helped me to my feet. We headed away from the river toward where the truck was parked. Tellico walked beside me. The people by the river were busy putting equipment back in boxes, getting ready to leave. That whole long walk, they all stopped what they were doing and stared after us. They acted like they'd never seen people cry before.

CHAPTER TWENTY-FIVE

Bryn

The hospital admitted Josh, taking chest X-rays, checking for concussion, splinting his wrist. They declared him extremely lucky, but his body was a multihued patchwork of bruises, and he looked tired and drawn. He said little, snuggling under a deep pile of too-thin hospital blankets, raising and lowering the head of his electric hospital bed, watching cartoons designed for a five-year-old. He didn't talk about his father. He didn't ask about his mom.

I called Landon that first night. I was exhausted from the episode on the river, worried about Josh, and confused by my flip-flopping feelings about Sawyer. His death had torn something loose inside, and the least little thing had me tearing up. As soon as I heard Landon's calm voice on the phone, I fell apart, and the whole story of the past twenty-four hours tumbled out. Spotting Sawyer at the Games. Carl's latest set of threats. Tracking Sawyer down. The news that Del might be in horrific shape. Josh taking the kayak. Sawyer's death.

Hearing myself say it all out loud made it feel a little less overwhelming, and it felt good to spill the whole thing to a sympathetic listener. "Seeing Sawyer alive at the Games—alive and running away again—all I could feel was anger. Listening to his self-justifying bullshit about taking all that money didn't help. But then he risked his life for Josh on the river. He saved his son. I wouldn't have been able to do it."

Landon stopped me right there. "Sounds like he stepped up, and that's great, but you're not giving yourself enough credit. You faced that river. You never thought you'd be able to do that again. Josh wouldn't have made it if you hadn't been there."

Maybe. He wasn't wrong, but I couldn't quite embrace it. There were plenty of things I was going to have to sort out.

"I still need to find Del and decide what to do about Carl." Had it only been that morning when he and his men swooped in on us at the campsite? Grabbing Josh and choking Tellico? It felt like a lifetime ago. "At least now we know Del is here. Assuming Sawyer was telling the truth. I guess that's tomorrow's project. At the moment, I'm too exhausted to move."

There was silence on the phone for a moment, and I pictured Landon looking out his window into the quiet darkness of the Blue Ridge. I, on the other hand, was huddled in the windowless corridor outside Josh's hospital room, squinting against the glare of the overhead fluorescents.

"I'm homesick. I miss the mountains and the animals and the garden. I miss the quiet mornings, watching the sunrise, walking down to check for the night's tracks at the creek. I miss you." I stumbled to a halt. That last sentence was totally true, but I was surprised I'd said it out loud.

271

"I miss you too." Landon said it so quietly, I thought I might not have heard it right. Then, in a normal voice, he said, "What can I do to help?"

I wanted his help. I wanted it badly. The temptation to share some of my worries and fears about Josh, about Del, about Carl was a physical craving. But if I let Landon in, I was risking more hurt. How could I do that when I already felt so battered?

Then again, Landon was right. I'd faced the river, survived Silver Run. If I could do that, maybe I could risk a little more. I wasn't looking to be rescued, but I sure as hell could use a friend.

How could he help? What I wanted most of all was to ask him to come out and join us, but that felt like too much. Our relationship had been so uncertain lately. Asking him to drop everything for days was a big request. I didn't answer him right away, debating with myself.

Landon spoke into the silence. "Do you want me to come to Colorado?"

I was both startled and touched. It felt like he'd read my thoughts, but I bit off the temptation of an instant *yes*. "I can't ask you to do that. I know how you hate to travel." Even thinking about leaving home must fill him with trepidation. He was the sort who liked to have his coffee in the exact same mug every day, and he wanted to sit in the exact same chair at the exact same table to drink it.

"Travel isn't my favorite pastime, I admit, but if it will help, I'll come. I can get one of Jim Stephenson's sons to stay at the farm."

Landon, someone I could count on, here in Colorado to help. A surge of relief at the prospect left me leaning on the hallway wall. To hell with worrying about what it all meant. I wanted him here. "Yes, that would be amazing. Yes. Please."

"Good." His voice was emphatic. "Give me a day to get things settled here, and I'll fly out. How long will Josh need to stay in the hospital?"

"They say at least tonight and tomorrow night so they can repeat chest X-rays and watch for infection. He inhaled a good bit of river water. I should know more tomorrow. Send me your flight information once you have it, and I'll pick you up at the airport." My relief at having some backup left me buoyant. Well, not just any backup. It was Landon I wanted in my corner. "Thanks. Thanks so much for coming."

He gave a deep chuckle. "No problem. It was the *'I miss you'* line that did it. See you soon."

* * *

That second day in the hospital was long and tedious and boring. Josh, withdrawn. Carl, snarling in his daily text. Me, restless, confused and feeling useless. I called the half-dozen rehab centers I could find listings for, but got nowhere. Well-trained voices informed me it would be impossible to acknowledge the presence of a specific patient. There were rules. Policies. Procedures. I learned exactly nothing. I needed to find something that narrowed down the location so I could go argue in person, but that would have to wait until I could return to Sawyer's house and search.

I also bowed to the inevitable and called Mom. She'd left multiple messages since we'd left Memphis—realizing belatedly that if Josh and I were searching for Del, it might mean Del was in trouble. I'd avoided answering since I had no real news, but I could no longer make that claim.

She answered on the first ring and jumped right in. "What's going on, Bryn? I know you're not telling me everything. I keep calling Del, and she doesn't pick up. I can't even leave her a message."

She hadn't started off with a detour into neighborhood gossip, and she sounded on the edge of panic. What I had to tell her wasn't going to help.

I walked slowly through the full saga, leaving out anything related to Carl and pausing every few sentences to let Mom vent. Colorado. Sawyer alive. Josh trapped in the river. Sawyer presumed dead. "Mom, Sawyer knew where Del is, and it doesn't sound good." I passed on what he had told me. "I'm not sure how much to believe, but Del has some issues. I'll learn more once Josh is out of the hospital."

Dead silence. I don't think I'd ever heard such silence from my mother. Even the television noise in the background was missing.

I waited. "Mom, are you still there?"

She blew her nose. "Find her. You can find her, can't you? And call me as soon as you know more." Her voice sounded like it belonged to a different person—uncertain, pleading, and intensely sad.

"I'll do my best." My mother's idealized vision of Del was pure fiction, but it was a fiction that had long provided her comfort. I hated the fact that I was going to be the messenger who ripped that fantasy away from her.

I could hear her sniffling, and despite the decades of friction that divided us, I wished there were some way to console her.

"Mom, do you remember that day when Del and I set up a tea party on the porch with all of your best china? I thought we'd get in horrible trouble, but instead you sat down and played with us." I'd pulled that memory out several times since I'd told Josh. A reminder that not only Del but my mother had been different once—gentler and more understanding. We'd been a family.

I don't know what I expected from her. A softening of her grief? An acknowledgment that I was trying to help?

Instead, she snorted. "Don't be ridiculous. If you had touched that china, you would have been grounded for a month. Get busy, Bryn. Find your sister. Call me as soon as you know more."

I felt like I'd been slapped, my attempts to focus on a more benevolent history discounted out of hand.

And with that, the call ended.

* * *

As predicted, Josh was discharged after two nights in the hospital. I walked beside him as one of the young nurses pushed his mandatory wheelchair toward the exit.

"After lunch, we'll pick up Landon at the airport, and then I thought we could head up to your father's place and see if we can figure out where your mom is. Hopefully, we can find records somewhere, so I can at least figure out who to argue with about access."

Josh grunted and gave a tired nod. I tried to ignore the flinch I'd noticed when I said the words *your father*.

"So . . . you're okay with going back to his house to look?"

"Sure." His voice was flat. "Why should I care? I just want to find Mom and go home."

I wasn't buying his studied indifference, but I didn't have a clue about the best way to crack through it. He had complained nonstop about the hospital food, so I took him straight to a hamburger joint. But even cheese fries didn't cheer him up. He took a few bites of his burger, then set it aside. "Tell me another story about when you and Mom were younger."

Not a request I'd expected. Apparently I wasn't the only one who would like to anchor into happier times. I flipped through dusty memories, discarding the ones that featured lies, arguments, and insults, finally finding one I could share. "I remember when your mom was about eight, and she came running into the house one afternoon during summer vacation, claiming there was a wild animal living under the garage."

Josh sat up straight, looking more alert than he had in days.

"I didn't believe her, but it turned out there really was a feral cat who had moved into the crawl space out there. Del decided she was going to tame that cat, and I've never seen anyone more persistent. She put out food and water. Used her allowance for cat toys. When she knew the cat was in there, hiding, she'd sit on the ground and read out loud so the cat would get used to her voice."

I was describing a different sister from the one I knew years later. A gentle sister who had disappeared into someone I hated. This gentle version was the one I missed. "At any rate, it took weeks, but that cat eventually trusted her enough so Del could pet her. She named her Sally and told everyone Sally was her best friend. Maybe that's why you're so good with Patsy."

Josh nodded, his face less tense, and he took a bite of his burger. "Mom always used to pet Patsy if she saw her. I like that story. Maybe you can think of some more sometime."

"Sure. I'll do that." I was glad Josh didn't ask what happened next, because when Sally got hit by a car and killed just before school started in the fall, Del was inconsolable. Now that I thought about it, Sally's death was when Del quit making any sort of effort to be nice—to me, to plenty of other people. It was as if she'd invested her full reservoir of kindness into that stray cat, and when the result was only grief, she decided it wasn't a fair trade.

Josh and I finished lunch and went to the kennel next to pick up Tellico, who'd been imprisoned there while I slept on a recliner in Josh's hospital room. He was wildly happy to see us, his tail a joyous blur. Sharp yips let us know in no uncertain terms that he hadn't liked being abandoned.

Josh thawed even more, petting the dog, and when we returned to the truck, he joined Tellico in the back seat instead of sitting in his regular place beside me. In the rearview mirror, I saw him clinging to the patient dog, soaking up a type of comfort I couldn't give.

"Airport next."

All I got in response was a grunt. I gave up trying to chat, and we traveled in a suffocating silence that got thicker every minute, each of us trapped in our own thoughts.

Landon's flight was on time, and we waited for him in front of the terminal. I couldn't help but think about our airport visit only a few days earlier when we'd confirmed Del had been here. Josh had insisted on switching the lanyard bracelet to his good wrist when they splinted his injured one, and he spun the bracelet while we waited, no doubt also thinking about his mom.

Landon came out of the terminal, and my buoyant reaction to the sight of him startled me. He tossed his bag into the truck bed and climbed into the passenger seat beside me.

"Hi there." His smile was quick and genuine, and his hug smelled like woodsmoke and pine trees, warm and familiar. Some of the tension I'd carried for days eased.

"Hi. Nice flight?" I felt suddenly awkward. He'd flown half-way across the country. For me. A step forward for both of us, and I wasn't sure how to navigate.

"Two flights. To be honest, it was two flights too many, but I survived." He turned in his seat. "Hey, Josh." He offered him one of his magical smiles. "I'm glad you're feeling better." He tact-fully ignored Josh's splint and his rainbow of bruises. Tellico pushed his head over the back of the seat for a pat, his tail thumping hard.

"If you're okay with a drive, I thought we'd head up to Sawyer's place next. See if we can figure out where Del is."

"Sounds good."

We started off. I followed the same route we'd used two days before, winding our way toward Sawyer's house, glimpsing the river through the trees where it ran close beside the road. It was Landon's first trip to Colorado, and he looked around with inter-est. "It's a completely different feel than at home, isn't it?"

"These mountains are so much younger, so raw. I like it, but you're right, it's not home."

278

We chatted about the scenery we passed, carefully avoiding any reference to the events of the past few days. For a few minutes at a time, I could even forget the purpose of this drive.

I'd been concerned the trip would bother Josh, and he stayed awfully quiet. He kept one hand on his phone, playing yet another game, and the other hand on Tellico. As we got closer, I was the one disturbed by the reminders—the rushing whitewater, my panic while searching for Josh, the moment when I seized his wrist and found no pulse. The horrifying news that Sawyer hadn't been found.

The policeman who came to interview me at the hospital had been willing to answer my questions. "No sign of a body yet, but that's not too surprising. That river empties into the Roaring Fork, and that in turn heads on to the Colorado River. Sometimes it takes days before a body reaches a spot where we can find it."

I'd seen how much Sawyer had to drink, and I'd seen the effort he expended to save Josh. He'd been in no shape to fight that river, but it still surprised me that the river had won. Everyone was convinced he was dead, and they were probably right. But still . . . Another death without a body? I had to wonder.

CHAPTER TWENTY-SIX

Bryn

We pulled up to the cabin and parked beside Sawyer's SUV. "I have no idea who any of this belongs to now. The house, the land, the car. Are Del and Sawyer still legally married? There was a death certificate. She collected widow's benefits for years."

"I don't have a clue," Landon said, "but I can guarantee it's going to take some work to get the legal side of things straightened out. I think it depends somewhat on whether Sawyer had a will."

"Something else to look for, I guess."

Landon and I got out of the truck. Tellico scrambled out of the back seat, and Josh came slowly behind him.

"I'm going to look around in the house. See what I can find out about your mom." I stepped onto the porch and opened the unlocked door, but Josh made no effort to join me.

He made a face, obviously reluctant, and Landon patted him on the shoulder. "If you'd rather wait out here, I can hang with you. We can take a walk if you feel up to it."

"Yeah, okay." Josh gave him a look of pure relief. He and Landon started slowly down the driveway, with Tellico snuffling ahead of them. Maybe Josh would talk to Landon in ways he wouldn't talk to me. I headed into Sawyer's house to begin my search, relieved to be alone.

The house still felt lived-in, and I looked around the large room, part of me expecting to turn and see Sawyer standing there. I shook the feeling off and tried to focus on the task at hand. Logically, any information about Del should be in the corner Sawyer had outfitted as an office, but I couldn't resist looking around the rest of the house first.

Bedroom—classic Sawyer, a simple platform in a corner of the great room. Bed made, water glass on an end table, clothing in the closet impeccably organized—dressy items on the left, outdoor clothing on the right. Nothing belonging to a woman. If he had a girlfriend, she hadn't spent much time here.

Kitchen—well equipped. Pantry items shouldn't have possessed the power to make me nostalgic, but they did. He still ate the same brand of granola. Bought the same kind of imported pesto. The spices were lined up alphabetically, as he'd always insisted. The familiar setup made his death feel real in a way it hadn't before. If we'd married, this was the way our kitchen would have looked.

I threw out the food that still sat untouched on the island, abandoned there when we'd left to search for Josh. Washed the dishes. Propped them in the drainboard to dry. It all felt invasive—this was Sawyer's domain, and I didn't belong here.

I moved on to the office—a walnut desk, a laptop, a long wall of bookcases. A desk chair and a separate recliner with a reading light.

What I needed was access to Sawyer's laptop, but he was always careful with passwords, so I didn't think there was any way to guess. I settled into the desk chair to search the drawers.

I found a checkbook with a blank register, pens, pencils, paper. Old bills, clipped together by category, each marked *Paid* in red ink. A folded handkerchief that carried the scent of Sawyer's soap and tossed me decades into the past when I had breathed that same scent from his skin. As far as Del was concerned, I found nothing, nothing, and nothing. But the deep file drawer in the desk was locked, and that struck me as unusual.

Had Sawyer carried the key with him? It seemed unlikely. I sat back in the chair and looked around the room. If his kitchen habits were any indication, the patterns of the past might predict the present.

When we were dating in college, Sawyer hollowed out a book to create a hiding place to store his cash. I could picture it, a fat book with blue letters on the spine, but I couldn't remember the title. I went to the bookcase and scanned the shelves, hoping I'd recognize something like it when I saw it.

Asimov and Bradbury sat side by side with titles I recognized as recent Hugo Award winners. National Park handbooks, bound collections of topographic maps, and a well-worn wilderness first aid manual filled a long row. I spotted what must be the hollowed-out book on the bottom shelf—*Atlas Shrugged*—and pulled it out. Inside was a thousand dollars in cash and a small key that slid easily into the keyhole of the locked drawer. It turned with a satisfying click.

I held my breath and opened the drawer, reminding myself it might contain nothing. But it was stuffed full, a bulging black pocketbook on top taking most of the space.

It had to be Del's. I riffled through the multiple zipped compartments, emptying as I went, stacking the contents on the desk. A wallet containing Del's ID and credit cards and forty dollars in cash. A cell phone, off. Comb, brush, and makeup case. A small cloth pouch containing a half-dozen pairs of earrings. Two chocolate-chunk power bars. And then, at the bottom of the main compartment, four large bottles labeled generic acetaminophen. This had to be it.

The front door opened, and Josh and Landon joined me.

"That's Mom's pocketbook."

I looked up, nodding.

Josh looked more settled after his walk. Or maybe talking to Landon had helped. He stood in front of the desk, his eyes on the stacked items. He picked up the wallet and ran his hand over it, his lanyard bracelet a bright spot of color. "Open the pill bottles."

A shame he understood that much, but of course he was right. "Cross your fingers."

I twisted the childproof cap on the first bottle, pulled out a wad of cotton, and tipped some of the tablets onto the table. They were the same size as the pill I'd found in Del's freezer, slightly irregular in shape, and they didn't have a manufacturer's mark. Something illegally made, perhaps something cooked up by Carl. I'd read about batches of opioids that were mixed with other things to make them more profitable, sometimes with disastrous effects. These pills were the reason Del had collapsed.

I checked the other bottles. They held the same kind of tablets. "This looks like most of what Carl is looking for. Maybe all."

Josh turned the wallet over and over in his hands. "Good. I didn't want him to burn down your house. Or hurt the goats."

"You and me both." I picked up two of the bottles, one in each hand. To Carl, they meant cash. To me, perhaps they offered safety. But these pills were what had harmed Del.

"What are you planning to do with it all? Just tell Carl to come and get them?" Landon hefted one of the bottles. "The street value of all this must be enormous."

I stared at the bottles as if they could provide a sensible answer. "I don't think we can just hand all this over to Carl. It could hurt too many other people. But beyond that, I don't have a clue. We still need to get Carl off our backs, and these pills are the key to that."

Josh set down the wallet. "Is there anything in there about where Mom is?"

"Maybe." I pulled a manila folder from the bottom of the drawer and flipped it open. Inside was a glossy multipage brochure from some place called Elk Creek Recovery Center. A business card gave the name of the director of the facility.

"This might be it. At any rate, it should be the first place we check." I handed the brochure to Josh, and Landon read it over his shoulder.

A sheet of paper was next in the folder, with a line of handwritten numbers across the top: $6 \times 4.6 = 276$. The numbers meant nothing to me, and the math was all wrong. I set the sheet aside to puzzle over later.

The final item in the folder was a page covered in Sawyer's small tight handwriting, dated the day we'd found him. It was addressed to me, and I held it at an angle to read, not willing to let Josh see it.

Dear Bryn,

This is a letter of farewell.

I knew someone would come looking for Del, but I didn't expect it quite so soon. My plan was to move fast and get things arranged before anyone arrived. My lawyer would have gotten in touch with you after I was gone, told you about Del, and asked you to look after Josh. But you're here now and I'm not gone yet.

Seeing you at the Games—seeing Josh so unexpectedly— all I could think was not yet, I'm not ready. I ran. I shouldn't have. My entire life has been screwed up by instant decisions, most of which have hurt other people. This was another one. I'm sorry.

I'm tired of regrets, and I'm tired of fighting myself. A bet-ter man would stay and face the consequences of the faked death, the safety deposit box, everything else. Instead, I'll take care of a few final things and then help myself to these tablets Del has so conveniently provided. I'll address this letter for the police to pass on to you.

Take care of Josh. Tell him I'm sorry and make him believe it. Give him all the love I should have been there to give. With Del as she is, he'll need you.

I've thought often of what our lives would have been if we'd stayed together, and that, too, has been a source of regret.

Through it all, I never stopped loving you. I have no right to say it, but that's the simple truth.

He had signed the note with his real name, not the one he'd changed it to. Sawyer Whitman. Josh's father. The man I'd once loved. The full meaning of what he had planned sank in, and a chill crawled up my spine and curled around my heart.

I read the page again. And then a third time. Even the fourth time through, every sentence was a body blow. When I'd seen him at the Games, I'd thought he was just there to play around and have some fun, but perhaps he had gone as a private farewell to the sport he loved.

He had planned to kill himself, and on the Silver Run, he'd had the chance to do exactly that. Sawyer knew how to keep himself safe in the water, but that also meant he knew how to increase his risk.

I closed my eyes for a long moment, the room suddenly far too bright. *Sawyer.* Could he really have done such a thing?

"Bryn, what's wrong?" I must have looked bad for Landon to sound so concerned.

So many things were wrong. I shook my head, uncertain where to even start.

"Did Dad write that?" Josh had shifted to my side of the desk, and he leaned over my shoulder, trying to see.

I flipped the page over on the desk so he couldn't read it. "Yes, he wrote it."

"Then I want to read it."

Let Josh read a suicide note? That felt cruel and out of bounds. "No. It's pretty personal. I can read it more carefully later and let you know what it says."

But Josh straightened and glared at me with eyes that already knew far too much. He looked older than he had only a dozen days earlier, and with all that had happened, I guess it shouldn't have surprised me. He pointed at me with his splinted hand. "Stop treating me like a kid. My mom is an addict. She's in a rehab center. I almost drowned. My dad faked his death and now he's really dead, and he died saving me. If my father wrote that paper, I should be able to read it."

His voice choked a few times along the way, but that last sentence was firm.

And he was right. "Okay."

We moved into the living room. Josh and Landon sat together on the couch. I handed Josh the letter and stood to one side, watching his face as he read.

He stared at the page long after he must have finished. Slow tears rolled down his face. I reached toward him to give him a hug, but he pulled away in a jerking movement. He handed the sheet of paper to Landon for him to read it.

I went to the kitchen and found some tissues, handed Josh one and took a few for myself.

Damn you, Sawyer. Suicide or unintended drowning, dead or simply skilled at creating another disappearance—the details didn't matter. He'd run away yet again. Abandoned his son for a second time.

I wanted to sit down with Sawyer and talk with him. I wanted to tell him that despite his mistakes, I understood. I wanted to tell him there were reasons to stay. I'd believed all those years he was truly gone, but now that I'd found him alive, I didn't want him gone again.

I swallowed a lump of bitter impatience. *Come off it, Bryn. Move on.* That story had finished long ago.

Josh sat, no longer crying, staring out the window, Tellico curled at his feet.

Landon set down the paper. "A sad letter. He sounds haunted."

An understatement. Restless, I went back to the kitchen and put some water on the stove. Dug out teabags. Isn't that what you were supposed to do in a crisis? Brew some tea? I waited for the water to come to a boil, trying to give Josh time to pull himself together. I carried two steaming mugs back to the couch and handed one to each of them. Landon nodded his thanks.

Josh's eyes were red, and he was still sniffling.

"Sorry, no coffee. But I put in double honey."

"That won't help."

"You're right. But it won't hurt."

He gave me a small tight smile, as if it was a betrayal that leaked out despite himself. He set the mug aside without trying it. "He wanted to die."

"Yes."

"Even if I hadn't taken that kayak. Gotten trapped. He'd still be dead now?"

I hesitated, unsure how much of my uncertainty about Sawyer's fate I should share. "I think he would be gone now, regardless of what you'd done."

Josh closed his eyes for a long moment.

Landon reached over and squeezed Josh's shoulder. "None of this is your fault. None of it. He had already made up his mind—the letter makes that clear—and it looks like when the opportunity came on the river, he took it."

Josh's face crumpled, he folded inward, and his tears started to flow in earnest.

My heart twisted. I could find no words of comfort. I sat on the couch, wrapped my arms around him, and held on tight. He clung to me for long minutes, his fingers digging in hard, as if their fierce grip would keep him from slipping away into the unknown. I tried to send him calmness and support, wishing I had more of it to offer, and his breathing gradually slowed to match mine.

He gave a long shuddering sigh. "It's not fair. I find my dad, and he's a thief and a liar. I want to get to know him, and I want to scream at him, and I'll never get the chance to do either one."

I wanted to change things for him. Protect him somehow from all of it. But it was far too late for that. "You're right. It's not fair."

He pulled back and looked at me, his face red and blotchy. "It sucks." He thought for a moment and grasped at the one thing we had some control over. "We need to go see Mom. I was supposed to take care of her, and we can't even find her. That's not fair either."

"It's not your job to take care of your mother."

He shook his head, defiant. "If I don't, no one else will."

Nothing in his life so far had led him to believe Del could take care of herself, that was for sure. "We'll finish things here, and then we'll go to this rehab center and find out what the story is. Fair enough?"

My voice sounded calm and steady, but my heart was going triple time. Landon, Sawyer, Del, Josh—my head churned—my feelings tumbled—it was all too much at once.

Josh nodded, but Landon gave him a worried glance before turning to me. "If it will help, I can go with you."

"Yes. Please. I'd like to have you there." I was dreading this visit. I could have gone out to look for Del the day before, when Josh was still in the hospital, but I'd avoided it. The luxury of having someone to back me up was too great an opportunity to pass up. "Let me pull things together in Sawyer's office, and then we can drive back into town."

I went to the desk to repack Del's belongings, and Landon came with me. I stowed away the full pill bottles. "I wish I knew what to do with this stuff. The sensible thing would be to turn it all over to the police, but I don't want to be the cause of Del getting arrested or landing in jail. Hopefully, I'll know what to do after I see her."

"You've got some way of reaching Carl?"

"I'm supposed to call him tomorrow morning to meet his revised deadline. At least he has no clue where we are at the moment, and that's been a relief."

I zipped closed the last compartment on Del's pocketbook. "Del first. Then we can deal with Carl. Let's head out."

I grabbed the pocketbook, the folder of information, and the garbage. I flipped off all the lights. The house had felt lived-in when we arrived, but after reading Sawyer's letter, it looked sad and abandoned. We headed outside. The front door closed behind us with a solid thunk that resonated in my chest. I was leaving Sawyer's house, but it felt like it was Sawyer himself I was leaving behind.

CHAPTER TWENTY-SEVEN

Josh

We drove down the mountain from Dad's place, through the town's streets, and up the other side of the valley to get to the rehab center where Mom was living. I expected either a hospital or a prison and dreaded seeing her there, but it turned out to be a big mansion with long wings of windows and one of those driveways that swoop right in front of the door. It sat high up on the mountainside, looking down toward Aspen.

Lots of flowers grew everywhere, shining in bright colors and smelling like one of Mom's perfumes. Two big wooden doors were in the front of the building, like something a butler would open in the movies. Everything was fancy, peaceful, and quiet, but none of it made me feel any better.

We left Tellico in the truck with the windows down and climbed up the long front stairs. No butler—we just opened the door and went right in. Bryn talked to a lady at a desk in front,

then we waited in big chairs that were crowded with little pillows. After a while Bryn went back into an office, and Landon
and I waited.

"You okay?" he asked.

I was getting tired of that question. I nodded because what
could I say? I just wanted to see Mom and find out when I
could take her home. Everything would be better when we got
back to the apartment. We'd be back to our own schedule and
our own food, and maybe Carl would leave her alone and
maybe her boss at Kroger would even let her come back to
work. Things would all go back the way they used to be.

We waited and waited. No TV or anything, just quiet, with
men and women down the hall talking in soft voices so I couldn't
hear what they were saying. My arm itched under my splint, my
head hurt, and I spun Mom's bracelet around and around on my
wrist. A bracelet for luck. I needed all the luck I could get.

Bryn finally came back, but she sat down to wait some more.
"She's here. They're bringing her up so we can talk to her in private. It took a while because the director called the police to
confirm Sawyer's death. Fortunately, Sawyer had put my name
on a list authorizing medical information, or who knows what
we would have had to do to see her."

Landon reached over and took her hand, and Bryn let him
hold it without even seeming to notice. "How is she?" he asked.
It was the question I'd been afraid to ask out loud.

Bryn frowned. "I'm not sure. He just focused on who we
were; what right we had to see her. Said the doctor would meet
us to discuss specifics."

We sat. Not quite so long this time, and then a woman wearing bright yellow scrubs came in. "Dr. Wilson will be available shortly. Follow me."

She led us to a room that looked like someone's living room on a TV show, with a fireplace and a couch and a coffee table. At the far end of the room, Mom was sitting in a big cushy armchair. She looked way better than I expected. Not bruised or wrapped in bandages or with crutches or anything.

I ran toward her.

"Mom." It came out with a jerk, sounding like I'd tripped over something, because closer up I could tell something was seriously off.

This was Mom and not-Mom. She wore a thick blue robe and blue slippers, but that wasn't the problem. She looked way too skinny and her face wasn't quite the right color, but that wasn't it either. It was her eyes. They were looking right at me, but they didn't seem to see me standing there.

"Hello." Her voice sounded rusty, and it was like she was saying hello to a stranger. A gasp came from Bryn behind me, but I didn't try to turn around and look.

"Mom, it's me. Josh. We found you, but it was really hard, and Dad wasn't really dead, but now he is, and . . ." I thought she could probably hear me, but that nothing look on her face didn't change.

I stopped talking and sat down on the soft carpet at her feet, the way Tellico always did when he knew I needed help. I reached up and took her hand, which was cold and sort of floppy. She let me hold it, but she didn't squeeze back. Her fingers rested on the stiff lanyard bracelet on my wrist, but she didn't seem to notice that either. "It's okay, Mom. I'm right here."

I was there. But she wasn't.

I tried to breathe slow, the air as thick as syrup. My chest hurt bad like I was back in the river again, pinned down, unable to move, and trying not to drown. Trapped. But this time no one was there to rescue me.

CHAPTER TWENTY-EIGHT

Bryn

I stared at the fixed, static face of my sister and clutched Landon's arm, too dismayed to move any farther into the room. "My god. I thought I knew what to expect, but this . . ."

I kept my voice down, but Josh was so focused on his mother, he would have been oblivious to anything short of an explosion. I had no worries Del might overhear—she didn't look capable of paying attention to anything going on around her.

The memories I'd held close to my heart for years rushed in, the images I took out and revisited on a regular basis. Del, stealing my favorite sweater in middle school and cutting it into postage stamp–sized pieces that she scattered around my bedroom. Del, spreading lies about me in high school, claiming I cheated on tests to get my good grades. Del, blaming me whenever my parents noticed cash missing from their wallets. Most of all, Del and the too-smug look on her face as she coolly informed me she'd slept with my fiancé and gotten pregnant as a result.

But Josh had brought other memories to the surface—that day of the tea party; Del and the care she took with that scrawny cat. And standing in that rehab center, looking at what was left of my sister, another memory pushed the others aside.

I was ten and Del was eight when our elementary school sponsored a fall fund-raising event at a park just outside town. There were games and food and carnival rides that should have kept us entertained, but the biggest attraction was a broad stream that ran through one edge of the park. The older kids dared each other to cross using widely spaced rocks as step-stones, and we younger ones gathered on shore to cheer the friends who succeeded and laugh at those who got soaked.

I hung back, analyzing the best path across, taking careful note of the boulders that rocked unsteadily, debating whether I dared to join in and give it a try.

Del didn't hesitate, moving quickly to the edge of the stream before I could stop her. She was a foot shorter than anyone else who had tried to cross, but she jumped from one rock to the next with a cat's grace, landing surefooted on even the most unstable stones. In the middle of the stream, where the current was deep and the leap was long, she threw her arms wide and stretched for the landing. In that instant, her face intent and her hair flying, she was suspended in mid-air above the water and haloed by sunlight. In that instant, years before she discovered boys and drugs and the knack of lying to get her own way, Del was totally, awesomely, breathtakingly alive.

My sister.

This empty husk of a person who sat so still in her robe in front of me bore no resemblance to that joyous child. A scalding pain radiated through my belly and left me gasping, the loss eating into my core like acid. It caught me off guard. No matter how bad things had gotten between us, a small unacknowledged part of me must have harbored a hope of reclaiming some version of sisterhood. A hope that now seemed absurdly naïve.

I stood there, shaking, and a woman with a stethoscope hanging around her neck came in behind us. She glanced at Josh, then gestured me toward the door. Landon and I followed her into the hallway, where I could look back and see Josh, still kneeling beside his mother. He hadn't been present when Sawyer described the full seriousness of Del's condition, and now that I'd seen her, I regretted not preparing him better for what he found here. I'd doubted Sawyer's honesty. Hadn't believed in the extent of this damage.

"What happened to her?" My voice sounded shriller than I liked. Sawyer had said drugs, but this . . .

Landon slipped his arm around my waist, and I leaned into him, more off balance from this visit than from anything else that had happened in the past crazy week.

The doctor held out a hand for each of us to shake. "I'm Dr. Wilson." She was tiny and birdlike, with sharp, quick movements and a doctor-in-a-hurry attitude that implied we were taking up valuable time. "You're Ms. Whitman's sister?"

I nodded, and she turned to Landon. "And you are?"

"A friend of the family." Landon's arm tightened around me.

Dr. Wilson nodded. "I'm sorry I didn't get the opportunity to talk to you before you saw her. Did she recognize you at all? Or show any response to her son?"

"No. Nothing. She said hello, but she didn't even look at us."

She frowned and tapped a quick note into the iPad she carried. "I had hoped seeing people she knew would reach her. But even her son . . ." She shook her head.

For a moment she seemed genuinely saddened by the situation, but that was nothing compared to my horror. I'd come to Colorado prepared to lecture. Prepared to spew out anger and recriminations. Possibly prepared to swoop in and fix whatever problem existed. This was far worse than anything I'd imagined.

The doctor reorganized her face, banishing any sympathy, and became briskly professional again. "You asked what happened. The short version is that Ms. Whitman lost consciousness and stopped breathing. Her husband attempted to revive her with CPR, but it wasn't until an ambulance arrived and Narcan was administered that respiration resumed. Her blood tests showed high concentrations of fentanyl, cocaine, and alcohol, and that combination severely depresses the respiratory system. Despite aggressive therapy, she stopped breathing twice after admission that first night and had to be resuscitated each time."

She sounded like she was reading aloud, but she hadn't consulted her notes. "Unfortunately, loss of oxygen like this can cause significant brain damage, and in the days that followed her admission, it became clear that had happened in your sister's case."

I looked back again at Josh. He was still clinging to Del's hand, but his head had dropped forward to rest against her knee. She gazed across the room without the smallest flicker of emotion in her expression.

Dr. Wilson cleared her throat and went on. "Ms. Whitman was transferred here at her husband's request following her initial hospital treatment."

"What's the prognosis?" I didn't want to face the answer, but I had to know.

The doctor frowned. "Difficult to say. Brain injury is hard to predict, and we can sometimes see gradual improvement over time." My hopes soared, and she must have seen it in my face, because she hurried to squash my optimism. "With this level of severity, however, I have to be very cautious. It's possible her condition as she is now is the best we can expect."

Alive but not living.

Dr. Wilson cleared her throat again, and I tried to focus on her words. "She's very compliant and easy to work with, but she takes no initiative in even the smallest tasks and is almost completely nonverbal. Her caregivers dress her, feed her, remind her of bathroom needs. She often becomes confused at night, wandering the halls when she was permitted to do so. We've had to place her in a secure ward."

"You're saying she could need this level of care . . . forever?"

"I'm sorry."

Forever. The word looped in my head. No Del to fuss at. No Del to take home. No Del to get into trouble anymore. Worst of all, no Del to take care of Josh. I buried my head in Landon's shoulder, trying to keep from losing it, and he pulled me in for a long hug.

When I finally straightened, I was somewhat surprised to find Dr. Wilson still standing there, scrolling through her iPad screen.

Forever brought with it some all too real practical consider-
ations. I looked around at the thick carpet, the tasteful paint-
ings, the ornate light fixtures. The entire facility reeked of money
and lots of it. Doctors, nurses, caregiving attendants. Secure
wards, drawing rooms, immaculate gardens. I couldn't even
imagine how much all this cost, but it was way out of Del's bud-
get. And mine.

"Thank you for explaining. I hate to bring up the subject of
money, but Del's resources are very limited. We'll need to evaluate the current bill and consider whether alternate arrangements
are needed." *Alternate arrangements.* The understatement of the
century.

Dr. Wilson looked puzzled, and it pissed me off. Didn't she
realize a facility like this was beyond the reach of the average
person? Had she spent too many years hanging out with Aspen
millionaires?

She rubbed her hands together and gave me a questioning
look. "I'm sorry, I must have misunderstood. I thought you were
sent here by Ms. Whitman's husband before his death."

Her phrasing didn't quell my irritation. "He told us she was
here. He didn't give details."

"I see. He didn't explain the financial arrangements he'd
made?"

"No."

"I can ask the administrator to make copies of the paperwork for you. You'll need them if you're now our primary contact for communication. You don't need to have financial
concerns. Mr. Whitman has transferred a significant sum into a

trust for his wife's care." She emphasized the word *significant* with raised eyebrows.

"Enough to cover costs at this place? How much money is involved?"

She cleared her throat. "Four point six million dollars."

"What?" It came out screechy. "Four. Point. Six. Million?" I couldn't even conceive of that much money.

The numbers Sawyer had jotted on the paper in his desk suddenly fell into place. Six percent of 4.6 million equaled 276,000 dollars. He had been calculating annual return on invested money, making sure what he set aside would provide adequately for Del.

"Correct. Don't worry, this was all set up through his lawyer. It's completely aboveboard." She chattered on, explaining contingencies if Del improved and needed less care, contingencies if she got worse, contingencies if she died. The paperwork specified an annual independent review of her condition and the therapies Elk Creek used. Every potential outcome provided for. The details passed by in a blur, but the bottom line appeared to be that Sawyer had set things up to provide care for Del for the rest of her life.

I couldn't help but give a moment's thought to what all that money might have done for Del if she didn't need it for care. Put her onto a better path? Or given her the resources for complete destruction? It was foolish speculation. Sawyer's guilt-ridden reevaluation of the mess he'd made of his life had been prompted only by Del's disaster. If he'd found her at the bar and she'd remained healthy, he probably could have paid her off for next to nothing.

"When were all these arrangements made?"

"He initiated the paperwork when he first transferred her here from the hospital. When he realized how guarded the outlook for recovery was."

Weeks ago. While Josh was hanging out with neighbors and I was at home, hating him, Sawyer was out here putting everything in place to take care of her.

The doctor checked her watch and took a step away. "I'll get you copies of the pertinent documents. If you have additional questions, I suggest you talk with the lawyer who drew up the agreement. I'll leave his contact information with the receptionist out front."

I nodded, feeling numb. "Thank you." She hustled down the hallway, and I turned to Landon. "I can't believe any of this. It feels surreal."

"Understandable. How much money did he originally steal?"

"He said two million. I had assumed he spent it all—he always wanted to be rich—but he must have invested almost everything to let it grow to that extent." Sawyer's aging SUV. The one-room house with its low-key furnishings. He'd spent little. His guilt over that money must have weighed heavily long before Del showed up.

"I can't bear this. I keep thinking I should have done more. Gotten in touch with Del after Sawyer's plane crash. Tried to offer some support. Maybe if I had, none of this would have happened."

Landon gave me an emphatic shake of the head. "Blaming yourself for this is the same as Josh blaming himself for Sawyer's death. Del and Sawyer made their own choices. They betrayed you, and that set up a chain of events that had nothing to do with you. You built a wall to protect yourself, and that's understandable."

Nice of him to believe all that. I wished I could believe it myself.

He rested a hand on my shoulder. "Don't forget, when Josh landed on your doorstep, you turned your life upside down to try to find your sister. That doesn't sound like someone who's walled herself off from life." He gave a wry smile, and I got the sense he was thinking about the barricade that still existed between the two of us.

I reached up and took his hand, then led the way back into the room where Del and Josh remained. Landon and I sat on the couch. Josh sat cross-legged at Del's feet. He was still holding her hand, but now he was talking steadily.

". . . and Bryn let me canoe on the lake. You'd like it there. It's not all that far from home, so maybe we can go there one day. The drive to get here took forever, but the camping was fun. We cooked on a Coleman stove, and I got to light it in the morning to make breakfast. Then, after we went to the Games . . ."

Del pulled her gaze away from an end table, and our eyes met. It was like looking into the eyes of a faded doll. I had wanted to punish my sister, but I would never have wished this sort of horrifying half life for her.

Landon pulled me tight against him. "I'm so sorry, Bryn. So sorry."

We sat for a few more minutes, then a nurse bustled into the room. "I hate to interrupt, but it's time for Ms. Whitman's physical therapy."

"Josh." I kept my voice quiet, and he turned to face me. "Are you okay leaving?" I didn't like pulling him away, but the calm veneer he'd pinned in place was beginning to worry me. "We can come back tomorrow if you'd like."

He closed his eyes for a moment, as if bracing himself for whatever came next, then he scrambled awkwardly to his feet, still holding his mother's hand. He leaned forward to give her a kiss on her forehead. "Bye, Mom. I'll see you tomorrow."

He came over to join Landon and me. The nurse took Del by the arm, and in response to a gentle tug, she rose to her feet and shuffled out of the room at the nurse's side, her movements stiff and jerky. She didn't even glance our way.

Josh watched her leave, then slumped forward, collapsing into my arms. "She didn't even know who I was."

CHAPTER TWENTY-NINE

Josh

We went from the rehab center into town to get some dinner, stopping at a restaurant with a flashing "Hot Food" sign and a six-page plastic menu. Nothing tasted any better than it had at lunch. I kept thinking about Mom. She looked too skinny. Maybe they didn't know what foods she liked. Maybe that was why she didn't recognize me. Maybe if I started taking her food, making sure she ate right, she would get better.

But maybe not. "What did the doctor say? What exactly happened to her?"

Bryn looked away before she spoke. "Maybe we should wait. Talk about this in private after we're done with dinner."

Bullshit. "No. Now. Tell me now."

Bryn's lips tightened up, and she didn't look too happy, but she nodded. "When your dad found her, she wasn't breathing, and even though he did CPR, it wasn't until the ambulance got there that they got her breathing on her own."

"You said I wasn't breathing when you found me in the river, and I'm okay."

"I got there fast, and you didn't have drugs in your system. To make things worse, after they got her to the hospital, she stopped breathing again. Several times. Oxygen levels in her brain dropped dangerously low, and that's why she's having trouble now. The combination of the pills she was taking and the alcohol . . ." She stopped, like saying any more would only make things worse.

I couldn't imagine how things could be worse. "Not enough oxygen in her brain. You mean she's brain damaged." I felt like a traitor saying those words. I didn't know exactly what they meant, but I knew it was the sort of thing people said on TV when everything was hopeless. Not blood and bruises and bandages like I'd imagined. Something far worse. "They can help her, right? She'll get better?" My whole world hung on the answer.

Bryn fiddled with the salt and pepper shakers and wouldn't even look at me. Any hopes of good news sank into my stomach and turned into concrete.

"They'll take good care of her. And they'll try to help her get better. But I have to be honest, Josh. The doctor didn't sound very hopeful."

A baby laughed at a table beside us. A clattering sound came from the kitchen. The lady in the front of the restaurant counted out five menus, spoke to a family who was waiting, and led them to a table.

Mom, not knowing me. I'd made a fool of myself falling apart like a little kid at the rehab place. I didn't want to do the same thing here in a restaurant. I picked up my fork, held it under the table, and dug the points into my hand until the tears that threatened slid back where they belonged. I told myself I needed to think about what was best for Mom, but how was I supposed to know what that was?

"There's something else you need to know." Bryn made sure I was looking at her before she went on. "Your father set aside money to take care of your mother. Lots of money. She'll be able to stay here where people can try to help her."

I hadn't even thought about money, which was dumb, since I was the one who always kept up with the bills. A place that fancy had to cost even more than our rent. "She's already been there a few weeks. It's enough to pay for that and let her stay longer?"

"It's enough to pay for her to stay there forever, if she needs to."

Forever. I'd heard all the words that came before, but she stumbled over that one, and it smacked into me like a sucker punch. It was one of those words that was heavy to say and heavier to hear. I could tell from Bryn's voice that *forever* was what she expected would happen.

I'd set out to find Mom so I could take care of her. Instead, I'd proven she wasn't coming home.

I pushed my plate away, two bites of the burger gone and the fries untouched. My wrist ached under the splint. My hand burned from the fork points. I couldn't ask anything more about Mom. And I couldn't face the question of what was going happen to me if Mom was staying here in Colorado.

Bryn had said *no foster care*, but that promise was made back in Tennessee, and that was when she thought we'd find Mom in just a few days and bring her home. A lot had changed, and none of the changes were good news. Right then in that restaurant, I couldn't look that far ahead. "So, what happens tonight?"

"We thought we'd find a motel for tonight that will take Tellico," Landon said. "No sense you two pitching a tent this late."

Bryn pushed the food around on her plate. "In the morning, I need to see your father's lawyer. Find out what he knows. Then we can go see your mom again. We'll decide what's next after that."

"What are you going to do about Carl?"

She did her finger-drumming thing, like she couldn't make up her mind. "Tomorrow is Wednesday, and I don't think he's in the mood to wait later than his noon deadline. He said he would text, and he wants us to just hand over those pills. At least we have them now to barter with, but it's not that simple. Maybe giving them to him would keep him off our case. *Maybe.* But after seeing your mom and how bad she is . . ."

A surge of burning anger warmed me as I understood what that meant. "Those pills. That's what did it right? That's what made Mom this way?"

Bryn nodded.

"Then this is Carl's fault. You can't give that stuff back to him."

Bryn reached across the table and squeezed my hand. "I agree. If we give them back, and they hurt someone else, then it would be our fault."

I hadn't thought about it that way. Mainly I just wanted to get back at Carl. He'd strangled Annabelle, and he might as well have strangled Mom for all the damage he'd done.

Landon looked serious. "You've got to get the police involved. Any other path isn't safe."

"You're right." Bryn's face had the same determined look as when she'd taken a kitchen knife with her to find Carl at her farm. "Talking to the police can't hurt Del now. I'll call Steven when we get to the hotel and lay the whole thing out—he gave me his cell number. We'll see what he suggests. See if he can give me the name of an officer out here in Colorado. We've got the pills. We've also still got that tracker in the glove compartment. Maybe the police can activate it and trace its signal somehow to find him. Or turn it on to lure him in."

For once, the cops sounded like a good idea. The way Carl had looked when he talked about shooting me was seriously sick.

The two of them finished their meal, and by the time we went outside, it was getting dark, the sun disappearing behind the tall mountains. Bryn pointed to the moon, which had already risen. "A waxing moon, almost first quarter. Always a good omen."

Waxing, waning, the solstice coming soon—Bryn was trying to teach me all that stuff, but I didn't get why it mattered. Good omen or not, the moon didn't even give enough light to see by as we made our way from the café.

Bryn's truck was parked in the back corner of the parking lot. I pulled out my phone to see if I had any texts, and Bryn clicked the unlock button on her remote. She was reaching for the door handle when a man's voice came out of the shadows.

"Time's up. You've reached your deadline."

We all three whipped around to face Carl. Bryn and I were on the same side of the truck as him, Landon on the far side. Tellico was in the truck with the windows half open, tense and watching. I looked into the shadows, expecting to see Carl's other two guys there, but he was by himself.

He smiled like he was pleased he had our attention. "A day early, but I saw you spent a few days at a hospital. Is that where Del is?"

Bryn shook her head like she couldn't believe he'd found us again. "That tracker. We turned it off."

Carl gave a scratchy laugh. "Yeah, nice try. I can turn it on and off remotely. Thanks for hanging on to it. I've known exactly where you've been every day."

My fault. I should have thought of that. With the tracker sitting in the glove compartment and Carl able to manage it from his app, it was the same as if we hadn't found it in the first place. That creepy feeling of being watched came rushing back, but it reminded me of everything that could be done from a cell phone. I quickly pushed a few buttons on my phone screen.

Carl stood ten or twelve feet away, his eyes switching back and forth between Bryn, closest to him, and Landon, who was blocked by the truck from doing much. Landon started around the truck to join us, but Carl reached his right hand into his pocket and casually pulled out his gun. Landon froze. My mouth got so dry my tongue stuck to the roof of my mouth. Like at the campground, Carl looked like he'd be happy to use it.

"Easy. No need for that. We found Del." Bryn sounded angry, but she stood very still, her eyes glued to Carl's hand. "We found your pills. They're all yours. Congratulations. They've destroyed Del."

"She deserves whatever she gets after running like that."

My hand gripped my phone so tightly my fingers hurt. *Mom deserved what she got?* All those months when he sold her pills. The way he held his cigarette next to Patsy and hit me when I tried to protect her. Carl followed us. Scared Bryn. Scared me.

I took a few steps closer without him noticing.

His hand with the gun never shifted away from Bryn. "A shame Del's not here so I can give her a piece of my mind. That bitch has been far more trouble than she's worth. You found all my tablets? All two thousand of them?" He sounded excited, like a little kid offered a treat. "I have customers waiting. If you're bullshitting me, I swear I'll laugh while your house goes up in flames."

Bryn got even more tense. "I haven't counted them, but it looks like we found everything. They're here in the truck."

I was breathing fast, like I'd been running to escape instead of standing frozen. I tried not to stare at the gun. Tried not to think about how Carl was going to win. Mom had lost everything, but Carl was going to get exactly what he wanted.

Bryn reached again for the truck's door handle, but her other hand was sliding toward the pocket where she carried Landon's knife.

Carl took a long stride toward her as if he realized she was up to something, and Tellico pushed his head through the open part of the window, snapping and snarling. Carl twisted to look at the dog, pointing the gun away from Bryn and putting his back toward me.

All my anger swelled up inside and made me bigger. Mom. Annabelle. Threats about fire. Carl saying so casually that Mom deserved what she got, like she was nothing, like she was dirt. Worse than dirt. Each thing I thought about made me stronger.

So I did it. I took two running steps and kicked as high as I could, as hard as I could, like I was trying to kick Carl over the top of the farthest mountain. My foot caught him right on target, directly in the crotch, and the toe of my shoe dug in deep. He screamed and doubled over, clutching himself. His gun hit the pavement and slid under the truck.

"You bastard! You hurt my mom!" I kept kicking him, over and over, even after he was on the ground, my kicks slamming into his ribs, his head, his arms. He curled into a ball, swearing like crazy. I'd been the one who told Mom Carl was a good thing. I needed to be the one who finished things.

"Enough, Josh." Landon pulled me away. He picked up the gun and pointed it at Carl like he knew what he was doing. Carl just lay there on the pavement, moaning.

I stepped back, out of breath. Bryn called the police, then came over to give me a big hug. "Thanks."

I was still pissed, but the hug felt good, and after a while I could breathe almost normal again.

The police got there fast, and things got complicated. Landon dropped the gun and held up his hands, Bryn pointed to Carl as the criminal and told them about the drugs, the tracker, the threats. But the cops weren't happy when they found the knife in Bryn's pocket and the drugs in Bryn's truck, and they made all of us sit on the ground while they tried to sort it out.

Carl had quit moaning by then and was acting slick again. "This is a complete fabrication. Those drugs aren't mine—I've never seen them before. I never threatened anyone. These people are lying. They were the ones who attacked me, not the other way around."

He was being ultra-polite, his voice smooth, his fancy clothes commanding respect. Bryn and I, in our dusty shorts and T-shirts, looked like nobodies. I was afraid the police would believe him. The head cop walked past me, and I called to him. He came over and squatted down in front of me.

"What's the matter, kid?"

"Carl's the one who's lying. He really did say all those things." I turned the volume on my phone super loud and held it up so Carl could hear too. I pressed "Play" on the phone's recorder, the recorder I'd turned on when Carl first showed up.

Carl's voice came through loud and clear: *You found all my tablets? All two thousand of them?. . . I've got customers waiting . . . I'll laugh while your cabin goes up in flames.*

I watched Carl's face while I played the whole thing. If looks could burn, I would have ended up a smoldering heap of ash, but the policemen on each side of him held him back when he tried to lunge at me. His voice didn't sound nearly so smooth when he was screaming profanity. The police stopped focusing on Bryn and Landon and turned all their attention to Carl.

"Good job with that recording." Bryn waited until it was just her and me and Landon to say it. "And that was a world-class kick."

"He deserved worse." I was glad I'd gotten the chance, but no kick in the world was hard enough to pay Carl back for hurting my mom.

CHAPTER THIRTY

Bryn

The next morning dawned bright and clear, the totally wrong tone for the day. Dark skies and a steady drizzle would have been a far better match to my mood. We needed to see Del again. I needed to arrange for some sort of simple service for Sawyer. I needed to meet with his lawyer. And I needed to let Mom know what was going on.

Carl no longer remained a constant threat, but so much remained uncertain, I couldn't relax. Landon, Josh, and I were expected at the police station late that afternoon to sign the statements we'd given the night before, and I sincerely hoped it would be the last time I'd have to think about Carl until his trial.

The lieutenant had inspected Carl's pills with interest. "We've had a spike in the number of people landing in the hospital, not just here, but in a ten-state area. It's been traced to counterfeit tablets like these—a mix of fentanyl and cocaine with a bunch of other crap thrown in. We'll have to get them analyzed to make sure, but I'd bet anything these are from the same batch."

I was only sorry Josh hadn't kicked Carl harder. I'd been reaching for my knife, but I'm not sure I would have had the courage to use it or the skill to have any effect. Josh at least had the nerve to do what I hadn't dared.

He was still subdued at breakfast, his eyes tired, but at least his appetite was better. He polished off a towering stack of pancakes and sat back with a sigh. "When can we go see Mom again? Maybe she's better today."

"We can see her again this morning." I was glad Josh wanted another visit but feared he faced more disappointment if he already expected a noticeable improvement. "I've got an appointment with the lawyer at ten." I gave Landon a questioning look, and he jumped in.

"Why don't Josh and I go up to see Del while you take care of your appointment? We can grab a rideshare, and you can meet us there when you're done." The two of them headed out together, deep in conversation.

The lawyer, a young outdoorsy guy who looked like he'd be more at home rock climbing than trapped in an office, expressed little surprise at the news of Sawyer's death.

"I didn't know him well, but he struck me as a man tying up loose ends. Organized and intentional but resigned and a little sad. I've seen people like that when they're terminally ill, when they know they have very little time. He transferred everything into these trusts—his house, his truck, all his investment accounts. He commented that the only thing he had left after signing the paperwork was whatever cash he had on hand. He was in a hell of a hurry too—paid quite a premium to get all this in place so quickly."

He walked me through the details of not one trust, but two—the one I'd already learned about for Del and a second for Josh. My name was all over the documents, giving me the power to change trustees, change money managers, review expenses.

"So, if Sawyer had died before I showed up out here, you would have, what, sent me a letter or something?"

He nodded. "Yes. He assured me you knew all about it."

I tried to imagine what it would have been like if Josh had not come to me for help. No Carl. No cross-country trek. No confrontation with Sawyer. Just an unexpected I-regret-to-inform-you letter that would have left plenty of unanswered questions. I certainly would have been happy to miss out on Carl, but I was glad I'd had the chance to see Sawyer one last time and get some answers.

The amount of money involved in the trusts left me gasping, dumbfounded by so many digits. When I expressed my surprise at the totals, the lawyer shook his head. "Apparently he had a knack for Bitcoin. I wish I had that kind of talent."

I took a deep breath before I asked him my final question. "Sawyer won't be officially declared dead for quite some time. They're hoping a body will turn up, but as rough as that lower canyon is, they tell me it may be days or weeks. If ever. Does that impact any of these arrangements?"

He didn't hesitate. "No impact at all. A death certificate affects distribution of an estate. But in this case, there is essentially no estate left, because all of Mr. Whitman's assets were transferred into these irrevocable trusts. Your sister's care won't be affected in the least."

A surge of relief buoyed me for a moment. If we had been forced to detangle the mess involved with Sawyer's false identity before we could access the funds, I'd be old and gray before the legal issues were settled. At least Del could count on staying where she was.

I thanked him, collected copies of more paperwork, and left to join the others at Elk Creek.

The whole drive there, I kept thinking about Sawyer. He had successfully faked his death in the plane crash. Was this a repeat performance? He'd told the lawyer he'd handed over every penny, but there was no way to verify that was true. If he was really playing around with Bitcoin to grow his money, he could easily have stashed assets wherever he wanted. And he'd made quite an effort to distribute his money in a way that didn't require a corpse.

Was he dead, or had he managed yet again to disappear into a new life? I was certain of only two things. First, I was going to keep my doubts to myself. I would never say anything to anyone—including the police and definitely including Josh—about the possibility Sawyer was still alive. And second, if anyone ever reported seeing Sawyer's twin alive and well in some obscure bar halfway around the world, I would be the last person on the planet to go looking for him.

I reached Elk Creek and parked, but I had little enthusiasm for going in to face Del again. I ran my fingers over Landon's carved version of my homestead, seeking some strength. I should probably sit right there and call my mother. Fill her in on everything that had happened in the past day, give her the details about Del's condition and its cause.

I picked up my phone, but I couldn't call. I knew how the conversation would play out—the anguish, the sobs. Maybe she'd retreat into her grief. Maybe she'd fly out on the first possible plane. But regardless of her reaction, she wasn't going to take responsibility for decisions about Del's care, and she wasn't going to reach out to Josh. Whatever choices had to be made about the future would fall to me, no question.

I slipped the phone into my pocket. There were things I needed to take care of before I could face that particular challenge. I gave Tellico a pat and headed inside.

The waiting area of the rehab center was empty, and the receptionist led me to the same room as the previous day. The sight of Del, once again in her dark blue robe, once again sitting calmly in a chair staring at nothing, caught me off guard, a gut-wrenching reminder of her new reality.

Josh sat in a chair beside his mother. Not talking. Just watching. Her gaze shifted every few minutes, moving from one object to another. When she happened to look at Josh, she gave him the same calm consideration she gave to a vase of flowers or an embroidered pillow.

Landon sat on the couch with a book in his hands, but he wasn't even pretending to read.

"Hey, how's it going?" I kept my voice quiet. The room's funeral-home hush made the lavish surroundings depressing instead of cheerful.

"Hey there. Josh filled his Mom in on the rest of the story he started yesterday." Landon's voice was normal volume, as if trying to include Josh in the discussion. "And then we've been hanging out."

I walked over to my sister, and this time I was the one who knelt beside her and took her slack hand. "Del. It's me. Bryn." She didn't react. Didn't even look at me.

There had been times growing up when I'd wished I were an only child. But now, tears streaked my cheeks, and a tightness squeezed my heart so hard I was surprised it could still beat. I'd added a new chapter to my history with Sawyer, and it had given me added peace. But I would never have the chance to do the same with Del.

Silence took over the room. Not the peaceful silence of a moonrise or sunset, but an expectant silence, as if each of us was waiting in vain for something—anything—to improve.

The air grew heavier and denser with each minute. After an endless hour, a nurse arrived once again to lead Del away to meet some sort of schedule. Josh kissed his mother on an unresponsive cheek. His jaw tightened and his head dropped forward, his face contorted with a wrenching, deep-rooted grief.

Landon, Josh, and I walked out of the building, and I held up a hand. "Let's sit here in the garden for a few minutes. I want to catch you up on what happened at the lawyer's."

They waited, and I detoured to let Tellico out of the truck. We followed one of the winding garden pathways and reached a long bench that looked over the valley. In the winter, snow would lie deep here, but now the dense green of the conifer forests was sliced by the lighter green of the summer ski slopes. The town itself lay below us, long rows of windows sparkling in the sunlight.

We sat. Josh pulled out his phone, but I gave his knee a tap to hold his attention. "Listen up because this is about you. I met with the lawyer, and like I told you last night, your father set aside money in a trust for your mother that will take care of her for as long as she needs. It's all down in writing—she can stay here, or we can find a different place for her if we think that's best. The lawyer is the executor of the trust, so he's the final decision maker, but it's stipulated that family input has to be considered."

"You mean she could live closer to home?"

"Yes. We can investigate treatment centers closer to home and decide what we think will work. But I think we should let her stay where she is for now. She's settled here, and we don't know what other options are out there." I paused for a moment to let it sink in. "The bottom line is she's not coming back to your apartment. Not for a long while." If ever.

Josh stared at his feet. "They'll keep her safe? They'll look after her?"

"They'll do everything they can."

"And we can come visit sometimes?"

"Of course."

He ran his fingers over the lanyard bracelet. I had considered suggesting he return it to Del, in the hope it would be a reminder for her, but I was glad Josh still wore it. He needed its comfort far more than Del now. After a minute, he gave a slow, defeated nod. "Okay."

He had lost his father, he had lost his mother, and in some ways, he had also lost his vocation. Taking care of Del had been far more than a part-time job.

Landon started to ask something, but I held up my hand. One more topic to get through. "Josh, your father set aside money for your mother, but he also set aside money for you. It's enough to pay for ongoing expenses, and it's enough to pay for college."

His eyes whipped up toward mine. "He did that? For me?" Tellico came over and nosed Josh's leg, alerted by the distress in his voice. Josh reached down to give him a pat, but not before I saw quick tears cloud his eyes.

"It's in trust, and it's set up to cover only the basics plus education costs, not crazy stuff. But it means you can make your own choices about your future."

He shook his head, disbelieving, then he got up and walked a dozen feet away and stood, staring out over the valley. I started to follow him, but Landon put a restraining hand on my arm. "Don't worry. Give him some space. He's not going to disappear this time."

I settled back to wait. "After things get wrapped up here, Josh and I will have to drive back east. It'll take a few days."

Landon nodded. "I can stay for another day or two if that will help, then I'll head back home. Don't worry about the farm—take what time you need. I can keep things going until you get back."

"Thank you. That would be wonderful." I'd been thanking Landon a lot lately. He'd arranged for security at the farm, taken care of things while I helped Josh, set aside his hesitations about traveling to fly all the way out here at the drop of a hat. Why had I held this man at bay for so long? Perhaps the emphatic *no* I'd given him weeks ago was no longer the right answer.

Josh returned, and I scooted over to make room for him on the bench beside me. His eyes were red-rimmed, but he was holding himself together.

"So," he asked, "what about me? What about the apartment?" He squared his shoulders and glared at me. "And don't start talking about Grandma, because I won't go live with her."

And there it was, the question that had hovered ever since I knew Del wouldn't be coming home with us.

I loved my homestead and my life there. The peacefulness of a silent morning, alone, before I settled into the day's tasks. No fuss. No interruptions. No surprises. I was at no one's beck and call, and I didn't have to maneuver around anyone else. It was a life I'd worked hard to create. A life I treasured.

The past two weeks had tossed all that aside, my real life on hold while I dealt with this unexpected nephew and an endless string of surprises. I was still reeling from it all, and Josh had it even worse. Regardless of where he ended up living, he'd probably be looking at a different school. Different friends. A different life.

To compound it all, he'd come close to death, and I knew exactly the ways such a narrow escape could haunt you. I'd never considered myself a candidate for motherhood, but perhaps I could make a difference for this particular boy.

"I think you should come live with me." It wasn't until I heard the words spoken out loud that I was certain what I was going to say. "We'll add a bedroom to the cabin. The school bus comes down my road." My voice got stronger as I went. "There will be a lot of changes for you, and it may not be easy. But I think we can make it work."

"Really? You would do that?" His voice choked. His disbelief was obvious.

"I'm sure there's some sort of paperwork involved for me to get temporary custody. Hoops we'll have to jump through. But, hey, I'm your aunt. I'll fight like hell to make it happen. I promise."

He looked calmer than I would have expected. Tired, but maybe a little hopeful. On my end, surging hope had trumped my fatigue. This decision might give Josh a chance of moving forward, but it opened a door for me as well. I was tired of building walls.

If I wasn't careful, I was going to start getting maudlin. "An unpaid employee, that's what I'm getting here. After all, I need plenty of help with those goats and the garden."

"Yeah, yeah. I'm seriously looking up those child labor laws." Josh gave me half a smile. "Can Marcus visit sometime? He'd like the goats. And maybe we could take him kayaking?" He paused, as if rethinking what he'd just said. "Maybe on a nice quiet lake?"

We both laughed. "Of course. We can shop for bunkbeds for your new room."

He reached for his phone and started texting madly, already spreading the news.

I glanced at Landon. The breeze ruffled his hair, and his strong workman's hands rested quietly on his knees. I was acutely aware of his physical presence. Aware of his body and the promise it held.

The shift in my outlook on our relationship may have come too late. My offer to Josh had just made my life far more complicated—maybe too complicated for Landon. He liked his independence as much as I did, and he didn't share my reasons for feeling an obligation to Josh. Adding a fourteen-year-old into the mix might have screwed up any chance at something more than friendship between us.

But when I caught his eye, he gave me a smile. "It'll be good to have both of you back home. I'm glad I'll have the chance to get to know Josh better. We've got a few months before school starts, and it will give us all the chance of some uninterrupted time."

I liked the way that sounded. The fears of the past still lingered, but I'd faced my fears on the river when the risk was death. If I had the strength to do that, who knows what else I could conquer?

Josh finished texting, and I reached over and took his hand. He gripped mine in return, holding on like he was determined not to let go. *A life without risk is no life at all.* Sawyer was the one who used to say it, and it was one thing he got right.

ACKNOWLEDGMENTS

It is with a sense of profound amazement that I usher a second novel into the world, and I must first acknowledge you, my readers, for making this possible. Your enthusiasm, emails, reviews, and book club discussions about *Wildland* have been a delight. You have my heartfelt thanks.

My writing group, the Iron Clay Writers, have once again midwifed this story into existence. Nancy Peacock, Agnieszka Stachura, Claire Hermann, and Barrie Trinkle—your friendship, your feedback, and your constant support mean more to me than I can express.

Sincere thanks go to those who've worked tirelessly to transform my manuscript into an actual book. At Spencerhill Associates, Nalini Akolekar. I am so fortunate to have you in my corner, offering wise counsel at every turn. At Crooked Lane Books, Terri Bischoff, Madeline Rathle, Melissa Rechter, and the entire team—magicians all. Zachariah Claypole White provided invaluable editorial feedback on an early draft. Margie Lawson helped keep my words on track at a high-intensity Immersion class. Thank you all.

ACKNOWLEDGMENTS

A special thanks goes to the authors who have offered me such amazing support along this writing journey, support that has ranged from kind words on a bad day to advice on the intricacies of the publishing industry. There are too many names to list here in full, but particular shout-outs go to Barbara Claypole White, Sharon Kurtzman, Diane Chamberlain, Lainey Cameron, Alison Hammer, and Barbara Conrey.

The Women's Fiction Writers Association has been an invaluable source of information, opportunities, and friendship over the years, and the North Carolina Writers' Network has provided workshops and valued connections to other local writers.

Thanks go to all the family, friends, and colleagues who've cheered my writing from the sidelines. Last, but definitely not least, thanks go to my husband, George; my sons, Austin, Daniel, and Carson; and my daughters-in-law, Rose and Bianca. I would be lost without you.

DISCUSSION QUESTIONS

1. Bryn has reacted to Del's betrayal by withdrawing from life. Do you think her relationship with the past is healthy? How should she have managed this differently? How have you dealt with difficult memories?
2. Given her deep-seated anger at her sister, why do you think Bryn makes such a serious effort to find Del?
3. How does Bryn change over the course of the story? How does her attitude toward Josh change? Toward Del? Toward Landon?
4. In many ways, Josh takes on the role of parent in his relationship with his mother. Where does the line belong between giving children enough responsibility and giving them too much?
5. Josh initially distrusts Bryn and hesitates to give her full information about his mother. How do his feelings toward Bryn change over time and why?
6. When Bryn is forced to face her whitewater fears, does she act as you would have predicted? How does this event impact her thinking?

7. Bryn has crafted a homesteading life that's a mix of animals, gardening, and remote computer work. How would you design your own "fantasy" life?

8. More than 46,000 people died in 2018 due to opioid overdoses. How has your community or people you know been impacted by the opioid crisis?

9. If you could change something about this story, what would you change and why?

10. If you were to write the next chapters of this book, what would happen? What do you foresee in Bryn and Josh's futures?